Wanderlust
Love & Hate

MADASIN MAYFAIR

Westland Park Press
P.O. Box 9594
Canton, Ohio 44711

First Edition October 2012

ISBN: 978-0-9884444-0-9

10 9 8 7 6 5 4 3 2 1

Printed in the United States of America

This book is dedicated to all the wanderers.

A WORD ON WANDERLUST

The Wanderlust series began with a concept that I have pondered over for years- things never change. The first book-Love & Hate was more than a book I wanted to write; I needed to write it!

The series explores the connection between the human condition, our deepest desires, convoluted and warring emotions, and the inner demons that shape and influence our lives. Wanderlust is the experience of living a tesseract life: forever trapped in the vicious cycle of distortion- a false reality. I wanted to expand on the idea that reflections of the past haunt our present state and the future likewise will continue in the same redundant and stagnant manner if we never conquer ourselves.

Wanderlust is a place of no escape- we travel through our lives, aimlessly, searching for purpose and meaning. Often times, I wondered how the devils and demons of our past effect the outcome of our present, when what we love is jaded, empty, and lost.

We wander for the unforgotten. We wander for our dreams. We wander because we can't let go. I've learned to embrace Wanderlust; I've relived it with ink and paper. In time we must all embrace our inner demons because things never change.

Madasin Mayfair

FOREWORD

In today's age, not many books carry a sense of purpose or literary depth as those penned by the classic writers of old. Few emerge with characters that captivate our minds, unraveling our own vices at the core; yet, Madasin Mayfair's character-David- wanders with pain and suffering as his only companions. Ironic how we, intelligent minds, find it necessary to fill our inadequacies with superfluous wants which sadly leave us yearning for more. Yearning and wandering seem symbiotic in the world that Mayfair creates- can one exist without the other?

Wanderlust: Love & Hate explores the frailty of the human psyche and the tendency to fulfill our fiendish wants and seductive desires. Unscathed from these iniquities, David surfaces through the thick ink- the darkness that many of our desires arise from- as the 21st century Byronic hero. David defined the false reality of not only Autumn Marseille but the other characters with the novel; thus, his reality became our own as readers as well.

Where does an individual draw the line between love and hate? Wanderlust plays on these emotions and the convoluted nature of our perceptions of the world. What trials must one endure to continue on the foretold path of righteousness? Mayfair exploits the everyday choices that could irreversibly leave one trapped in a false reality- where the everyday is a systematic routine, created in our minds, to cope with the life we've chosen to live.

Regrettably, we are all wanders, trapped within ourselves, searching for meaning in the choices laid out before us. Juxtaposed, David would simply smile and take you by the hand and whisper- *follow me.*

Mike Wright
Westland Park Press

CONTENTS

Part III. *Recompense*

ACKNOWLEDGMENTS

My publisher, Westland Park Press, for making this all possible, and especially Mike Wright for his literary criticism, and insightful discussions which helped propel things forward.

A special thank you to my mom for her endless support.

Liannette Morris, for the wonderful artistic contributions that have brought Wanderlust to life.

Mike Swanson, for all the help in making things a success.

And all the others who wandered with me- Thank You

PROLOGUE

I haven't decided as of yet which is worse, to live with a **broken heart** or to die because of it. It's still a mystery to me how he appeared, as if out of thin air, the human embodiment of all things divine. How ironic it seems to me now, looking back, that such a lasting impression was stamped across my life.

Day after day my mind races through thoughts stored in **secret compartments**, and I go blind as the good slowly fades into the bad. To love and to hate, over time, turns bitterly into loving to hate. My heart is constantly wandering, traveling effortlessly, searching for a glimpse of his loathing familiarity.

Wandering: you find it everywhere, and wandering you find it nowhere. I live my life only in the hope of seeing him again. But, I only imagine the same glitter of the eye in the store clerk behind the cash register, and the same twisted smirk from the older gentleman who delivers my mail, and the same deliberate swagger in the young detective seeking to ruin me.

Ever since that terrible night, he left me- that devil- with a heavy black cloud following and continued wanderlust.

Part I

False Reality

"And out of the darkness came the hands that reach thro' nature, molding men." Lord Alfred Tennyson

A BRIEF INTRODUCTION

May 24, 2002

I hoped that Adrian would not try to call me. It was a muggy Friday night and the end of my junior year was nearing at last. Tonight marked the opening of the Osnaburg Township 52nd annual summer festival hosted by St. George's Preparatory Academy Student Council. The three nights that were to follow; similarly, were filled with community driven events and activities which highlighted the social calendars of all 3,712 residents of our rural town. As President of the Student Council body, an immense amount of pressure had been upon me over the course of the final quarter to ensure that no detail, no matter how small, was overlooked.

I sank lower in the worn; zebra print upholstered seats of Stacy Loughton's Escort and watched the cars wiz by the twists and turns of Big Bend, a dirt country road four miles south of St. George Prep. Metallica's Enter the Sandman blared at an inconceivable decibel, and my eardrums throbbed from the abuse. I silently cursed the fact that I had accepted Stacy's invitation for a ride. I would have much preferred to meet her and the rest of my friends at the festival, driving my blue Audi, and saving myself from probable, permanent ear damage. I sighed, at least this way Adrian would think I was at home if he, just so happened, to come looking for me. I had practiced my lines over and over, as every good actress does, in order to prepare for what I would say to him. I would lie through my teeth.

I had worked tirelessly to promote the festival and elevate it to a level never achieved before. I deserved to enjoy myself tonight- with my friends and committee staff, but Adrian had said the day before that I was not permitted to go. In his selfish way, he had declared that he didn't care it was my responsibility as Student Council President; I was not going without him. It was unfair that he never let me do anything; he always had to control me. He hated all my friends, and they in return hated him even more.

As the car rolled to an abrupt halt at the corner of Big Bend and Main Street, I nervously peered out of the window and prayed that I would not see him walking, on his way to Eric and Steve Wise's house which stood directly on the corner. Thankfully he was not, and as Stacy hit the gas, leaving the country roads and serenity of rural Osnaburg behind us, I finally was able to exhale. We had been silent, immersed in our own thoughts, but my constant nervous twitching must have given away my hidden fears.

Stacy eyed me cautiously. She must have guessed what was going through my head because she sighed and shook hers. Her stiff chocolate colored curls were tied securely in a low ponytail and her meadow green eyes squinted in the fading sun. "Why are you two still together?" she questioned. "I just don't get you Autumn. He isn't cute or smart, nice or funny. You are way too good for him."

I didn't say anything in reply. I had heard this a thousand times over the years that Adrian and I had dated, and at this point, I don't think that my friends expected an answer.

"I mean what an ass. Here you are riding in my car to the festival because you're worried that he will find out that you went out with your friends. Tonight you won't even be able to enjoy yourself because you're going to be freaking out that he will find out you aren't at home."

"You see it that way, but Adrian and I have a lot of history. I can't just break up with him," I snapped defensively. "Things aren't always bad you know."

"Right, like the time he ditched you at the football game against Local because you spoke to Tony Greggory. Or what about the masquerade ball last month when he made you cry right there at the dinner table because you accidently knocked his steak knife on the floor and got it dirty? Seriously Autumn, you can't fool me," she replied with a knowing air.

"Well, maybe things will change between us. I really don't want to talk about Adrian right now," I said in an almost whisper. We drove on quietly for half a mile. "I talked to Tony early this morning," I began again. "He said that he was planning on attending the festival tonight and that there was someone he wanted me to meet."

"Tony is so much more your speed. You deserve to be with an intelligent athlete, just like yourself," Stacy mused.

"We are just friends," I emphasized. Although we never had attended the same school, I at St. George's and Tony (and Adrian) at Local- the public school just a few miles away- Tony and I had been friends since middle school. Stacy was right about Tony, as she was about so many things, he was perfect for me. He was the elite wrestler and football star at Local, and a very strong pole-vaulter as well. Whenever I wanted to see Tony, I simply opened the Sports page of the newspaper and I was sure to see his handsome face smiling back at me. He was an honor student who was very talented in mathematics and sciences; he volunteered at the church and was active in the community. I was sure that he would earn a scholarship to a top university and do well for himself- and deservedly so. I compared him to Adrian and snickered. Tony outmatched him in every possible category: brains, brawn, and beauty. Maybe I was pathetic for staying with Adrian…but how could I ever break up with him? He would never let me go.

Stacy slowed the car as we approached the parking lot in the rear of St. George's carefully maneuvering her Escort

3

between Cameron's Civic and Lauren's Impala. I glanced about quickly; checking to make sure Adrian wasn't waiting to sabotage me.

"So, who is ready to party?" Cameron squealed throwing her arms in the air. Cameron Richmond always looked as if she were ready to party, with her short hair crimped wildly and her makeup dark and bold. She was always determined to play up her scant features and draw attention to her streaky blonde/black locks and attractive petite frame.

"No Adrian today Autumn?" Lauren said flashing her sandstone eyes at me.

I hated when she made comments to that effect- when she mocked me. I knew she was trying to steer a wayward reply from me. "Not today," I glared back at her, shooting her a look that said I didn't feel like playing her game. Lauren Vanderbilt was one of my best friends, but her pessimism and narcissistic personality, sometimes, was too much for me to bear. If one were to look up the word narcissist in the dictionary, a picture of Lauren would be found. She would, no doubt, take up the entire page! Her lovely face complete with a fake smile would expose a set of gleaming teeth and a pair of calcareous eyes lined with silver sparkling glitter. Glitter and Lauren always went in the same sentence- she loved glitter hairspray, glitter nail polish, and glitter lotion. She was the Glitter Queen and everyone loved her for it. "Let's go," I said slinging my rhinestone embezzled purse over my shoulder.

"Aren't we going to wait on Vicki?" Stacy called after me.

"Yeah, you guys stay and wait for her. I need to get going and meet up with Tony. I haven't seen him in nearly a week and I want to know who he brought with him."

"Let her go," I heard Lauren say. "She doesn't get much time away from the psychopathic tyrant."

I pulled my waist long, sable hair into a sloppy bun and flipped Lauren the middle finger as I trotted off in the general direction of the fresh squeezed lemonade stand where Tony had asked me to meet.

Butterflies began to rise and flutter in my stomach as I crossed the walkway into the quad, a sprawling grassy area in the middle of campus. Spanning nearly two acres, the quad served in many ways as a recreational site for school and community activities. Anxiety over the success of the festival was daunting. Tonight's kickoff was the most important aspect, always organized by St. George's and decorated by members of Student Council. As Project Manager, I was quite pleased with the outcome. Arrays of contrasting colors were used this year, thanks to the adopted theme idea submitted by Cameron- Vanity Fair. We had read Thackeray's satirical novel in British Literature class last quarter, and her inspiration, to turn this year's festival into lively Russell Square, was both elegant and theatrical. The light posts, which lined the path, were wrapped in fantastical colored scarves. Rustic wooden booths were stationed intermittently between food vendors and carnival tables that were radiant and whimsical: henna, fortune tellers, local art works, makeup designers, photography, and crafts. To my right, picnic table's setup in a spiral design pattern provided an ample eating area. Cameron said the idea was so vanity and so fair- whatever that meant.

I spotted Tony half way down the second aisle of food booths, at the lemonade stand as he promised, leaning on the edge of a picnic table top. I decided to circle back around so that I would pass him from the opposite direction. I desired for him to see me first, so that he could be the first to speak. I discreetly glanced at him, but kept walking; ready almost to pass him, my face was ruddy with humiliation over my near faulty plan. But…at the last second he grabbed me by the arm and pulled me in for a hug.

"Hey you," he said in a hushed voice.

"I was worried that I wouldn't find you," I lied. "There are so many people here and of course you aren't even that close to the lemonade stand."

"It's right over there," he said pointing and releasing me from his tight grasp.

"I'm glad I finally get to see you. It seems like forever."

"So you said it was girl's night out. How the hell did you manage that?"

I sat down on the picnic table next to him and mumbled, "I didn't figure Adrian would look for me here."

"Really? Why wouldn't he look for you here? You aren't with him and everyone in town is here," he asked darting me a curious look.

A hundred amperes spiked through my veins in a jolting blast- he was right. If Adrian called me and realized that I wasn't home he would come here. *Shit!* A horrified expression settled on my face as I weighed out my limited options and thought of the most efficient escape route.

Tony placed his arm around the small of my back and turned my head toward his. "Don't worry Autumn," he reassured me. "Nothing bad is going to happen while I'm around."

I breathed a sigh of relief- Tony always had a way of making me feel protected- and I loved him for that. "The girls should be on their way any minute," I added.

"You forget this is Vanity Fair. I'm sure they have gotten themselves enchanted by now and are wandering aimlessly, absorbed in their own vain existence."

"Aren't you feisty today," I said giggling.

He pulled his cell phone out of his pocket, glanced at it intently, and then placed it back in his pocket. He stood erect- all five feet eight inches of him- and leaned in toward me. "Our friendship means a lot to me you know," he started looking down, "I just want to know that you are safe and happy."

Our eyes met and in a faltering tone I replied, "I'm fine really... and our friendship means a lot to me too." I had perjured myself. Just as I was about to concede that I didn't want to be with Adrian anymore, I stopped. A perplexing sensation enveloped me. It felt as if I was suffocating. For a moment I was dazed, the world around me slowed, and an intense and tightening knot formed at the base of my stomach. I gulped in raspy mouthfuls of humid air, panicking, I was confused by the gripping emotions that pulsated through my body. I felt that someone was watching me. Frantically, I searched the faces of the people around me; however, no one was paying me the slightest notice.

"Autumn," Tony said shaking me. "Are you alright? You look like you've just seen a ghost."

"I'm fine... I think."

"Ah... there he is," Tony said pointing across the quad toward the stage where several punk rockers from Local were tuning their guitars.

As the stranger approached our table, a feeling of calmness warmed me, just as my grandmother's patchwork quilt does through the blustery Ohio winter nights. His piercing eyes, blue as the sky which dawns the morning star, latched on to my heart. I could feel them burrowing deep within, and though I tried, I could not break my eyes away from his. He was an angel I was sure. I had never seen someone more magnificently perfect and bewitching in my entire seventeen years on Earth. His hair was pure sunshine which paired with his smooth milky skin. I took him in, awed by his graceful appearance and intrigued by his gregarious; yet, striking demeanor. I wondered if everyone else was as smitten as I by the newcomer, but I was too mesmerized by his cogent eyes to tell. I thought I saw a smirk peek out from the corners of his full ruby lips, but I couldn't be sure. Slowly, the noose was loosened from around me and I bashfully turned away.

"This is who I told you about," Tony said nudging me in the ribs, "he's new to town and started at Local earlier this week."

I inwardly snorted. Of course he attended Local- I couldn't be so lucky- I was sure that if he ever did grace the mosaic halls of St. George Prep – he would be deemed, by Sister Mary Thomas Bernard, the last archangel. "Autumn Marseille," I said coyly.

"David Huntsmen," he said, quite cavalier, "I've heard a lot about you.

FURTHER EXAMINATION

May 24, 2002

Just as I was about to inquire what he had heard about me and from who, my purse began to vibrate under my arm. "I have to take this," I said.

Tony shot me an apprehensive look; we both knew who was calling.

I fumbled through my purse frantically, afraid I would miss the call all together and spark unwanted suspicion; and finally, I found it near the bottom of my bag. I flipped it open and took a few steps away from the table to distance myself from Tony and David. "Hello," I said wearily.

"Where the hell are you and what are you doing?" Adrian growled.

I instantly turned defensive; I knew that he had planned on going over to Eric and Steve's house after school, and it angered me that he always thought it was okay for him to do exactly as he pleased but it wasn't okay for me to do anything. "I'm at home," I lied convincingly. Over the years I had become a perfectionist at masking the truth and deceiving him. I hated that after all our time together things had gotten to this point; Adrian was jealous and hypocritical. Sometimes I wondered if he could sense the hate I too often felt for him. "I'm packing my things for the track meet tomorrow."

"I had forgotten about all that actually," he replied sarcastically. "I guess you want me to come, huh?"

For some reason I did. The track meet tomorrow was going to be a big day for me, I was going after the school record in the long jump and this was my final attempt for the year to grasp the title which I had worked so diligently to achieve. My personal best, so far this season, was only 2 inches shy. "Yes, I was hoping that you'd be there for me. If you don't mind coming early I could give you a ride."

"Nah, that's okay," he said shortly. "If I do come, I'll get a ride from Steve and Eric."

I felt David boring holes in the back of my head. *Had he been staring at me the whole time?* Self-conscious, I looked around auspiciously, but only noticed a table of three young girls in pleated skirts and white tailored shirts looking my way. *Why was David so interested in me- in my conversation?* I decided to try and cut things short with Adrian. "Okay, that's fine I guess. Let me know in the morning if you change your mind."

"Yea, well I'm going to get off of here. Eric just got back and we are about to start playing this new videogame he picked up. Maybe I'll come by your house later and say what's up," he said in a voice reeking of contempt.

"Fine, I will probably be in bed though, so don't go out of your way."

"Right…you want to look your best to impress that pole-vaulter from my school," he spat with jealous anger. "Don't bullshit me Autumn, and now that I think about it, I will come just to show him what the deal is."

I tried to image Adrian, who at five feet- ten inches tall and one hundred and forty-five pounds, telling Tony the deal. It was hate that had been brewing for several years: but one so far, I had been able to persuade Tony out of. "I'm not trying to impress him," I insisted. Adrian slammed the phone down and the line went dead. Breathing a sigh of relief, I returned my cell phone into my pocket and strolled casually back over to the picnic table. Tony had disappeared, and the seraph, David, was standing right where I had left him. "Where did Tony run off to?" I asked barely able to form a coherent sentence while standing next to him.

"While you were on the phone with your boyfriend, your friends wandered by and he took off with them."

I wondered how much of my conversation with Adrian he had overheard. "You know my boyfriend?" I asked surprised.

"Yes," he answered slowly, never unlocking his eyes from mine.

I could feel myself blushing. It was uncomfortable to have someone so sublime stare at me the way that David did.

"He's a bitch."

My face flushed with embarrassment. "What do you mean?" I asked. Tony had told me that David had just moved into town. There was no way that he had come to that conclusion in a week. *Was there?*

"I mean that anyone who hits on girls is a bitch. I mean that Adrian is a puppet and he does just as he is told," he replied with an air of knowledge.

I turned away mortified. *Who had told him that Adrian was violent and had hit me before?* Even Tony didn't know about that, I had definitely kept that a secret from him. I wanted to change the subject- badly. "Do you want to walk around too and see if we can find Tony and my friends, or maybe get something to eat?"

His lingering glare said that he knew- that I knew- that he knew everything. He made me stand there, wallowing in shame for what seemed like an eternity; then boldly, he took my clammy hand into his. "I'll walk with you anywhere."

My stomach began a series of acrobatic somersaults. Never in life had I felt so blissful and secure; but at the same time, I was worried that someone would see me walking side by side with David, and that somehow, it would get back to Adrian. Nevertheless, we strolled hand and hand down the walkway lined with greasy food booths and cotton candy stands. Periodically I would check my blind spots, in vain, for my group of friends. Once I found them, I would at least be in a small cluster and would draw less attention to myself. David was taciturn, lost in his thoughts, and seemingly unconcerned with what anyone else was thinking or what gossip was being brewed. We glided around the festival, as if on a cloud, wandering aimlessly, until we stopped in front of a shabby tent advertising itself as Madam Therriot Fortune Telling.

"Did you see them?" I questioned peering around a group of middle school students who were shouting excitedly and tossing plastic rings at small bottles which bobbed back and forth in a tank filled with water.

David shook his head.

"Miss Marseille…Miss Marseille," a young man with creamy beige skin, spiky auburn hair and who was dressed in a navy blue soldier's uniform called out to me. He appeared to be in charge of a military recruiting booth that offered free T-shirts and lanyards for completing a set of chin-ups within a sixty second period.

I vaguely remembered meeting him, along with several other entertainment vendors at an informational gathering which took place in the school gymnasium a few days ago. I waved at him and smiled.

"Miss Marseille, come try your luck. Come try your luck at some chin-ups," he called out and gestured for me to come over.

I paused and waited to gauge David's response. I glanced up at him but his attention was diverted elsewhere- as if he had not heard the soldier at all.

"Come with me," David said in a virile tone and guided me through the parse flaps of Madam Therriot's modest, enclosed canopy.

A delightful aroma of lilac and rosemary stormed up my nostrils, and I spun around to take in all the mystical sights before me. The tent was drab and from the ceiling hung dozens of sparkling bulb ornaments of all shapes and sizes. In the far corner, a reading table was adorned with an ivory laced cloth and a stately crystal vase which held several roseate plume feathers and a large vibrant orchid flower arrangement. A musical symphony played in my ears; for there must have been over twenty rustic bronze bird cages which cluttered the cramped entryway and were filled with bright yellow canaries who all sang the same tune, in varying octaves. "Wow," I breathed aloud. I had never been to a clairvoyant before, but this certainly was not what I had expected.

"Be with you two in just a second," a rickety, old voice called from a distance. *Could this be the mysterious Madam Therriot, and if so, how did she know there were two of us waiting for her?*

David looked at me as if he had read my mind. A slight grin reappeared on his lips. "She is psychic you know." He winked at me as he browsed around, sifting through the arbitrary displays of tacky jewelry, fortune reading how-to manuals, incense, and racks of yarn woven frocks.

I had no intention of exploring Madam Therriot's lair and all its oddities. I wanted to flee- I wanted my fortune to remain untold, but sensed that David was content, and in a strange way that made our current predicament perfectly fine with me. The beaded curtain, which hung behind the checkout counter, swayed in a rhythmic motion and Madam Therriot appeared.

"May I help you?" she asked in a thick eastern French accent.

"Yes, we are here to have our futures told," David replied leaning over my shoulder. He had come up behind me and as he spoke, his cool breath tickled the nape of my neck and sent a rush of chills down my spine.

"Ah yes," she said eyeing us from behind her oval spectacles. "I've been expecting you."

I had no idea what she meant by that. *How could she been expecting us?* I pondered that thought for a moment and finally came to the conclusion that I had met her at the vendor's meeting and that she expected me, as Project Manager to stop in on her. I choked back a laugh as I took in her golden braided turban and flowing embezzled gown. "I love your costume," I said jeeringly. She did not look offended, but rather puzzled, at my snide remark.

"Follow me," she said and motioned for me to proceed behind the counter.

I felt David's firm hands wrap around my waist. Electricity flowed freely through my body and an intense heat burned my cheeks and chest. "Aren't you going back there with me?" I pouted.

"I think we should go back separately."

I protested, but it was no use. "This was your idea," I whined. "I didn't want to come in here."

"Well," he said in a hoarse whisper. "Would you agree to have your fortune told if I told you it was for your own good?" He gave me another nudge- this one more forceful and direct.

"How so?" I spat. I was tired of everyone telling me what was best for me. When was I ever going to be free to make my own decisions? I had heard in a movie the saying 'fate is what we make', but for me-in my life- it never seemed the case.

"I just didn't think that you wanted Adrian finding you here at the festival...and certainly not with the likes of me." He cocked his head toward the opening of the tent. "Go!"

My knees had turned to putty, and the afflicting knot returned to my stomach. I was in a catastrophic fuck mess. Excuses swirled through my head- racing one after the other- but none of them would save me if Adrian found me. Conquered, I parted the dense drapery and followed the sound of Madam Therriot as she hummed Edith Piaf's La Vie en Rose- a cherished melody from my homeland. *How in the world had David known that Adrian was at the festival?* I seethed as I inched down the tapered and musty corridor and considered the possibility that he had fabricated the story to lure me back into the enchanted wonder-world of Madam Therriot. After several steps more, I stumbled into an open area.

"Here we are my darling," sang Madam Therriot as she pointed to a chair in the center of the room. "You sit there.

Try to relax your mind and I will tell you what lies ahead in your future."

I swallowed nervously and watched her begin to dance fluidly around me. She strutted and twirled, slowly at first, but gradually she increased in speed. Her frayed, flowing gown swooshed about her feet and the haystack turban shifted on her head from side to side. If I were not completely taken aback, I would have laughed at her. She babbled and chanted for several minutes and swayed her arms up in the air and then brushed her long, gnarled fingernails across the grass at her feet. I sat in mortified silence, thinking of all the ways I would kill David when this was over. There was no doubt in my mind that after this blatant display of foolishness, he had set me up for sure.

"Hard as you try, my darling, you can't escape the pain. It will be sometime before the nightmares will stop."

Was she referring to Adrian? I was not impressed- a lot of people have pain and nightmares.

"You will never be able to let him go," she trailed off. "It's impossible."

"Who?" I asked, "Who are you talking about?"

"You know very well that I mean the one that you love to hate."

Adrian that bastard! Madam Therriot's visceral prophecy caused an unsettling feeling to encompass me. It was not true! The Student Council hired these people for god's sake! She slowed her dance until she stopped in front of me. She looked down on me and extended her hand slightly above my head. Her dropping eyes closed, and for what seemed like an eternity, all was still. When she opened her eyes again, a startled expression filled her wrinkled face. "What?" I demanded. "What did you see?"

"No matter," she cooed. "I sense that you believe this all a farce. There is nothing to worry about." Abruptly, she turned her back to me and adjusted the tilted hat; so again, it was situated properly on her full head.

"No, tell me," I pleaded.

Madam Therriot was motionless. "I understand what you see in him, but he is no good for you. If you stay with him…you will die soon…too soon."

I was stunned. I tried to ask her for clarification, but I stammered badly, and after several moments, dazed, I followed the sound of the chirping songbirds and the concentrated scent of the fresh picked herbs back down the dim hallway. I didn't know what to make of Madam Therriot's predictions of my future. No matter how much Adrian hated me, there was no way possible he would ever kill me- *would he?* I shook the deranged thought out of my head; we had too much history, and nothing that Madam Therriot, or anyone else, could say would ever dispel the hardships that we had endured together. It became increasingly difficult for me to breathe. I paused at the end of the hall, sucking in rapid gulps of air; I tried to tame the anger that flowed inside of me. A sound just beyond the beaded curtain made me stop and strain to listen.

David was saying, "I just got here myself." There was a pause. Hard as I tried, I could not make out what the other person said to him in reply. I inched closer and delicately swept a small portion of the hanging valence to the side to better ascertain the dialogue between the two. "A lot of people at Local talk of her, but no, I've not had the pleasure," David responded. I had to know who David was talking to and I desperately wanted to know who he was talking about. Just as my curiosity teased me to emerge from behind my cloaked position, something inside of me told me to stop. Nervously I took a step back. "Tony Greggory? He is walking around with a group of girls from St. George's." Pause. "Yea, I'd like a Catholic school girl myself, but no, I'd remember if I saw someone like her," David laughed.

I saw a shadow shift and sweep across the adjacent tent wall and then, Adrian's figure became visible. I shrank down in an attempt to better conceal myself. *Damn!* He had come to the festival to search for me. If he did run across Tony or my friends they would vouch for me I was certain.

"Alright, see ya around then," Adrian said. His glance

lingered on the entranceway, for just a second, but he coolly turned and left.

David let out a low and mischievous chuckle as he ducked behind the parted curtain. "Come here," he said lifting me effortlessly from the shadows. "I just had a nice talk with your boyfriend- he is looking for you." The left corner of his perfect mouth was curled up into an amazingly attractive smirk. "He asked me if I had seen you and I told him I didn't even know who you were. He then proceeded to describe you to me, and let me add he didn't do you justice at all."

"I told him I was at home and going to bed," I groaned.

"He seems pretty insecure," David asserted backing me against the wall. He placed his hands on the wall above my head and seductively hovered over me. He was a good six inches taller than me, putting him at six feet- one inch, which caused me to raise my head slightly in order to meet his gaze. In such close proximity, I was intoxicated by the heavenly fragrance that lingered around him. It was spicy and sweet: cinnamon, oak, and citrus- a perfect combination of sex appeal.

"Do you love him?" David asked dipping his head closer to mine.

It took a moment for his question to register- I had been lecherously daydreaming about wrapping my fingers around his sculpted neck and drawing him in for a kiss....

"Autumn, do you love him?" he said again. He was tugging at my vulnerable heart-latching on for the kill.

I couldn't decipher my mixed and bleeding emotions. Of course I loved Adrian, in my way, but I hated him too. "I don't know." The sincerity in his expression lured me in deeper, as he gently brushed the tip of his nose across my cheek. It felt like a strand of silk- sweeping and smooth.

"Let me know when you figure it out," he said pulling himself away and taking my hand once more into his. We then exited Madam Therriot's tent and entered back into the moonlit scene of Vanity Fair.

"I think I better get home," I said tugging on David's

arm. He ignored me and rounding another corner of food vendors we stopped in front of a group of art booths. "David," I said beginning to panic. "I really shouldn't be here. You said yourself that Adrian is here and he is looking for me."

"I'm not concerned, so you shouldn't be either."

Perturbed I said, "no offense, but you really have nothing to do with my situation."

He shook his head, "I said don't worry about it. Adrian's got more on his mind tonight than looking for you."

Madam Therriot's terrifying omen still rang clearly in my ears. *You will die too soon.* I wanted nothing more than to leave the festival and evade all the negative energy that surrounded me. I was on my phone again, this time ringing Stacy, hoping to find out where they had gone. I let the seconds roll, one after the other, but she didn't answer. I cursed under my breath, irritated that I was trapped, and presently being hunted by the person who I was supposed to love.

"What are you thinking about?" David inquisitively asked.

"I don't know," I lied.

"I heard that you were a pretty intelligent girl, but tonight, there is a lot of stuff that you don't know."

"What else have you heard about me?" I asked cautiously, afraid of what he might say.

"A lot of things really. You're charming."

I didn't know what to say in response to that, so I said nothing for some time. "We need to find Tony and my friends," I said instead.

"They are down that way," he pointed. "They went to hear the concert."

"Figures," I said, "nobody can hear their phone."

"Do you want to go that direction and look for them?"

Listening to a group of wannabe rock stars was not something that I was remotely interested in doing. *Damn them.* "I'd rather just get out of here," I uttered.

"Let me call Tony and tell him that I'm going to take you home; that way, they won't be worried about you," he replied.

I nodded in relief and tried to remain inconspicuous as he placed the call- Adrian could be lurking anywhere and my tense nerves would not settle until I was removed from danger. At last, he snapped the phone closed and we wandered back, through the maze of Vanity Fair, toward the main parking lot. The idea of being completely alone with David was troublesome. The entire evening, I had wanted nothing more than to grab him and kiss him and... I couldn't trust myself with him. Whenever his eyes met mine, a tightening feeling stirred within me- I had never experienced anything like it before. We crossed the avenue and zig zagged around the endless rows of cars until he finally released my hand. "Wow, nice car!" I gushed, dazzled by the sleek and sexy peril white beauty with ebony race stripes, which accented, from hood to bumper, the exterior body.

"Thanks," he said proudly as we settled in. "It's a 1967 Chevy Camaro- completely restored."

"It's amazing," I said noting the custom interior restoration- the carpets, the fabrics, the gadgets, and the wood.

"Want one?" he asked, thrusting a pack of cigarettes in front of me and exhaling a thick cloud of hazy smoke.

"I don't smoke."

"I know that, but you should, it will relax you."

Reluctantly, I accepted one and reached out for the lighter.

"They say a gentleman always lights a ladies cigarette," he said sparking the end.

I sucked on the filter, allowing the rancid smoke to fill my lungs. I gagged. A fit of coughing followed, and when it finally subsided, I caught David snickering back at me.

"Good shit," he laughed. "Now that I have you alone and the nicotine is loosening you up, tell me what the old sibyl said in regard to your future?"

I shuttered, reflecting back on the dancing French woman. "She said she knew what I saw in Adrian, but if I stayed with him I would die too soon."

David flinched and the twisted grin that accented his lovely face disappeared. "Are you sure that is what she said?" His thin arched eyebrows crinkled in doubt.

"Yes, she said that she could understand what I saw in him, but I would never be able to let him go," I replied exhaling a mighty lung full of menthol smoke.

"Shit," he said in disgust. We sat for several minutes saying nothing, smoking our cigarettes.

"Aren't you worried that someone will see us out here smoking?"

He flicked his Newport out the window. "Just worry about what I think of you." The tires rotated rapidly, spitting gravel, as he jetted from the parking lot.

"What do you think of me?"

"I think I'd like to keep you around for a long time." His voice was extremely inviting: deep, consistent, and pure. I nearly fainted. As we raced through town, I couldn't help but notice the way the passing lights gleamed off his flawless skin. I wanted to reach out and graze my fingers across his exposed forearms, but I restrained myself. We turned off of Main St and fishtailed onto Big Bend. The engine roared and screamed, and the faster we accelerated the more I wished we could spend more time together.

"What do you think of Madam Therriot's vision?" I questioned, afraid of his reply.

He sighed and drummed his fingers on the wood-grain steering wheel. "I think what she said will take further examination." He broke eye contact and redirected his focus on the winding road ahead of us.

"I live just over this next hill," I said with a reluctant air. I loved the time that I was with David, and I hated that it would soon commence. A radiant smile spread across his face, exposing two playful dimples. He whipped the Camaro down my steep double driveway and we sat in the darkness, where all was still except for the low hum of the mighty V-8 engine.

"Tomorrow then?"

"Oh, the track meet," he grinned. "Yea, I told Tony I

would be there to support him."

"Great," I said relieved. At least I would get to see him again; although, it would make it rather difficult to concentrate on hitting my mark, knowing he was watching me. *Quit being so egotistical. Who is to say that he even will be paying attention to what events I'm doing? He just said he was going there for Tony- pole vault is more entertaining anyways.* I stumbled out of the car and slammed the heavy door shut behind me.

"Now I have more important and pressing reasons to go," he said in a serious tone.

"What reasons?"

"Do you think that I would miss you, sporting a pair of skin tight spandex shorts?"

My mouth fell open in shock. I couldn't believe that David had been so imprudent, and before I could give him a feisty reply, he flipped the car in reverse and I could hear him laughing as he sped away into the darkness.

ATHLETIC ENDEAVORS

May 25, 2002

I slipped into the house quietly, passing my father's study on the way down the secondary hall in our restored Tudor home. He was at his desk, smoking a Cuban cigar and drinking a tumbler of brandy. I could hear him mumbling to himself agitated. I sighed- another speech he was preparing for. The hall branched off again, and taking a short cut through the library- my favorite room of the house which owned such marvels as a first edition copy of Pride and Prejudice, a hand scrawled manuscript of Alice's Adventures in Wonderland, and my favorite, a first British edition of Virginia Woolf's To the Lighthouse-I made my way up the ancient stone steps which wrapped up and around the back portion of the house and led to the second floor. My room was the second door on the left, one of six bedrooms on the upper level.

     I began my typical routine of packing my sports bag for the track meet tomorrow. It was as if I was in a trance, systematically placing item after item in its proper place. I quickly scanned my email to see if anything interesting was waiting in my inbox, but no such luck. My conversation with Adrian was dull and brief- he had decided to spend the night at

Eric and Steve's house and said that he would see me sometime tomorrow- he mentioned nothing of crashing the festival and looking for me there.

That night I could barely sleep. I tossed and turned for what seemed like hours, but each time I glanced across the room, allowing my eyes to focus on the alarm clock which was positioned on my computer desk, only a few minutes had elapsed. Inwardly I was content- knowing that the festival was a great success. I would have to thank Cameron tomorrow for supplying a wonderful theme idea and all her hard work bringing Vanity Fair to life. Around 3:00 AM I finally fell into a deep sleep.

David is in front of me. He is only an arm's length away. I reach for him but he is just out of my reach. I am drifting away from him. No….I am so close. Further and further- the gap between us widens. Out of the sky soars a massive black raven. It swoops down and grabs me at the waist. Its powerful talons dig into my flesh. We glide through the air. With a painful thud, I'm dropped to the ground at David's feet. The sooty bird bobs its head at me. A forceful thrust- David is on top of me…kissing me…touching me… inside of me.

I jumped- something vibrated under my pillow. *It had to be my phone.* I found it at last and checking the caller ID I recognized the number blinking across the screen. It was Tony. "Hello," I said groggily.

"I should have known that you were sleeping," he said softly. "I just wanted to make sure that everything was okay and that got home safe. I talked to David a little bit ago and he told me what happened at the festival. Adrian came looking for you?"

"Yea, everything is fine," I replied a little more coherent. "I had a really nice time with your friend David; except, he talked me into getting my fortune read by some old French gypsy, Madam Therriot.

"Madam who?"

"Therriot," I repeated. "Don't tell me that you didn't see the obnoxiously purple tent with the big sign in front?"

"No, unfortunately I missed that one. I'm kind of upset

by that too. I wanted to have my fortune told."

"Trust me," I said dryly, "the only thing you missed was her babbling and dancing like a genie in a bottle."

Tony laughed heartily and when he had recovered said, "I would have loved to see your face while all that was going on."

"If I recall, you were too busy sticking your nose up Vicki Tinsdale's ass," I said coolly.

"Okay, where is this coming from?" Tony asked turning defensive.

"I know you like her. I can hook you guys up if you want me to."

"Vicki is a cool girl, but she isn't really my type," Tony replied.

Our tense conversation lasted only a few minutes more. I wanted desperately to fall back into my virile dream; but again, I couldn't sleep. Mentally frustrated, I lay awake cursing my current emotional dilemma. I was stuck in a relationship that I desperately wanted out of. Although the thoughts of hating Adrian snaked through my head, nothing preoccupied my mind as much as David. It felt as if I had known him all my life, as if all this time, he had been an intricate part of it. I had met him only a few short hours ago, but I could not deny the fact that from the moment I laid eyes on him I loved him. I shivered and pulled the covers closer to my chin. I love him. I was absolutely certain that I did. His beauty was unsurpassable: the crystal eyes of his had lured me in like the cerulean ocean-swallowing its victims and never letting go. I had never met someone so ethereal.

I couldn't help but smile as I replayed the night's events over and over. His fervid face burned fresh in my mind, and I could not help but wonder what it would be like to wrap my arms around him. I wanted to breathe in his divine smell; I wanted to feel his warm smooth hand in mine. I wanted more than anything to be with him again. My heart raced as I thought to tomorrow- he had promised to see me then. As I closed my eyes, for the final time that night, I firmly decided that David must be an angel. Every hair on his delicate head was a strand of glistening sunlight. Every inch of his skin was unblemished and fair, as if he had gone through his life escaping the common cuts and bruises of childhood. His proportions were distributed exactly, as if a mathematician had applied a complex formula in creating him. The elevated manner in which he walked was notable, though it reeked of neither pride nor condescension. I drifted off to sleep knowing that I would love him for the rest of my life.

I awoke the next morning to a fine northeastern Ohio spring morning. The sun's beaming rays peeked through the window blinds across from my bed, and I shielded my eyes from their blinding light. I was up before my alarm had sounded, an occasion strictly out of the ordinary. I sludged out of bed and made my way to the cluttered computer desk in the corner. A mural of photographs hanging on the adjacent wall greeted me. There were several team pictures, ranging in years- volleyball, track, basketball, and cross country; there was an array of candid shots: Cameron hanging out the window of her boyfriend, LJ's car, Lauren hugging Stacy in the school cafeteria, Vicki at a drama recital in the auditorium, and Tony flexing his muscles for the camera, holding his shoulder pads in one arm and his helmet in the other. Several photos were grouped together of the winter homecoming and St George's annual masquerade ball, and then there were the pictures of Adrian and me. We looked happy together in all of the pictures- a convenient façade.

I decided to check my instant messenger before showering and eating breakfast. Like so many things in my life, it was a routine. AOL instant messenger was the only place that I did not have to hide. Adrian didn't have a profile so I never had to worry while chatting with friends. I had several messages and read them all quickly. Most were from my friends at St. George's wishing me good luck at the track meet today. Tony had also left me a message asking if I wanted to come to his house that night for a party the wrestling team was throwing. *Hmm...I would have to think of a way to do that.* I grabbed my uniform and warm ups and headed to the bathroom to get ready for the day. I emerged twenty minutes later; my hair wrapped securely in a towel, and began doing my makeup. I had plenty of time before I had to leave, and in the hopes that today would be my big day, I took extra care in applying my makeup and tying my hair into a stylish ponytail. Despite what I had said to Adrian, I always did want to look my best at the meets that Local attended because Tony and his friends would be there. When every strand of hair was in its place, I grabbed my track bag and spikes to head out the door. As I turned to leave, a message popped up on my computer screen.

Huntsmen12: did you think about me last night?

I blushed and sat down once more at my desk.

Autumnallstar: who is this?

I waited impatiently for a few moments until the reply came, and my heart jumped into my throat.

Huntsmen12: DAVID…did you forget me already?

Autumnallstar: how did you get my screen name?

I ignored the second part of his response.

Huntsmen12: Well let me see…not that I needed help attaining it, but I got it from Tony.

Autumnallstar: I see…it's nice of you to check up on me

Huntsmen12: Sarcasim- I love it

I rolled my eyes in frustration. Why was he so hard to interpret?

Autumnallstar: Yea, I was just getting ready to get some breakfast and head over to St. George's

Huntsmen12: I figured that. Big day for you. For some reason I just have the feeling that you are going to do outstanding today.

I smiled, he was so sweet. I was glad that he was so confident because in the back of my mind I knew today would be a very difficult day for me. I was up against the best long jumper in the state and our relay teams would struggle against Local.

Autumnallstar: I hope you're right. So I'll see you there?

Huntsmen12: No…I will see you in ten minutes because I'm coming over to take you to breakfast.

I froze. There was no way possible that I could go out to eat with David. I shook my head. Didn't he get that I had a boyfriend?

Autumnallstar: Not a good idea. I'm with Adrian remember?

Huntsmen12: I don't forget anything. See you in a few.

I sent him a message reiterating my concerns, but he had already signed off his computer. I cursed David and his deviant intentions. If he only he knew how bad things would be for me if Adrian found out. Worried, I dialed Adrian on his cellphone and let it ring for over a minute before I hung up. It was no surprise that he didn't answer. It was nearing 8:00 AM- much earlier than his lazy ass ever got out of bed. I descended the stairs with my bag over my shoulder and my CD player in hand. I bounded into the kitchen and plopped down on one of the tall chairs behind the breakfast bar.

"Good morning sweetheart," my dad said barely looking at me from behind his newspaper.

"Are you all set for your big day today?" my mother asked placing a steaming bowl of oatmeal in front of me.

"I guess so," I said eating a spoon full.

"Of course she is Denise," my father replied peering over the paper for a brief second. "Don't you look just lovely today."

A waxy smiled smeared across my mother's face as she primly sat in the chair next to me, "your father is a little

28

preoccupied this morning."

"Why?" I asked disinterested.

"I received a call this morning from Washington," he said happily, "they want me to speak at the black tie gala at the Embassy tomorrow night."

"That's great dad," I said insincerely, pushing my oatmeal away. My father, Dr. Bellino Marseille, had been a State Representative for the 51st District for over fifteen years and was well respected in Osnaburg Township as well as highly connected in Washington D.C.

Folding his paper, my father looked at me and said, "I expect great things from you today my dear, and your mother and I both regret that we won't be able to attend today."

"I wouldn't expect anything different."

"Autumn, you barely touched your food," my mother scolded.

"Mom, I'm going to breakfast with one of my friends." I grabbed my bag and headed toward the front door.

"We won't see you this weekend either dear," my mother said following me to the door. She was involved in so many charity organizations and clubs that I could never keep them straight.

I didn't remember. "What do you have going on now mother?" I shot her a questioning stare.

"Well, with the gala in Washington tomorrow night tonight and the benefit for the Southern Ohio Wildlife Conservatory the following evening in Marietta, we decided to make a weekend of it."

I nodded.

"We'll be back in a few days," she cooed stroking my hair.

I rolled my eyes at her. "Great, I will see you later then," I replied and shut the door behind me.

David was already waiting for me in the driveway. A distressing knot formed in my stomach and I suddenly had the urge to vomit. I was nervous to see him again, even though I had spent all night tossing and turning over him. I approached

29

the car dubiously and pretended to fumble for something in my bag as I sank into the car's plush leather seats.

"Good morning princess," he said grinning.

I had planned on staring ahead and diverting my eyes from his, but his smooth, enticing voice drew me in and I turned to face him. I nearly fainted. He was more beautiful today than he had been yesterday, if that were possible. His flaxen hair was covered with a light blue baseball cap and his skin looked almost translucent paired with a cream and light blue polo shirt. I was in complete awe, and sensing that my jaw was gaping open, I quickly looked down, acting as if I were still preoccupied with finding something in my bag.

He laughed, and we pulled out of the driveway. "I was thinking we could go to that little diner in Meriton. I know that you don't really want to be seen with me, but humor me Autumn."

His comment stung. *Did he really think that I didn't enjoy his company?* "It's just that you are new in town, and you really don't understand my situation," I said avoiding his cutting eyes.

"I fully understand your situation. You are with someone that you hate. You stay with this person out of guilt and unintelligible regret." It was as if he had known Adrian and me our entire lives. Tony must have told him about us.

"Why are you doing that?" he questioned.

"Doing what?"

"You never look at me," he said vexed.

We were nearing the diner and the closer we got to our final destination, the more the knot inside of me tightened. My mouth was dry and my hands were beginning to sweat from nervousness. "I don't know what you mean," I said deliberately meeting his glance. "I was looking for something in my bag."

"I know I'm not much to look at so I don't blame you."

What did he mean by that? His modesty was false and his attempt to pacify me only added to my frustration. David was, by far, the most attractive person I had ever met. He certainly did not appear to have low self-esteem or insecurity issues.

Maybe he was simply trying to come down to Earth with the other peons- like me. In so many ways it did not fit- he was too perfect- he had to know it.

As we pulled into the diner's parking lot and made our way inside, I was determined to uncover as much as I could about David. The diner was already busy, filled with mostly cute little senior citizens enjoying their morning coffee and bland breakfast bagels. The fans above our head circulated a welcoming, cool breeze and the noise of the kitchen staff could be heard over the soft riff of the juke box in the corner. I barely acknowledged our waitress as she approached our table. I didn't hear what David ordered, but I nodded that I wanted the same. As she waddled away, I turned to David and said. "So you moved to Osnaburg from where?"

He flashed his hiemal eyes at me and I could almost feel their sting. "Here and there. My family and I are kind of wanderers."

I waited for him to continue but he didn't- he continued to stare. "I see, so do you like it here?"

"There are some things I like and some things I don't like."

He was being curt, avoiding directly answering my questions. "Have you made many friends?"

"Friends? Friends are never hard for me to come by," he said shooting me a devilish grin.

"I can see why," I retorted accepting my coffee from the waitress who had returned with a tray of beverages and toast.

"I doubt that," he said helping himself to a piece of toast and pouring cream in both of our coffee cups.

The waitress said she would return shortly with our meals and smiled toothlessly at David. He nodded at her in return.

"I bet most of your friends are of the female gender," I said playfully.

"Why do you assume that?"

"I'm sure most girls find you handsome."

"I have just as many girl friends as guy friends."

"Well aren't you popular!"

"They are all jinn," he mumbled, "people see what they want to see."

We were silent until our food arrived: eggs over medium, bacon, and hash browns. I wanted to ask him so many questions, but his flat and non-descriptive answers intimidated me. He smirked at me from across the table and said very little the remainder of the meal. I stepped outside the diner for some much needed fresh air the moment old Helga, as her name tag declared, cleared the plates from the table. I was beginning to think it an opportunity lost; not to press him further, I wanted to know everything about him, but he wasn't letting me in. I was disheartened. It felt as if I had no choice but to open up to him, but in return, he remained guarded and coy. I watched him from the car as he lit a cigarette and gazed keenly at the people walking across the boulevard. I thought I could discern an occasional change in his demeanor- his lips would slightly purse and a hint of amusement would cross his face.

I tried dialing Adrian again but got nothing. It was after 9:30 AM. I shrugged, he probably was still asleep.

"Who are you calling?" David asked getting into the car and snapping on his seatbelt.

"Adrian, but he still isn't answering."

He sniggered and pulled his ball cap lower on his brow. "No surprise there."

"You seem to know a lot about him."

"You have no idea."

I stood on the elevated platform and accepted my medal graciously. I had won the Regional track meet, on my home turf, with a distance surpassing St. George's school record by over a foot and a half. The speakers crackled to life and the announcer hacked his way through my French surname, announcing me the victor of the long jump and Regional Championship MVP. The winning distance, my second jump of the semifinal flight, had come only moments after Trisha Pritchard, the most consistent and talented jumper in the State, was walked out of the sandpit with what appeared to be a grave meniscal injury. But, I had won none-the-less- and that is all that mattered-except the pretension that rose up and shouted- David was watching!

My eyes wandered through the crowds of spectators standing along the fence which stretched the circumference of the track, the opposing teams' tents that dotted the hillside beyond the visitor end zone, and the vast wave of supporters who flowed in and out of the bleachers like the steady ocean tide. I hadn't seen him since the long jump semifinals and with all the commotion of athletic trainers and ambulance personnel assisting Trisha, I had lost track of him. I had hoped that because Adrian hadn't shown up, he would have approached me- spoke to me, but instead he was blatantly avoiding me. I didn't understand why. We had such an enjoyable time last night, and he had taken me to breakfast too. *Maybe he was offended by our conversation earlier?* I caught a glimpse of his gleaming blonde hair and settled my roving eyes on him. He was across the field in the concession stand line, and I was determined to make my way over to him and instigate a conversation. I felt compelled to be near him again and hear his low and deliberate words. I couldn't stop thinking about him; he had charmed me from the moment I laid eyes on him, captivated my heart and my thoughts, and even knowing this I couldn't get enough of him. Hastily, I grabbed my belongings and dusting the sand from my bronzed legs; I cut across the two hundred meter start area and headed toward the concession stand.

David was leaning against the outer stadium fence with his back turned to me. Just behind the fence, in the gravel parking lot stood a couple and another young man who were conversing with him. The couple looked to be in their early twenties and very much in love. The girl, who had chin length black hair with white globby streaks, had her arm affectionately intertwined with her mate. She was tall and voluptuous, with deep-set sod eyes, a leather corset, and matching shorts which screamed for attention. Her boy-toy was athletically built, with matching green eyes, a comic tee, black leather pants, and fiery, artificial red hair. The second male was older, perhaps in his mid to late twenties, and towered over David. His dark chocolate skin seemed to be pulled tightly over the bulging muscles which accented his thick figure. I shuddered as I looked past David and connected with his eyes which hosted corneas that were so light they drowned into white.

I heard the redhead say, "I'm sorry we couldn't meet last night but there were urgent matters to attend to."

Zebra girl added, "we were all very busy."

The three of them looked down to the ground, as a young child does when they are chastised.

"As you can see, I've been busy here today. I'm always busy, but there are important things to discuss."

White eyes nudged David through the fence. "We have company," he mouthed.

David jerked his head around and glared at me. "We can finish this discussion later. In the meantime, I want you to back off."

Something in his reaction caused me to repeal back in uncertainty; but to my relief, his three acquaintances- with their heads bowed low sulked away.

David shook his head at them, disgusted, and then casually walked toward me.

"Were you ignoring me on purpose because it certainly felt that way," I said wounded.

"Autumn, you would know if I were doing something to you on purpose. I have a lot going on right now, but that doesn't mean that I am ignoring you."

"Who were those people you were talking to?" I asked pointing to the three disappearing out of sight.

"The royal pair: Mara and his wife Lamia, and Stolas. They are close friends of mine," he said and a twisted grin spread over his face.

"I've never seen them before. Are they here visiting you and your family?"

"They just can't get enough of me," he laughed. "Yes

they are visiting and will probably be around for some time."

"You were being modest earlier when you denied that people are attracted to you. I mean, you have been in town less than two weeks and your friends already are flocking in for a visit."

"I figure why be honest with you when you aren't honest with me."

"What does that mean?" I said in a shrill voice. I was beginning to see that David was quite proficient at convoluting the things I said to his better advantage.

"It means that what you really want to say is that you are attracted to me, and you are looking for a way to be with me."

I decided to go along. "You're exactly right. I want to be one of your close friends too."

"I won't let you."

Honestly...you tease? "I'm surprised that you associate with them, they try too hard to be perfect like you, but they are so beneath you."

"I've never been picky about who I associate with- them or jinn, but you're right, they are beneath me."

"What is jinn? You said that earlier at the diner this morning too."

"Oh, that is what my friends and I call everyone and anyone. Or would you prefer John and Jane Doe?"

It took all of my inner strength not to lunge out and bite off his luscious lips. "You are perfect," I whispered to him.

"I'm just for you," he said seductively.

I was about to ask him if he truly meant what he said or if he just wanted to play on words and my emotions, when I heard someone calling my name. It was coming from the side of the concession stand diagonal from us.

"Hold on," I said to David and jogged toward the outcry. I stopped outside the women's restroom. The line wrapped around to the back of the building and ended at the sidewalk. A few meters away I saw Eric and Steve Wise sitting on one of the benches, and as I drew closer I could distinguish a look of panic on both of their faces. "What's the matter?" I asked collapsing down next to them.

"You aint gonna like this," Steve said reluctantly.

"Where the hell is Adrian?" I shot back. "There better be a damn good reason he wasn't here. He knew how important this was to me."

"There was a problem last night," Eric said sheepishly.

"What kind of problem?" I asked, but it was beginning to sink in. Adrian had got himself in trouble with the police…again. "What the hell did he do this time?" Eric kicked several loose rocks from the sidewalk back into the crowded lot and Steve jammed a half smoked cigarette butt into a wide crack in the cement. They were silent. "For Christ sake!" I screamed. "I am so sick of bailing him out." I stood up and paced in front of them. "What the hell did he do this time-assault, underage consumption … what?"

Steve stood up and grabbed my arms to hold me still. "It's pretty bad this time Autumn."

A group of three middle school aged girls brushed past me, giggling, and headed for the restrooms- the same girls I had seen the night before at the festival with pleated skirts and white button shirts. At that moment, I wanted to turn and follow them inside- so I could puke, or scream, or both.

"We went with Adrian to pick up some stuff last night," Eric said.

"What kind of stuff?"

"Drugs," Eric said sheepishly.

"Holy shit!" Furious, I threw my arms in the air.

"Yea, he got the stuff but it was a setup. We were in the truck waiting for him and then the cops busted in for the raid.

"They got a warrant for us too," Steve added.

Unbelievable. I covered my face with my hands and tried to keep from hyperventilating with rage. "What are the charges?"

"Probably felony drug possession, disorderly conduct, assaulting a police officer, and god knows what else," Eric said quaking with fear. "We got to get out of here though. They've got to be looking for us now too."

"Felonies? He's a minor they can't be serious."

"This aint the first time that Adrian's been taken in," Steve retorted matter-of-factly.

"Don't remind me Steven," I said through clenched teeth. "Who do you think was always there to pick up the pieces? Let's go."

I sat in the driver seat of Eric and Steve's rusted F150 and waited for David to wander past us. Eric and Steve were engaged in a frantic dispute about what the next course of action should be. I tuned them out as David wandered past the driver side. He didn't slow. *Come here. Come here. I want you.* A sagacious expression was painted on his brow and an appetizing smirk slithered across his angelic face.

OBSESSION POSSESSION

May 25, 2002

I silently fumed as I drove to the holding station. I was relieved that we didn't have far to travel, Steve and Eric bickered loudly back and forth and a part of me contemplated slamming on the breaks, sending both seat beltless passengers through the windshield. I was quite familiar with the Osnaburg Township holding facility- I had been there on numerous occasions before. Six months ago Adrian had been caught at a party, one I was not invited to, intoxicated and I had been called at four in the morning to pick him up. Before that, he earned himself a complicity charge and community service. Two years ago he and a gang of his friends had assaulted a 13 year old boy, beating and robbing him of twenty seven dollars in a Wal-Mart parking lot. Every time I had come to his rescue and called my father who pulled more than one string to get him out of each mess. I was always the one who cared about him- even when his drunken father, abusive step-father, and bi-polar mother did not. Perhaps I always felt sorry for Adrian.

Walking into the holding station, I debated whether or not to call my father for another favor. In my way, I loved Adrian but my once unconditional love had bitterly turned into hate over the years. Each fight, each nasty and hurtful word that had ever vomited from his mouth, rushed through my mind at once with Madam Therriot's heinous omen echoing in my ears. I decided not to involve my father this time. If things were really as dreadful as Eric and Steve said, I certainly didn't want either one of my parents knowing about it. My father, in the past, had dismissed Adrian's rebellious behavior as kid stuff- boys will be boys mentality; my mother had always pitied him saying it was a shame that his parents had ruined him the way that they had. A part of me agreed with them-for years I empathized with Adrian and his poor upbringing- but today, the darker side of me prevailed. I would not help him this time. I would finally teach him a lesson.

"May I help you?" The heavy-set officer behind the counter asked.

"Good afternoon officer," I smiled sweetly, "I'm here to see a friend of mine Adrian Waters."

"Captain Murmur," he said grabbing a sign in sheet from a wire basket behind the desk, "can you escort Miss Marseille back?"

I scrawled my name on the sign in sheet and looked up to see the young soldier from the chin-up and recruiting booth moving toward me.

"Small world," he said. "We didn't have the opportunity to talk yesterday, but as fate would have it, we meet yet again." He opened the sliding gate and ushered me to follow him.

We had taken no more than fifteen strides before we reached the first holding cells.

"I volunteer here from time to time and I believe the last time I was here I had the pleasure of meeting Mr. Waters."

I spied Adrian in the third cell on the left. "I'm afraid that if you continue to do so, you will see him again as well," I replied.

"We are going to hold him here until tomorrow morning."

I reached out grabbing the sleeve of his course navy uniform. "Where are you taking him tomorrow?"

He scoffed, "That little bastard is finally going to get what he deserves. He's going to juvenile hall tomorrow and I've got a feeling he will be staying there for a while." He shook me off, leaving me standing in the back of the dirty little station staring at Adrian behind the rusted steel bars.

Adrian's wrathful eyes danced after the Captain who strutted back down the hallway whistling as we went. "Pig," he said directing his foul comments to Captain Murmur. He spit on the stained cement floor. "It's about time you got here."

"I just heard about what happened," I said leaning on the bars and reaching my hands through the narrow gaps. "Eric and Steve came to the track meet and told me you got into some trouble last night."

He rolled his eyes. "So what are you going to do to get me out of here?"

"Adrian, I don't even know, officially, what you are charged with. How the hell do you expect me to get you out? You can't keep screwing up and think, every time you are going to walk away with no consequences."

His face turned scarlet and slowly he rose to his feet. Harshly he grabbed my wrists and pulled me against the bars. "I know your daddy can make a couple of phone calls and put an end to this Autumn. People skate on charges much worse all the time."

My wrists burned from the pressure and I begged him to let me go. This only enraged him further, and he twisted his tightly clamped fingers back and forth blistering my skin. "Okay...okay," I pleaded. "Let me go and I'll see what I can do."

Reluctantly he released me. "Let daddy know I need help. I know that my assault and drug possession charge can be bumped down to a misdemeanor or something."

Fury and hate simmered inside of me and glancing to my swollen wrists I retreated and said, "I'm done Adrian; I can't do this with you anymore."

He gave me a confused look. "You can't do what?"

"I can't be with you anymore. I can't bail you out of

every shit storm you create for yourself," I wailed. "Every six months you do something completely senseless and end up here. You probably won't finish high school because you won't even show up. You hang around a bunch of losers who I'm almost ashamed to be seen with, all you want to do is sit around and play video games and do drugs, and you can't even hold down a lousy summer job because you're too lazy to wake up and go. I mean what did you think Adrian- that I was going to be okay with this forever?"

Abhorrence gradually surfaced in Adrian. The color drained from his sallow cheeks, he bit down on his lower lip angrily, and glared at me saying nothing.

Tears rolled down my cheeks as I stared at him and said the words that had been suppressed for too long. "Things change," I said hysterically divulging my true feelings. "We were just kids when we got together. Do you remember back then? Things were pure, simple, and good between us. We had so much fun then- what happened to that? Can you even remember what it feels like to actually care about me?"

His eyebrows crinkled and deep ceases formed across his forehead. "You are the one who doesn't care about me. What do you plan to do, leave me in here?"

I grabbed ahold of the bars to steady myself. "Adrian, I've done all I can for you. What have you ever done for me? I'm always the one making sacrifices and I'm tired of it."

"You're tired of it?" he squinted at me with unfeeling eyes.

"Yes, I'm tired of always giving and giving and receiving nothing back in return. Is it that hard for you to have one nice thing to say to me every day?" It took everything that I had not to reach through the bars and strangle him. "I'm the one who takes you to school every morning and picks you up afterward. I'm the one who gives you money all the time... and you just blow it on booze and drugs and god knows what else. I'm the one who bails you out every time you get in trouble and I'm the one who cooks for you, buys your clothes, and makes sure you have everything you need and want. I'm sick of providing for you Adrian. I'm not your mother and it's not my fault that you never had one."

"You bitch! Everything is your fault. All you do is try to control my life- don't even act like you do anything from the goodness of your heart. You are selfish and only give a damn about yourself. You think you're God Autumn but let me tell you, you're not nearly as great as you think you are."

Frustration overpowered me. *How dare he talk to me like this!* I had heard these and other painful words from him for years. Each one pricked my heart, time after time; the wounds remained acute and unhealed. His hatred had left a void in my life, and at this exact moment, I felt it expand even further. I stood for a moment and thought of David-his ocean eyes, his delicate skin, his sensitive and mysterious countenance. At that very moment, while hating Adrian and loving David, I had an epiphany. *I deserved to be happy. I deserved to love someone and I deserved to be loved.* I wasn't sure if David loved me the way that I loved him, but I was willing to let go of Adrian just for the slight possibility that maybe he could. "I'm sorry you feel that way about me," I whispered. "I'm sorry you don't see my worth- you never did." My pride was crushed by the realization that he never loved me- he only loved the idea of me. The anguish inside turned vengeful and I thirsted to retaliate against him. "It's good for you that you feel the way you do though," I said sarcastically. "It will make it that much easier for you to get over me. You're nothing but a sloth Adrian...a lazy...filthy...leech."

"Get over you? You're not going anywhere," he shot back.

"Watch me Adrian," I said rejoicing in the fact that he was behind bars and I wasn't. I turned to leave but his chilling words stopped me.

"You always take the easy way out Autumn- now and then. You wanted me to do it; you just never had the courage to do anything about it yourself. I did what you couldn't do," he sneered, "I know that you are not giving up on that dream that easily. You want another chance, and you need me to give that chance to you."

I swallowed the lump that had formed in my throat and I hated him even more. It was his way to always throw things- particularly that one thing- in my face whenever I dared speak of leaving him. This was not the first time that I had said I was breaking up with him. The last time I had, we had fought bitterly, and I ended up with a black eye. I had told everyone that I had accidently gotten hit at volleyball practice- a wild spike gone wrong- of course my parents and teachers believed me and my friends had not.

The thick metal bars served well as a barrier between us and for once I didn't fear Adrian. "You're obsessed with me Adrian. You don't really want me but you sure as hell don't want anyone else to have me. You think that you can keep me with you by reminding me of what a monster you are and how you mean to make things up to me. Well, let me fill you in on something- what was done in the past is in the past. I'm not going to live my life in the present, or base my future decisions holding on to the false hope that you are ever going to change. You are a liar; you are a terribly miserable, abusive, controlling hypocrite. All you've ever done is bring pain and suffering my way, and I'm not going to give you the chance to ever hurt me again. You ripped out my heart and you stomped all over it. You live with your decisions and I will live with mine."

"You will do whatever it is I tell you to do," he raged. "You aren't going anywhere. You are with me and that is how it always will be."

I shook my head at him and said nothing more.

The moments that followed were neither unexpected nor unentertaining. Adrian's temper finally gave way and the tantrum that ensued was nothing short of completely pathetic. He cursed and threw things about the holding cell. He kicked the walls and beat his fists against the bars. He tried to spit in my face. I stood there taking in his violence and inwardly agreed with Captain Murmur- *little bastard was going to get what he deserved.*

"You're mine," he cried. "You think you can just walk

44

away from me you dumb bitch? You're wrong! You're lucky...so lucky right now. I bet if I punched you right in your mouth you'd shut it and that would be the end of the conversation. I swear Autumn if I even hear that you are running around while I'm locked up you'll regret it. You will regret it when I get out!"

"I'm not your possession Adrian, and since you'll have a long time to sit and obsess over me while you're in juvie think about this- I'm in love with someone else."

I sat on the curb outside the tiny Arab owned convenience mart- the Duke- that was on the corner of 16th St. and Grace Ave. Eric and Steve had left me, the cowards, stranded and with no means to get back home. I had wandered across town going nowhere in particular- reflecting on my latest and most grandiose triumph- leaving Adrian. It hadn't been that hard, but I knew the worst was yet to come. The drug charge would be harder than he thought to overcome and with him being 17 I highly doubted that at this stage, the judge would show leniency. He would be locked up for a year at least. The notion of that was relieving, and for the first time in years, I felt a massive weight lifted off of my shoulders. *I was free! I could do whatever I pleased!* I sat and daydreamed about what I would accomplish. *How can I be with David?* It was disturbing, that my mind constantly drifted toward him. I thought about David nearly every second of the day. I could hardly keep him out of my mind long enough to speak or to eat. His luxuriously delectable scent lingered on my uniform and I instantly drew the front fabric of my shirt closer to my nose inhaling deeply. I could feel the void in my chest begin to shrink. I debated whether I should call David now- maybe he would come give me a ride. I was too nervous; it was unbearable to think about calling him. I was bound to be awkward, stuttering and stammering stupidly on the phone- it was a chance I wasn't sure I was ready to take.

I wouldn't have to, as it were, for as I looked down the lonely sidewalk, it seemed to illuminate with his glorious presence. I studied his walk intently as he neared me- every movement was graceful and strong. I wasn't even sure his feet touched the Earth, but if they did, I was sure to worship the ground he walked on. I was determined to breech his reserved exterior; I wanted to be invited in to his world. He, above anyone, could make me happy, and I was convinced that if given ample opportunity I could make him happy too. I would do anything to be close to him- I could live in his wonder- I would go wherever he would take me. He was my obsession and I longed to be his possession.

THE SILVER NECKLACE

May 25, 2002

"What are you doing on this side of town?" David asked. "You left the track meet with those guys in a hurry. Is everything okay?"

"No, not really," I mumbled keeping my eyes focused on my feet.

We paused in front of a two-story brick colonial with a wide wrap around porch and steep steps which led from the street and connected to the front entrance way. A large birch provided ample shade to the side of the house and porch where a rickety swing swayed in the afternoon breeze. Thick shrubbery lined the solid foundation and grew wildly alongside its base. Healthy rose bushes accented the slight walkway and flower beds which twisted alongside the rear of the establishment.

"Will you tell me what happened at least?" he pressed. "Maybe I can help."

"Maybe later," I replied and began to ascend the steps. A thunderous growl froze me in my tracks. The ominous sound intensified, the rumble produced, deep and heinous. Petrified, I began to slowly back pedal down the step.

"That's just my dog, Cerberus," David said reassuringly. At the sound of his name Cerberus emerged from the shadows, and to my surprise, he was far fiercer than I had imagined. At the withers he measured over three feet tall and weighed, I'd guess, over one hundred and fifty pounds. His body was long, muscular, and lean and the thick, short fur that covered his body was the deepest black. Red markings dotted his confident almond eyes and lined his strong muzzle. Pointed ears crowned his massive head and solid jaws exposed a set of razor sharp teeth. Cerberus inched closer to the edge of the porch, jutting out his wide chest that too was marked with red which flamed out and crept up his thick neck. The rusty markings on the lower region of each of his legs contrasted against his midnight coat and brought about a certain recollection of my old homeland- France.

I stared into Cerberus's unflinching eyes. "David... he reminds me of the French Shorthaired Shepherd I had as a child. Hero was his name, but he was only half the size of your beast."

"A Berger de Beauce," David confirmed taking my hand again to comfort me, "and your Hero- what became of him?"

"Another story for another time."

Understanding my uncertainty in the presence of his canine and suppressing the unspoken hurt surrounding my own childhood pet, David led me up the steps and onto the porch where we sat on the creaking swing. Cerberus had stepped aside, letting us pass easily enough, but now stood only a few feet away, his eyes intently fixated on me.

"Easy my un loyal... easy loyal one," David called softly. Cerberus dipped his mighty head and submissively approached us. Immediately, the great dog relaxed and the dense, raised fur on his back flattened, his ears dropped back, his lips uncurled from his teeth.

"My loyal bas rouge," David said approvingly rubbing between his ears. With Cerberus at ease, David pulled me to my feet and lovingly embraced me. We kissed- sweetly- passionately- lustfully. The sand in the hour glass ceased to fall for those precious moments, and even Father Time himself stepped aside. That first kiss was one of many experiences with David that I would bottle up, preserve, keep safe, and manically love for the rest of my life.

Cerberus circled me, still cautious, turned and led the way up to the front door.

"I had no idea you spoke French," I said to David while still eyeing his loyal one.

David chuckled as he unlocked the handle. "Yes, that and many others."

I shook my head amazed. Not only was David gorgeous, intelligent, and kind; but he also reminded me of everything I missed from home. As I entered his century home, I wondered what other intrigues I would learn about him.

The house was old and still, the white plaster walls were a discolored shade of corn flour and the hardwood floors beneath our feet creaked and moaned beneath our weight. From the foyer I could discern the general layout of the first floor- there was a spacious living room, a cozy sitting room that branched off the far side of the house, a rather grand dining room equipped with a crystal chandelier and an antique curio which displayed a fine set of plate and silver. A winding staircase was situated on the right side of the living room and curled its way to a sizable landing on the second floor. David's home was not at all what I had expected; it was a hidden gem amongst the other decaying homes in the neighborhood. From the outside it was nothing more than a sagging, turn of the century colonial, but on the inside it was bursting with charm and charisma. Each room in the house was breathtaking and encompassed a unique genre, age, and style.

"Did your mom do all this?" I asked touring the various rooms on the first level.

"No. I did actually."

The living room resembled the 19th century Victorian era, complete with bold, floral print wall paper, crown molding, decorative archways, and beautiful area rugs. "This furniture seems to be a perfect replica of the 1800 English style," I said recalling all I had learned in my British Literature class and running my hands over the rich fabric of the straight back chairs that were placed conveniently in front of the fire place.

"That's because they were made in 1817 by the best craftsmen in Kilburn England at the time- Old Topps," he said matter-of-factly.

I noted the dated photographs which hid behind thick bronze frames, and various decorative pieces that cluttered the mantel piece. "These pieces are priceless," I said in awe as I explored the various porcelain figurines, vases, and wall hangings. "They must have been in your family for decades."

"A small piece of my history," he said taking a seat on the velvet embroidered chaise lounge near the center of the room. Cerberus, the loyal bas rouge companion, sat at his master's feet and continued to eye me closely without any signs of outward aggression; thus, putting me at ease to further probe the treasures of the historic abode.

The dining room was fashioned after the elegance of old France. The color scheme of gold and black provided the dining room with a reserved feel, and the assortment of fine china and crystal contrasted nicely against the dark table linens and tasteful tapestries which adorned the walls. Beyond the dining area was a small sitting room modeled after the 1970's American mod era. Everything was black and white, from the shiny black marble floor to the swirling white painted ceiling. The couches were sleek black leather and were situated on top of a lamb white shag rug. Although the sitting room was not styled after my taste, I was impressed by the precision and care in which it was designed. In contrast, the kitchen was updated with the very best that 21st century technology could afford. Cherry cabinets paired with speckled granite countertops were focal points in the room along with matching stainless steel Whirlpool appliances.

Just as I approached the bathroom, I felt a chill and turning abruptly, I was astonished to find myself nose to nose with David. Flustered, I sucked in a rattling gasp of air, I was frozen, mesmerized by wide blue eyes and his seductive smell.

"So what do you think?"

"I think this house and everything in it is absolutely amazing."

"It is an extensive collection isn't it?" he agreed. "You haven't seen the half of it. Sometime I will have to show you everything, but not today, I don't think you have time today to see it all."

"How is it that your family was able to keep all this stuff and pass it down through the generations?"

"Possessions…we are always able to keep what is truly important to us," he whispered leaning in and brushing his soft cheek against mine. His full lips pecked my cheek and slid down my neck. I could feel goosebumps begin to form on my arms as David caressed my neck and chest.

Had I died and gone to heaven?

"It all comes down to obsessions Autumn. The things you own, always come back to own you."

I had just had a conversation with Adrian about this very topic. How was it that David was now talking to me about the same thing? I wanted to ask him, but my thoughts were hazy and unorganized.

"Follow me," he said taking my hand.

I will follow you to the end of the Earth and back.

The open floor plan of the house allowed us to circle back to the living room quickly and we ascended the archaic spiral staircase to the wide landing of the second floor.

"Won't your parents be mad if they come home," I asked worried. "They've never met me before and I probably shouldn't be up here, in your room, while they're out."

The devilish smirk was back, "I'm my own keeper."

"No really," I said, "I don't think this is a good idea." I was more anxious of being alone with David than being caught by his parents, but it sounded like a better excuse.

"Is that what's really bothering you?" he asked climbing on his bed and majestically reclining on the pillows against the headboard.

Cerberus positioned himself in front of the window

which faced out toward the street. He nuzzled his way behind the long damask curtain and seemed content to watch the empty street below.

"Of course," I lied.

"We all are free to make our own decisions Autumn. It should never be the opinion of others that concerns you, as long as you are prepared to live with your consequences...well it will always be worth it."

"Do you really believe that?" I asked.

"I didn't believe it for most of my life, but now, I can honestly say that I do," he motioned for me to sit next to him on the bed.

"You have an odd way of looking of things," I said sitting next to him and placing my head in the nook that formed between his chin and chest.

"I'm not alone in my presumptions about the world."

"Is that what you care about in life?" I asked curling myself closer to him.

"My interests are love and loyalty because everything else slowly fades away."

His sagacity was both insightful and clever. David was by far the most intriguing person I had ever met, and I felt blessed to be in his presence. I could have spent all of eternity in this way- snuggled next to him. When I was with David, time seemed to speed by and juxtaposed we were jarred and stored in the moment. In my vulnerable state, I lay with David and told him about my volatile relationship with Adrian and cried as I explained our bitter break up.

He clutched me tightly and listened, he softly stroked my forehead, he was the perfect shoulder for me to cry on. "I'm sorry for that princess," he said when I had finished.

"It's not your fault," I sniveled.

"Be with me then," he said unwrapping my arms from around him. "Be with me forever."

I sobbed uncontrollably. *Is this real? Is it possible that David could love...me?*

"I wanted to give you this," he said reaching into his

pocket.

I opened my hand, and into it he placed a dazzling silver necklace. It was extremely heavy, fashioned into the shape of an Old English letter D, and accented with hundreds of diamonds in various dimensions. The chain that hung from it was equal to the pendant in weight, age, and splendor. "It's gorgeous," I gasped, "it must have cost you a fortune."

"Its price reaches far above the intrinsic," David sneered fastening it around my neck.

"It's so heavy," I said admiring the way that the diamonds danced with the light across the bedroom walls.

"Like the weight of the world. But don't fret my love, after some time; you will barely notice that it's there."

I doubt that! "I will always remember it's there because you gave it to me David. I love it and I love you," I said swinging my arms around him. *How could someone so perfect and beautiful want me?*

Effortlessly, David pulled me on top of him. He unzipped my warm-up jacket and began to softly massage my shoulders and arms. He cradled my chin in his strong hands and pulled my face close to his. We kissed and my hands roamed uncontrollably over his face and chest, and my desire to feel his skin underneath his polo shirt caused my hands to shake. *Am I too bold? Go for it...do it!* I latched my lips onto David's neck and forcefully began to suck.

"Show me how you really feel," he teased.

Thoughts of David's naked body flashed through my mind and I almost urinated with excitement. I had never felt this type of attraction before. My fingers trickled down his collar bone; I tapped them rhythmically past his nipples and across his firm stomach. I paused as they reached his belt buckle, and I waited for him to voice any opposition. I could feel myself losing control. *I want you in so many ways- not just sexual ways- I want you until the day I die.* After loosening his belt and undoing his pants, I pulled his shirt over his head, exposing his bare chest.

"You're beautiful," I said kissing his heart shaped lips.

"Beauty is in the eye of the beholder," he smirked lifting my uniform top over my head. "Trust me, you are more than beautiful- beautiful means nothing- you Autumn," he whispered nibbling on my ear. "You are very special to me."

The throaty eruption from Cerberus caused me to jump. His slightly hunched body was rigid, and his austere barking alert grew louder as seconds elapsed. I leapt off of David's lap and frantically searched for my shirt, aware that my behavior was not what it should have been, and disappointed in myself for allowing my sensibilities to rule my actions.

"Wait here," David instructed heading for the door and whistling for Cerberus to follow. Nervously, I fingered the beautiful silver necklace which hung like lead around my neck. Several minutes passed and curious to see who was outside, I snuck to the window and parted the curtain. David stood on the porch, Cerberus at his side, bare chested- his chiseled body lucent and breathtaking. I began to doubt whether David and I could be together after all. *I don't deserve him. I am inferior.* The three that I had seen talking with David at the track meet were circled around him. I secretively watched David smoke his cigarette, and while he spoke, stroke the head of the bas rouge who guarded him protectively by placing himself between Lamia, Mara, and Stolas.

I tried to twist the knob at the top of the window in a failed attempt to open it. I wanted to hear the conversation, but as hard as I tried I could not pry the window up. Frustrated, I watched David flick his cigarette at the three and slam the front door in their faces. They stood for moment, blankly, after he retreated and in unison they all turned their heads to look up at me in the window.

CHIMERA

May 25, 2002

I shuddered and turned my face from the window, afraid to look back down upon the three infelicitous hostiles. Preoccupied by the thud of my heart crashing against my chest, I had not heard David sneak up behind me and wrap his chiseled arms tightly around my waist. I turned in surprise. "You seem to have fallen out with your old friends. Why did you turn them away like that?"

"It's no concern of yours princess," he said insouciantly and drawing me in close, kissed me on the forehead.

"They seem really angry," I said drawing the curtain back, but to my relief, the porch was empty.

"Those three breed rage. That's why I didn't let them in; I don't want them around to rub off on and influence you."

"I thought they were friends of yours? Why can't I meet them at least?"

"Yes, they are old and very close friends of mine; but, not all friends of mine can be friends of yours my love."

I started, "but David I don't see why," but he interrupted me before I could finish.

"I should take you home. You have a party to get ready

for."

I nodded, pulling myself away from his grasp. With the scattered and emotional events that had transpired, I had forgotten that the wrestling boys at Local had orchestrated a party that night at Tony's house. David's sweet fragrance tempted me to hold my ground, linger a while longer in the moment, but I fought temptation and reluctantly followed him back out into the spring sunshine.

I was relieved that my parents had been called out of town on business. A forced conversation about the track meet and my plans for the evening was not something I would have enjoyed. My conservative father would have frowned upon a night of frivolity. Having my parents out allowed me the solitude to reflect further on what had transpired earlier in the day. I searched the refrigerator in vain for several minutes before deciding to order a pizza from the small mom and pop shop on the edge of town. After showering and applying makeup, I changed into a pair of tight, dark blue jeans, a silver studded white tank-top, and matching silver studded strappy heels.

Ring…ring…rrriiinnnggg. The phone on the kitchen counter erupted in a series of increasingly annoying alerts. I checked the caller ID and sighed. It was a collect call from Adrian. "Yes, I accept the charges," I said into the receiver.

"I can't believe you showed up today just to tell me that you didn't want to be with me anymore," Adrian spat the moment the call was directed through.

"Can't you," I said slightly amused. I imagined Adrian huddled close to a germ infested public telephone in a dark and dirty hallway and almost burst out laughing. *Maybe he'll catch hepatitis in there. Sweet revenge.*

"Now that you say it like that, I actually can believe it Autumn. You always were a cold hearted bitch!"

You're right about that. My heart belongs to another. "What do you want Adrian?"

"You…I want you! I want you to say that we are still together."

"You're calling my house collect to ask me to stay with you? We haven't even been broke up a day Adrian!" *You weak-stupid-pitiful fool and all your envious anger.* "No, I will not say that we can be together. That's not what I want anymore." *Not even a little bit.* "I told you this already."

"You will always be mine."

Your wrathful love obsession is never ending. Goosebumps slowly rose on my forearms and uncertainty lingered. "There is nothing you can do about it Adrian." *You are in there and I'm out here.* "According to that handsome young soldier who volunteers at the holding station, Captain Murmur, you are going to be in the Pinehurst Juvenile Attention Center a long while, and guess what else? *I'm so glad!* I'm going to Tony Greggory's house tonight for a party he and the wrestling boys are putting on, and I think I have a date," I slammed the receiver down before I could hear Adrian's cursed response.

The sound of the doorbell startled me. I contemplated running upstairs to hide under my massive oak frame bed until I heard, "Vercelli's Pizza!" *Ahh...the pizza. I forgot I ordered that.* I fumbled to uncrumple the wadded bills that had been stuffed in my back jeans pocket. I swung open the front door, and before me stood- not Nicky our usual delivery boy- but the melancholy Captain Murmur. He said nothing, and in my state of utter surprise no words escaped from my lips either. *What are you doing here?* Before I could inquire as such of the steadfast soldier, he, in one fluid motion unholstered the nickel plated pistol which hung handsomely on his waist, placed it into his mouth, and pulled the trigger. Blood paint sprayed and with a glossy coat covered the front of my top, and brain matter dripped into chunky piles from his mouth cavity which was now blown completely open. Chards of thin burnt flesh flapped in the gentle evening breeze. That was all that was recognizable of the poor Captain's face. I witnessed in horror the small frame of the martyr finally give way and collapse. Trembling and unable to remove my eyes from the dead soldier's body, I watched as three young girls, clothed in plaid pleated skirts and starched white button shirts- wild and vagobonish- ambled down the drive. They moved like cockroaches, creeping on all fours, and snapped at one another as hungry hyenas do.... *God please help me!*

"Hey Autumn," Nicky the pizza delivery boy said shaking my arm concerned. "Are you alright Autumn? You kind of zoned out on me."

I wiped the beads of sweat from my forehead. There was no blood, no brains, no dead Captain Murmur, no ravenous beast-girls. There was only Nicky Vercelli and the green pepper, mushroom, and anchovy pizza I had ordered. "Sorry about that Nicky," I said relieved but still shaking. *Thank you.*

"Are your parents not home?" he asked trying to peek past me and into the foyer.

"No worries Nick, they left me some money. Certainly enough to cover a pizza."

"Look at you," he laughed.

"Yea, look at me," I said slapping a five dollar tip into his hand.

"Red eyes, paranoid, agitated...I won't tell your parents that you were smoking pot while they were gone," he said retreating to his delivery-mobile.

Go to hell. "Great Nicky, I appreciate that because I don't do drugs," I shouted back to him.

"Sure, that's what they all say."

Again I heard ringing in the background, and wrestling the oversized pizza box onto the dining room table, I lunged once more for the phone. "Hello," I said wincing in anticipation.

"You sound worried princess," the voice on the other end said. David's unexpected voice caused me to bobble the phone, my shaky hands failed, sending it plummeting onto the floor. I grabbed it quickly from the floor scrambling to recover.

"David, hi."

He was laughing, "I just called to tell you that I was planning on picking you up tonight...if that's okay with you."

If it's okay with me? Are you serious? "Of course," I gushed trying to mask my extreme delight but failing miserably.

"Everything okay love?"

"Yea, everything is fine. Better than fine actually," I said pushing the delusion of the wild she-beasts and the suicide of the noble Captain out of my mind. "I just told Adrian that I was going out to a party and that I thought I had a date."

"You thought you had a date? I told you before, I want so much more than that. I want you to be more than you ever can be."

Woodside Ave was lined with cars. My fellow classmates and those from Local had no regard for the other residents of Valley Hills, the small allotment in which the Greggory home was situated. Little consideration was given to Tony's neighbors, the short paved driveways were blocked and 50 Cent blared from the open windows of the first level Cape Cod. I immediately knew that tonight would be one that I would never forget. We were greeted at once by Tony's closest friend, the fellow wrestling extraordinaire Ramsey Sanders- or Ram as he was better known by, who sat on a worn folding lawn chair and balanced with all the grace six beers could afford, an open case of Natural Light. He was short and slim, muscular and lean- as many wrestlers are. His cappuccino skin, deep brown eyes, high distinctive cheek bones, squared chin and short wavy hair reflected his African American and German origin. It always amazed me that though boyishly handsome and athletically gifted, Ram was popular with both guys and girls alike. He was odd in his rudimentary mannerisms and even more so in his strange dress and general appearance. Daily, from 6:00 AM to an hour past, Ram could be spotted throughout Osnaburg running barefoot, shirtless, and in a pair tiny shorts resurrected from 1972. Rain, snow, or shine, Ram would run- it was rumored he ran over twenty miles a day. Tony claimed he ran eight every morning, before returning home to shower, dress in a tight polo shirt, sweatpants, and ratty Timberland hiking boots, and go to school.

"Welcome to the party mon," he said in his best Jamaican accent.

David and I laughed as he struggled to tame the fake dreadlock wig he often wore without falling from his seat.

"Beer?" the Rasta offered.

I hesitated; I had never been much of a drinker. *Would David think I was lame if I didn't drink it?* I felt a sharp nudge in my ribs.

"Drink up," David said flashing me a sparkling grin, "let me see what you've got".

I popped open the can and downed it. A single stream of fizzing hops ran down the side of my mouth and self-conscious, I quickly wiped it away with the back of my hand.

"Way to take it like a champ," the Rasta said slapping his knee with amusement. "Everyone has to down an introductory beer to get in, and let me tell you Autumn, you were the first to chug it all in one gulp." Next he presented David with a can, "for the newbie," he said still giggling and granted our passage.

I grabbed David's hand which was unusually cold and clammy and followed him up the driveway and around the pebble path leading behind the garage. Together, we wandered toward the back screened in patio- David lost in his thoughts and I wandering in his footsteps. We paused for a romantic kiss beside the small vegetable garden that was blooming with vine ripe tomatoes, string beans, and juicy summer squash, and then David pushed open the door and I followed him inside.

The music was gone, the people had disappeared- David and I were alone. Fear embraced me. I had been to Tony's home on several occasions before, his mother and my mother sat on the town's Garden and Lifestyle Committee. *We aren't at Tony's house at all!* A sickening feeling saturated my body and mind as I glanced around frantically trying to regain my bearings. We were back at David's house. *How could this be?* Colors began to bleed before me: reds, blues, and greens. The ceilings and the walls streamed color and the rich wood floors faded to black as the deep brown hues formed puddles and were eventually evaporated up. Color drained from the fabrics and furnishings, the china and draperies. It hung in the air-little droplets of life- and became smaller and smaller until there was only black. I screamed and closed my eyes and after waiting several moments, I opened them again.

I was on the floor in David's living room; surrounding me were the towering silhouettes of a crowd of people-hundreds and hundreds of people. As if in a zombie trance they groped for me, lashing out viciously, a wave of unstoppable cannibalistic fury. Frantically, I clenched my eyes shut. *Why am I on the floor? What the hell is going on?* David hovered over me shirtless and dipping his head down massaged his moist lips on mine. *Am I drunk? Maybe I blacked out at the party. Did David bring me back home...to his house?* He kissed me more passionately a second time. I allowed my impulses to take control over me. I closed my eyes and savored David's sweet kiss and warm embrace. I opened my eyes, but David was ...gone.

The game room in Tony's basement was alive with activity. Groups of students from Local and St. George's mingled next to the bar, which was loaded with fattening junk food and a bowl of spiked fruit punch. A competitive game of pool was underway in the back corner near the laundry area and the wrestling boy's simulated a match in the practice ring Tony's dad had assembled- before he left.

"I can't believe he called you after you broke up with him," Stacy said shifting her sizable weight on the bar stool and snacking steadily from a bag of Cool Ranch Doritos.

"I so can see him doing that," Cameron said turning her white dusted nose away from us to sniff down another fix.

"What an asshole," Lauren said touching up her makeup in the small mirror of her ivory compact.

"I can't believe you went down to the holding facility. What's next? You gonna visit his sorry ass in jail?"

"I know right," Vicki added, "I bet it was scary in there."

"What did you say to him?" Stacy asked with a mouth full of chips.

"I would have died to see his reaction," Cameron said with new found speed energy.

Sliding off her coveted seat, Stacy joined in circling around me.

No…no…no…not again….

Cameron, Stacy, Vicki, and Lauren had conspired to corner me somehow. I took several steps back until my back was pressed tightly against the wall. My eyes wandered back and forth slowly, I could see only in limited shades of black, grey, and white. My mouth fell open in complete disbelief as I stared at the altered state of my closest friends. I dug my fingernails into the drywall, I desperately needed to escape.

"What's wrong?" Stacy's skeleton asked. The skin hung in folds over what was left of her starved and wasted body.

"You don't look so good," Vicki's mouth stated. Her gaping skull was split across the forehead and in her hands she cradled her prized, mushy brain.

"Autumn…are you alright?" Lauren's mutilated figure asked as they closed in on me.

I was back on David's living room floor, naked and glistening with perspiration. Are bodies were meshed together- David and I. The floor was hard and cold, but I barely noticed. David was on top of me and was saying how much he loved me. His supple skin glided over my bare chest, over and over and over. *Is this real?* I stared into his soul penetrating eyes and nearly drown in them.

"You're amazing," David said after pulling his red polo shirt over his head and tightening his belt. *What is going on…what the hell is going on?* I sat up abruptly. It was just David and I alone in his big empty house. "I think I'll hide these," he said slyly picking up my jeans and tank top and devilshly dangling them just out of my reach.

I'm afraid…why is this happening? "David, please let's go," I begged tugging on the tail of his shirt. Tony's basement walls spun around me in disturbing shades of mud and silt as fiendish laughter filled my ears. *It's just a hallucination…it's not real…this is not real!*

62

"No, I think I'll have those back," I said snatching my loose clothing from his fingertips. I dressed hurriedly in the main bathroom and tried to make sense of the sudden changes that were happening to me. *I'm caught in a tornado, a destructive, unforgiving, and evil storm.* I splashed cold water on my face and hoped that it would help ground me. The entire night blended together into one magnificent cataclysm.

"Newport?" David asked lighting his and maneuvering his striped Camaro from the parked vehicles lining Woodside Ave.

David was waiting for me outside the bathroom door. He leaned in and placing the silver necklace rightfully around my neck said, "you took this off in the car and forgot to put it back on."

I watched Valley Hills allotment fade behind us. "Come back to my place," David enticed. His words were two times slower than normal, low and drawn out.

In rapture with you. "You gave me this gorgeous necklace and you tell me that you love me and want to be with me. Why me?"

As we turned off of Woodside Ave and onto East Maple, I cupped my tired head into my hands and focused on breathing slowly and calmly. We passed Local and continued down East Maple until we came to an idol stop light at the intersection of Maple and Main St. South. Suddenly, a vast shadow rose from the top of the street lamp, engulfing it and diffusing its light. Smash! My harrowing scream hung like London fog in the near summer's night. A massive raven, with greased feathers and a hook curved beak feverishly pecked at the windshield. "David!" I screamed out again. "Do something please!" Desperate, I turned to him. "My God!" I wailed. Crimson trails of nearly coagulated blood oozed from the hollow sockets of his bored out eyes. *I'm trapped in the horror again.* I wanted to scream and run- run far away, but I couldn't. Apart of me could not escape. I was ensnared in darkness, unable to flee my new-found reality.

I've waited an eternity to find someone like you," he

replied swooping me into his arms. I absorbed every possible sensation- from his sweet and spicy scent to the rhythmic beat of his heart. I was certain that David and I were a match made in heaven.

We screeched to a halt in front of David's house. Unable to move or speak, I remained in the vehicle in a state of shock.

"Here we are princess," David said opening the car door on the passenger side and lifting me over his shoulder. I was paralyzed with fear and did not protest. Raised purple veins slithered underneath the weathered skin of his gruesomely disfigured face. I vomited.

David paused at the door, and placed me on my unsteady feet again. Underneath the dim glow of the porch light, I realized that his skin was just as white and smooth as it had ever been. His face was clear, shining, and bright. His eyes deeply set, sparkling, and blue. *What is wrong with me? There is nothing wrong with David. Had there been no black bird set to try to kill me? My friends are alive and well- not disturbed and walking dead as I had thought. It is all just a chimera. Sleep…I just need sleep.*

That night, and two blue Xanax pills later, I was able to relax. I found comfort lying next to David. I forgot about the party, the delusions, and my love and hate relationship with Adrian. I nestled myself tightly in his arms and buried my face securely in the aroma of his feather down pillows. The room was dark and unfamiliar but I had never felt such tranquility and sanctuary. I had more than I ever dreamt could be possible; I had David. He was the substance that filled my void; everything pure, beautiful, and blissful like the twinkling morning star. I stroked my beloved silver necklace and found, because of David, there was more in my life than just love and hate. I fell asleep knowing I had love and loyalty.

INCUBUS

May 26, 2002

How innocent you look just lying there. Your weakness is most pathetic. You are beautiful, desirable, twisting and contorting as you sleep. Wait until they learn of the limited thoughts your mind possesses.

I will tell! I will tell…and if given the chance they will eat you alive.

I am a servant. You are a servant too.

You think you know. Think you have it all figure out. You haven't a clue. There is so much for you to see. What you have and hoard. Thank The Reign.

Until now.

It's gone too far and the masters are worried. You should be worried. They've seen your broken heart open wide and in just days you've indulged, swallowed, and had your fill. The power of treachery over your feeble soul. I fear somewhere along the way things have changed.

Our consumption- our gluttony has been suppressed. Devour you up!

Devour you up!

Devour you up!

What would you do if you saw me- hovering over you? Disturbing your dreams? Would you pass me off as just a nightmare? A terrible occurrence of the worst kind. The day trips you've taken are nothing. The things that haunt you now. You dismiss them as fantasy.

It's your reality.

You are unaware of my presence.

We all have a purpose.

We all have needs.

You think you are in love with him. Ah yes, you're watched from a distance. You know not love- you are just under his spell. His beauty is as fleeting as the wind.

The pleasure of how he torments you. Your blind love. Your selfish affection triggers a sense of pride.

Your lust.

Your commitment makes you all the more sexually appetizing.

But a link in the chain has been broken. You are the tested and I am the tester.

Recompense!

Your toxicity has polluted the natural order. For that I know you will have to pay. But that- like all things must come to an end.

The addiction.

My suspicion.

And you know too little of it. I will show you.

The monster that I am is the origin of the monster you have become.

What... what is that hanging from your neck? I must climb down from my perched position above you and examine it more closely. Could it be? It's heavy- it has born the weight of the world. Shiny silver, linked, ancient. Bearing the letter D and embezzled in diamonds.

He has given away the silver necklace!

The suspicions have been confirmed.

I now know what your heart is capable of and it is delightfully sickening. I shall make a habit of this- if they allow it- visiting you nightly.

Order shall be restored to our misery- our disarray.

They will…and I will help!

I can feel your sweet breath. His scent lingers on you. You wallow in it.

The time to strike is now. Now- on top of you.

Fragile and delicate.

Nightmare.

In your head.

I'm inside of you.

I know you feel me.

Don't fight.

Don't resist.

Nightmare.

Just despair.

It's happening.

Nightmare.

Right Here! Right Now!

And yes, I enjoy your pain- your fear.

This is only the beginning.

The Reign is here.

They rule over me.

They exist to destroy you.

I must make a thorough report. It is deeper…it is darker than anticipated.

Death.

Passion.

Decay.

Pity.

Sin… and much of it too!

In these challenging times- we must all learn to prey.

Wait!

He's coming. I'd know that stench anywhere.

Nightmare.

He's seeking me out.

There will be punishment.

You're protection.

Nightmare.

Your guardian is upon us. And I must flee.

The place beside me is cold, vacant bed.

David- gone- only the voice in my head.

WAKE UP MY LOVE.

There is distant shouting but it's too unclear to make out.

Scratching and clawing at the door too persistant to doubt.

HASTEN TO THE DOOR.

Quietly I obey and welcome in; my one and only true best friend.

FROM ME TO YOU.

Into my arms bounds Hero, excitedly wagging his tail.

Stroke his face, hold him tight, remembering I was the one to fail.

IT WASN'T YOUR FAULT.

Protectively my Hero growls at the shadows above.

Reassure him, he's safe, we are together again, forever loved.

FOLLOW WHEREVER HE GOES.

Through the door- down the hall.

Hero pauses- looks up at me- then disappears through the wall.

COME DOWN TO ME.

Voices loud, shrill, and angry float in the air.

Faintheartedly, I descend the stair.

DON'T YOU BE AFRAID…

DON'T BE AFRAID…

DON'T BE AFRAID!

David's at the fireplace, his back turned to me.

Clenching the mantelpiece and listening to their plea.

He stares into the fire; he curses and screams.

He damns them to hell; he crushes their dreams.

There are three on the floor quivering with fear.

One in the chair with many at his rear.

Cerberus, the loyal one, is a three headed beast.

Rabidly attacking, enjoying his feast:

Mara the pretty red-head, and Lamia his faithful one.

And another that David claims does it just for fun.

The tall, thick, black figure in the chair remains still.

Commands his Legion to do his will.

The floor opens up beneath all their feet.

The flame spreads from the hearth and raises up heat.

Down below Cerberus drags the three guests.

The Legion- the many- absorb into the dark figure's chest.

Then transforming into the wicked, dark raven:

He glides from the window seeking safer haven.

The floor closes up- it's just David and I.

He turns to me and asks me to try.

To love him, and trust him, now and forever.

In dreams- my life- because he is stellar.

Morning Star- awake or asleep.

"Wake up my love," I sleepily hear David repeat.

REPRISAL

May 26, 2002

"Tell me about Hero," David asked gently.

I had awakened, shaking and sweating and in between harsh tremors mumbling about nightmares, ravens, and Cerberus the three headed monster. David smirked down at me and claimed it was nothing more than a fever, and diagnosing it as such mixed a formulaic tonic of Paracentimol and seltzer. I told him of all the terrible things that had occurred over the past several days: the way in which reality as I'd known it had changed. I explained the hallucinations, the malign terrors that had become more present and more severe. David said it was a false reality- that something had stirred up these awful fits, and if I would just talk about them, they would go away.

The notion of Hero appearing in my dream and coming to my rescue intrigued him, and again he urged me to tell him about my bas rouge.

"He was courageous, brazen, and devoted. He was my closest companion. When no one else cared or had time for me, I could always count on him, and even now, he is still here to protect me."

"How could someone not care for you...or have time for you?"

"It was easy enough," I sighed. "When we lived in France things were different; I try to forget my childhood altogether, I've tried adamantly for so long- I thought I succeeded- until last night when I saw Hero again."

"And your childhood, what was it like?"

"Painful."

"I can empathize with that, but I don't understand why you would masquerade as if it never occurred."

"It's easier to forget than forgive," I said as the medicine began to take effect.

"I'm here for you," David said smoothing my messy hair, "you can confide in me."

Knowing that his persistence on the matter would not wane, I interlocked my fingers with his and began. "I grew up in northern France, in a city called Caen, just inland of the English Channel. I remember it being mild and humid. Caen is a splendidly scenic place with the thriving and historic La Porte Oceane not far off. The coast was only a few miles away from the chateau where I lived."

"It sounds pleasing," David said impressed. "Was your home as illustrious as the tudor you live in now?"

"Was it?" I gasped feeling my health quite recovered. "It was everything a French estate should be." Excited and suddenly loquacious, I continued. "The main dwelling was over four centuries old, and the property was built upon years later. There were more narrow hallways and rooms than you could imagine. I remember playing hide and seek in the mansion for hours with sweet Lenoir, my young nanny, before she was driven away by the jealousy of my mother. After Lenoir left, I truly had no one. My father was the President of the General Council and was always away on business- and now, even though his title and position has changed- his absence never has. When he was at home, he preached only of education. Even as a child of five or six, he would have me sit across from him at his desk in the study and read or write for hours. I grew to enjoy his being away, except I was then left with my predacious mother."

David intently gazed into my eyes and squeezed my hand. He coaxed me to sit between his legs and lean my back snuggly against his chest. He played with my hair and kissed my neck sensually. "They say like mother like daughter love. She can't be as horrid as you claim."

"I'm nothing like her," I snapped. "I spent all my waking hours outdoors when I wasn't with my home tutor. I knew every square inch of the five acres of grove and pasture, and spent more time with the servants, following them from outhouse to outhouse and from the stables to the garages. I would sneak to the cellar and play on the empty racks and pretend house with the tall unused wine barrels. There was a lake too and in the spring I would sit in the little row boat for hours and feed the swans and wish I would float away. I was a wretched and lonely child. It took years for my self-important parents to notice…to notice me."

"I'm sorry," he whispered.

"I'm sorry too," I admitted. Talking about the past was an inner tug-of-war. One pull relieved me by sharing the experiences- my hurt- that I had repressed for so long, but the sharp tug of the atonal truths widened the emptiness that had always been inside of me. "I was nine years old when we first vacationed to Saint Chamas. I was thrilled by the chance to escape the prison of everyday life I was trapped in. The Provence Alps were so quaint and quiet, with a high beveled cliff separating Etang de Berre from the mainland. The villa we acquired for the summer had a sprawling park, a diamond shaped pool, and a terrace that was perfect for sun tanning. One evening, my father and I snuck away, leaving my mother in a vodka induced coma, to stroll the banks of the Berre Lagoon. He had promised to take me the day we arrived, and that evening, six weeks later, he finally kept his word. We walked along the countryside on the only paved road that existed in the whole town. I was exhausted from the walk and the poor choice of footwear I had worn that day. My father lit a cigar and lectured me on wearing flip flops- they ruin your feet- he matter-of-factly preached, adding he had read it in a medical journal.

As I rested underneath the arched passageway and leaned against the stone pillars which marked the city limits, the lecture paused long enough for him to admire a pair of swart, short-haired shepherds that walked their owner. My father commented on the pair and proceeded to strike a conversation with the handler who turned out to be a middle-aged, Dutch, market tycoon with five illegitimate children and one eighteen year old wife. I massaged my swollen feet while my father and the tradesman became acquainted and worked out an arrangement to the meet the following day to inspect the latest litter. Apparently, between swindling thousands out of millions of dollars, the Dutchman also found time to breed Beaceron herding dogs."

"Good man," David said with a sly chuckle.

"I wouldn't go that far," I replied joining in the laugh. "He did have a lovely litter of dogs for sale, and my father, showing me regard just once, bought the king of the lot. I named him Hero because he was truly the hero of my life-until you came along of course."

"So it was just you and Hero?"

"He was my pal. Every day it was he and I against the world."

"I'm sure it was arduous, being an only child and having such a proud father and disinterested mother. Yesterday you wouldn't answer me when I asked you about Hero. I want you to know and believe that you can trust me with your secrets and your distress. Your scars have broken open again love, and I don't know if you're ill, depressed; or worse, but you can open up to me and let me wipe the darkness from your face."

Leaning forward I reached for the pack of cigarettes and the lighter that were innocently laying on the nightstand. My hands rattled as I tried, unsuccessfully, to light one. I wasn't sure if it was indignation or acknowledgement of my own weaknesses that has raised my pulse and a sudden rush of blood to flow to my brain, causing the onset of a throbbing migraine. With the filter pursed between my lips, I finally lit the tip and took a long, thoughtful drag. "What happened? My father and the Dutchman really hit it off. They found that they had more in common besides the love of pretty French Shorthaired Shepherds- they shared the desire of pretty, young girls."

"Oh…shit," David said under his breath.

"His affair nearly ruined us and it sent my mother on a drinking binge that she hasn't ever been able to stop. The papers reported the affair lasted over a year and was with a nineteen year old Russian ballet dancer who was a friend of the Dutchman's wife. The scandal caused such uproar in town my mother recommended that I be shipped off to a boarding school, not for my protection of course, but so I would be one less thing she would have to deal with. She only cared about herself…her image…her bottle of vodka. She didn't give a damn about me! She only wanted time alone so, in her inebriated state, she could pretend our family didn't exist. My father didn't have the balls to stand up to her; he was vexed over the impending divorce he feared would leave him penniless and with only an inconsequential title. My mother comes from an old aristocratic family, with old refined ideals, who would never pardon such impropriety- and he would be left with nothing," I said smashing the smoldering butt into the ashtray in disgust.

"So they sent you away to Paris, I presume, for your education?" David asked, wide-eyed and engrossed.

I sank back into his alabaster arms and closed my eyes. "No, unfortunately not, I was sent to the most prestigious fine arts school in Europe."

"That doesn't sound so bad."

I rubbed my eyes in frustration. "You want to know what was bad. At the age of ten, I learned that my father was a spineless sociopath and my mother a deceitful, manic depressive. They threw me out like a mound of trash. They took me away from Hero- the only one who ever loved me.

My father had the audacity to ship me to Belgium, the god forsaken place, to attend the same school as the Dutchman's bastard children. Brussels was foreign to me because I didn't speak the language and didn't understand their customs; but even when you're ignorant to most everything, you are aware when you are being mocked and cursed. I had no one and nothing. Worldly as my mother was, she sent trivial gifts and supplied me with an excessive amount of money; I think it made it easier for her not to love me. I spent an entire school year there and was brought home only twice. It didn't bother me not to see my parents, but I missed Hero terribly- he was my un loyal. He was everything to me…the only thing in the world that truly made me happy. My father's political career in Caen was rapidly declining, he had burned all his business relationships and his unethical behavior caused him to lose favor with the General Counsel, his constituents, and the people.

My second year at boarding school started off the same as the first, but I was a year older, a year tougher, and a year wiser. I secluded myself away from everyone. I remember…it was the end of August and I had taken a walk outside of the school courtyard that day. I was wandering alongside the flower carpet, which consists of about a million bright colored begonias planted in the middle of the square downtown near the Grote Markt, only a quarter mile from the school boundaries, when the headmaster summoned me back to the grounds. On the way back, he instructed me to go to my apartment and pack my things immediately- I was going home.

Six hours later, I was standing at my own doorstep, knocking, but when the door was opened, it was only my mother: red eyed and thick tongued- but no Hero. I remember asking her where he was and her telling me, disingenuously, that she didn't know. I brushed passed her, anxious, because it wasn't like him to not be there to greet me excitedly when I came home. I searched all over the house for him, but when I couldn't find him, I frantically entered my mother's sitting room. I found her sprawled out on one of the sofas, martini in hand, with an ice bag covering her forehead and eyes. I inquired as to why I had been brought home, and she explained that we were moving to the United States, to a small rural town in northeast Ohio where we could start over. Again, I demanded after Hero…and…she laughed. She actually laughed at me when she told him that he had run away."

"She was drunk out of her mind Autumn. You can't hold that against her forever."

"She is a liar," I spat. I paused a moment to collect my over-driven emotions. "It was decided that we were to leave Caen in a month, and for all thirty days, I slept outside in a make-shift tent and waited for Hero to return. I walked the woods surrounding my house every day, I searched for him downtown, and I put up fliers, placed ads in the paper, and even called the authorities on a daily basis, pleading for them to keep their eyes open for him. Every day for a month I waited…waited and prayed that he'd come back to me. I didn't understand why he had abandoned me- why he wouldn't come home. The day that we were to move, I threw a frightful tantrum! I swore to my mother that I would not move! I refused to travel to the United States without my Hero. What if we left and he came back? I was prepared to be left behind. Later that night, my mother called me to her, and annoyed and aggravated with my moping and crying, she told me the truth. Hero hadn't run away. He had been sick…caught an aggressive respiratory infection…he had been sick for weeks. Hero…was…dead."

David cradled me like a whimpering, newborn baby. "I didn't know princess. I'm so sorry."

"She never told me he was sick. She was too heartless to take him to the vet. He could have survived. He could have been treated. She should have at least told me. She could have brought me home to see him in his final days. She blatantly deceived me. It was her fault that Hero died; she neglected him, just like she neglected me."

"It's okay Autumn, let it out," David soothed rocking me gently.

Tears rushed down my flushed cheeks in warm salty streams. "They were both too selfish to give a shit about anyone but themselves- their own hollow needs. My father was greedy and impulsive. My mother was miserable because she chose to be miserable, and in her depressive, impious downfall, she was oblivious to the fact that Hero died painfully and alone. I never even got to say goodbye."

Cerberus crawled onto the bed beside me and licked my hand. I rubbed underneath his chin affectionately the way I always had done to Hero.

"I see why you say that your childhood was painful. I would have never guessed that you had those types of skeletons lurking in your shadow. You conceal them well."

"It's the only way I've learned to deal with it. Push it down deep and try to never let it surface."

"So you moved here when you were still in grade school?"

"Yes."

"And what happened?"

"Zen happened. My parents got exactly what they deserved," I said fighting back my hidden pleasure.

"How so?" David asked intently.

I slid off the bed and stretched my legs. I drew up the chair that was positioned in front of the computer stand and rolled it next to the bed. Spinning it around, I sat down and leaned my arms against the padded back. "All the lies and the bullshit followed us here. My father decided to run for a State Representative seat in the 51st District. He began his campaign strong, but within a few months, an avalanche of unfortunate events crashed down upon us. All of a sudden, around town fliers were distributed with my father's picture and the word adulterer. A few weeks later, my mother went into town for some shopping, and when she returned to the car the word drunk was spray painted on the back of her window. The intensity of the pranks only increased over time. Once my father was elected things got much worse. He would come home humiliated after a long day at work and complain, at the dinner table, that collections agents were harassing him over fallacious bills and credit blunders. One day, someone called him while he was in a meeting, and with the setting on speaker-phone, inquired as to when he planned to return to the free clinic to discuss his medical treatment options for the syphilis he had recently contracted."

"What!" David exclaimed in awe.

"The only thing my mother cares about, other than her bottle of vodka of course, is her lawn and garden. Actually, that is how I met Tony. His mother and my mother are garden committee members. Anyways, the summer of my eighth grade year I woke up to my mother screaming and throwing things out on the deck which is directly below my back window. Our lawn was burned out in a splotchy design that read 'fuck you', and all the flowers and plants had been trampled and destroyed. Over the years our home and my parent's cars has been toilet papered, egged, and vandalized."

"You can try to run from your past, but it always catches up to you. It sounds like the same is true for your parents. They left France and came to Ohio but the truth of who they really are was exposed anyways. It sounds like someone is still very angry with them both," he said thoughtfully.

"It would seem, but your right, and they are getting exactly what they deserve. Just the other day, two packages came in the mail- one for each of them. The one addressed to my father was sent to his office and was filled with all sorts of compromising things: a whip, handcuffs, leather open-backed briefs, anal beads, lubricant, a vibrator, and who knows what else. You should have seen his face when he came home...priceless. My mother had received a fed ex delivery, which she tearfully explained, came in a plain box. She had anticipated the contents to contain her regularly scheduled shipment of fall perennial bulbs. Instead, she found a container filled with fresh cow manure and a set of plastic eating utensils.

David smirked, "eat shit huh?"

"You have to admit that's a good one!"

"I'm more curious to know who is behind it all. Have

they thought, perhaps, it could be the dancing Russian beauty?"

"I doubt that."

"Why would you doubt it? She has a reason to be angry, does she not?"

"I doubt it because though she may have the motive, she did not have the opportunity this morning to fill my mother's favorite, mint scented, shampoo with hair remover or spike my father's coffee travel mug with a week's worth of laxatives. I hope they are enjoying their trip…and as my father stands at the podium to give his speech, while he struggles not to shit his pants, I hope the audience enjoys the clips of my mother in her alcoholic glory that…my father…of course… spliced into his presentation just to scorn her."

"Autumn, I never knew you had it in you," David said amazed.

"Reprisal is complete," I said abandoning my chair and climbing on top of him.

We laughed harmoniously. We let our passion rule.

DECONSTRUCTED

August 28, 2002

Stacy

"I'm so glad that lecture is over," Autumn said unclipping her pager from her belt and smiling.

"Let me guess, you got a page from David?"

"Yes," she said giddy with excitement. "He must be in study hall or lunch or something because he wants me to call him."

My stomach grumbled at the sound of food. We had just sat through two hours of senior orientation on our first day back to school. The only thing worse than the sermon, performed by Sister Mary Thomas Bernard, about the obligations of stewardship, was the buffet table positioned directly behind her lined with a delicious assortment of sandwiches, chips, cookies, salad, pizza, and desserts. I could see her lips moving, but couldn't make out the words. The aroma of lunch meat, cheese, and chocolate saturated the air making it impossible to concentrate. No matter how many times I scolded myself to pay attention, no matter how often I shifted in my chair to divert my cravings, no matter how hard I tried…I only could think of eating. I had felt myself begin to salivate as the good Sister warned us against procrastination in our studies. *When do we get to eat?*

With the lengthy parlay behind us, and my belly stuffed from lunch, I suddenly felt guilty. *Why am I such a fat pig?*

"Are you going to call him back?" *I already know that you are.*

"Of course," she replied already reaching for her cell phone.

"I'm going to head to next period. You girls have fun," Lauren said.

"Meet you in gym," Autumn called after her.

Cameron and Autumn walked ahead, giggling, and turned into the bathroom. I trudged behind them, unhappy that they were happy. *If only I were tall and thin like Autumn, who had swooned the most beautiful boy any of us had ever seen, or short and petite like Cameron, who always had the college guys in the palm of her hand. That will never be me because I'm fat…fat…fat!* The bathroom was empty and at Cameron's urging I shut and locked the door behind me.

Autumn climbed on the sink vanity and pulled herself up on the ledge which ran along the exterior wall and pushed open one of the four plexi-glass windows. She scooted her tiny bottom across the shallow lip, placing her foot against the top of the stall for support. She lit a cigarette and dialing her phone, seemed carefree and content to smoke and chat. I entered the stall directly across from her and to the right of Cameron. Staring at the toilet in front of me, I sank to my knees and wrapped my arms around the rim of the bowl.

It feels good. Satisfying.

The first rush of semi-digested matter pushed itself up. My esophagus burned as it spilled forth, my stomach rejoiced as it was emptied. I gagged and heaved. My eyes watered from the effort of expunging every ounce of waste. *Why did you have to eat? Why couldn't you resist? Resist the need to binge? To engorge yourself?* I stared at the heaping pile of mush that floated in the dirty water. Red, green, and brown. *It feels good to be clean again.*

It felt so good, knowing that even though I had faltered…again- I was able to make things right. I wiped my mouth and struggled to get back to my feet. Next to me I heard Cameron sniffling loudly. *She's coking her nose again.*

"Were you puking in there?" Autumn asked as I rinsed my mouth out in the sink.

"Yea," I laughed. "It's the only way to lose weight." *Don't you dare judge me.* She was off the phone now, and stared at me with her condescending eyes.

"You shouldn't do that," she said concerned.

Easy for you to say Miss Perfect.

"No need to do that," Cameron said exiting her stall and reaching into the front pouch of her book bag produced a sandwich bag filled with white powder. "Snort some of this and you will be going so fast, you won't remember you're even hungry."

Autumn shook her head as I accepted the gift and stuffed it into my purse.

"Where do you get it from?"

"Just some boys I know," she said heading for the door.

"Great, now I have two of you that I have to worry about," Autumn replied following her. "I will just stick to these," she mumbled tucking the Newport pack into her messenger bag. "Stacy you are just fine the way you are. You don't need to be a toilet hugger or a coke-head."

You disapprove, but you don't know what it's like to wake up every day and hate yourself. I'm so fat…disgusting and fat. I just want to be like you…or Cameron. At least she is willing to help me. All you do is judge. "That's easy for you to say."

"Tell her Stacy," Cameron said smiling and kissing Autumn on the cheek. "We got this."

If you say so. "Let's go to gym."

September 20, 2002

Lauren

"So I know Cameron will appreciate my latest efforts." I adjusted the mirror on my vanity table. *Why is no one paying attention to me? Autumn is too busy sucking face with David, Vicki is engulfed in Tony's latest wrestling tall-tale, and Stacy is pretending not to look at the open bag of Reese pieces on my dresser.*

"Tell me," Cameron said running the wide tooth comb through my hair.

"I found us a place to go tonight!"

She dropped the comb and spun me around in my chair. "Where? Where?" she exclaimed.

"I'm not saying until everyone is listening." *I will raise my voice if I have to. I didn't invite you all over to my house to ignore me. Everyone wanted to go out and do something. Enjoy our Friday night off from school, and sports, and our lame ass parents. I found something totally cool and no one is even paying attention to me.* I proceeded to apply another thick coat of glitter to my upper eyelids as Autumn, Vicki, and Stacy honed in- finally- to what I had to say. I pretend pouted and relished their accelerated pleas and inquires.

"You little trickster," David said flashing me a perfect grin.

I can't believe he is so into Autumn. I am just as pretty, if not prettier than her. I could have him…if I really wanted him…but he's not my type…and why narrow the playing field? There are so many to choose from. "I met some college frat boys online." I dabbed a layer of glue on the string of fake eyelashes I had just removed from the packaging. *I could so have him. But, David is good for her. So much better than Adrian that piece of shit.*

"Nice," Cameron said hugging me.

I bet you're trying to think up ways already to hustle them out of money.

"Sounds fun," Tony chimed in.

"I knew you weren't that beautiful for nothing," Autumn said happily. "Are there going to be alcohol beverages there?"

You better be careful. You are turning into a drunk just like your mother. Smoothly my hair meticulously and angling the mirror to reflect the different angles that the shadows had concealed, I replied, "of course."

"Do you really think that is a good idea?" Vicki whispered to Tony leaning into him intimately. "Do you remember the last time we went to a party in Meriton? Lauren had four shots of Everclear and was on the roof claiming she was Superman and could fly."

Tony burst out laughing which caused the others to laugh at me too. "I think she was snorting some of your fairy dust Cameron."

"I'm just saying…we don't even know these guys…they could be serial killers posing as frat boys for all we know," Vicki said defensively.

I rolled my eyes. *You're trying too hard to impress him. Loosen up and have a little fun. No one says you have to be like Cameron, floating on the clouds twenty-four seven, but be spontaneous once in a while. He sees your weaknesses. Be daring…be fun…like myself. Cameron's too wild for him…and ridiculous, Stacy is too damn fat- who can take her seriously? And Autumn…his glance always lingers on her, but I know the heart of the matter. Tony and Ram have secretively been feuding over me for years! I could have either one of them whenever I want. This year is different. Everyone has changed…and for the better I think. Senior year has brought out the best in all of us. Except Vicki. Her jealousy is nauseating. We've paid our dues; studied, done everything we were told. Why can't we enjoy ourselves? Why does she have to ruin it? We all had loosened up and learned to go with the flow. We've figured out that there is fun to be had, and I of course am the one to lead the way and show them how it's done. Everyone, but Vicki, is on board. They all followed my lead. I haven't figured her out…she openly disapproves of the parties, the drinking, the boys, the sex, and the drugs. Is the only thing keeping her around Tony? I will find out and I swear if I'm right, as I always am, there will be hell to pay. I will squash it…I will steal him myself just because I can. He really wants me anyways.*

"Are you ready yet darling?" David asked and jokingly grabbed a fistful of mascara, eyeliner, and bronzer and ran out my bedroom door.

"Oh…you are asking for it," Autumn shouted above the

hum of constant conversation. "You should know better than mess with her cosmetics."

"Give that back!" I chased him out the door.

"I guess that's our cue to head out," I heard Stacy say.

Good job mama whale, get those kids in line. "David says he's ready to go." I listened to confirm that everyone heard me and was following my directions. They were. I led the way to the vehicles and delegated who was driving and what cars we were taking. I was in charge...as I should be.

October 31, 2002

Autumn

You're gorgeous sitting there- statuesque- and brilliant like the morning star. My morning star. I want to take a break from the fun and just be with you. I want to climb on your lap and take in your luscious smell. I want to taste your full lips and run my fingers through your platinum hair. I'm undressing you with my eyes...I know what is underneath that shirt...those jeans...because I've had it, but you're a mind race and it's all I can think about.

"Autumn, come take another," Tony called out to me from the raised dining area in Cameron's tiny trailer.

I can't see you. The space- all 500 square feet- is packed with bodies. I know he means another Dixie cup of syrup with a Coors Light beer as a chaser. Tony had bought the Tussin and the other Local boys had bought the beer.

"Go for it princess," David said sneering.

I want to make this experience more enjoyable. Right here in the moment. I fought my way through a small crowd of Local students who were shooting dice and dong Copenhagen until I found Tony.

"Last one," he said pulling me onto his lap. "I don't want you doing too much."

Thick and sugary, the syrup coated my tongue. *It's gross. Why I am doing this?*

"My roll," Tony shouted out and discreetly kissing the back of my neck, he helped me to my feet and resumed his spot in the dice circle.

Stumbling down the two steps, I fell onto the couch next to David. He stared down at me for a moment as if to assess my condition. *I'm fine. I will show you.*

"Autumn, come on," Cameron yelled from the driveway. "We are car skiing again!"

The only thing I want another go at is David. David and that paralyzing body. I mustered all my strength and rose to my feet. David's eyes met mine, and licking my lips seductively, I motioned for him to follow me. *You can do it Autumn. You can make it. Two steps to the door. Through the door. Two more steps. Turn right. Through the door.* I fell through Cameron's bedroom door and onto the leopard print pillows that were stacked on her bed. *My head is pounding. Damn…what did I do?*

"You must be feeling pretty good," David said sinking down on the bed next to me. He touched my temple nurturingly.

Ouch…that hurts!

"You're bleeding love," he said taking off his shirt and applying it to my open wound. "Caught the corner of the dresser on the way down," he added concerned.

I want to touch it…your ghost white chest. Trail my fingertips over the outline of your ribs. I know what you taste like. It's so good. I need more…and more…and more. Can't get enough. Of you. I push David down onto the cheap, thin mattress. *Your hair is silk through my fingers. I've molested you with my eyes. All night. I want you to rape me. Make me beg. I know you like it too…but not like I do. Ahh…those rib bones…move down…move down. I tease myself more than I can ever tease you.*

"Are you sure you're up for all this love?" David asked pulling my hands away.

"You're already up for it." *Shaking with sexual desire. Anticipation. The naughty things I want to do to you. You make me crazy.* "David…your body makes me insane." *I have you right where I want you…naked again.*

October 31, 2002

Cameron

"Here's how it's going to be boys. You bring the drinks and the drugs. "I'll have the pretty girls. You bring the cash and I'll bring the ass. Got it?" I hung up the receiver. *They better make it happen.*

"Who was that?" Lauren asked adjusting the new push up bra I lifted from Victoria's Secret earlier that day.

"The Meriton boys of course. They are on their way." *They better have cash too. If they think they are going to get a free show they will be disappointed. I need some dust…need a drink…need some cash. My first private party! This is how you make money! Doing a show for one client is bullshit. I'm going to have at least ten older guys here tonight…they've got to have some cash. I know they will pay to see some skin…especially if I can get Lauren and Autumn to strip for them too. Vicki is lame. Why is she here? Maybe I'll spike her drink. Dumb bitch can't be ruining this for me. I need the money. Where's the rock and roll? We need something to loosen up a bit. To break the ice.* "Hey Tony. Why don't you and your buddies run down the street to the gas station and get some cough syrup?" *Better than nothing. Let's trip!*

"Cough syrup?" he asked scrunching up his face. "How about some Copenhagen?"

Don't knock it until you try it. "Yes whatever you want that will get a buzz going." *There is money to be made tonight if we can impress the college boys. Think about it. You will get a free show.* "Autumn come here."

"What's up?" she asked popping her head in.

"Smell this." I shoved a nail polish remover soaked napkin in her face.

"Ugh," she said coughing and drawing away.

Don't be a bitch. "Inhale it deep." I placed it up to her face again.

"Huffing are we?" David said from the other room. "I smell that shit in here."

"Come try it!" *If you do it; she will too! That's it Autumn. Breathe it in. I owe you one David. I knew she'd do it if you did. Thank God Tony's back with the syrup. Vicki's preoccupied with him. If she sees us huffing this shit she will throw a tantrum like a baby. Why come if you're not down for a little fun? The syrup…where is the syrup?*

"We got beer too," Ram called out.

We'll down that too.

"Let me try some of that," Lauren shrieked at the sight of the chewing tobacco.

There you go. Let that go straight to your blood stream. Syrup is nasty but it's working already. Get cranked up. I want to go faster. Faster. Faster. Faster. Faster Faster. Faster….I need real speed. No sense of time. Those Meriton boys should be here by now. I've convinced Lauren and Autumn to take off their shirts. I want to do something crazy….and yes! They're here! Spike Vicki's drink. Dumbass passed out on the pre-heating stove. We burned the pizza. Lucky she didn't burn too!

"Where are the skates?" Autumn asked searching through the pile of clothes, bags, and shoes that were stacked in the corner.

Skating? Where are we going to skate? I love skating! As long as we party. I'm up for it. Let's go. Let's do it. I'm ready. Let's go!

"Here they are," Stacy said tossing them to her.

"What the hell are you doing?" Ram asked.

Have no idea. "Going to have some fun." I rolled toward the door and free jumped from the porch to the gravel road below. *How the hell did I make that without falling on my ass? What is Autumn up to?*

"Hitch me up," she called out to a group of frat boys who were smoking pot and leaning on the hood of David's car.

"Car skiing!"

Autumn laughed uncontrollably and fell onto the dusty pavement.

"What's car skiing?" one of the frat boys asked.

What do you think it is asshole?

Autumn secured a rope to the trunk of the Camaro and hooked us both up to it through our belt loops. "Let's go," she

89

screamed spinning around on her speed skates.

"You've got to be shitting me," he replied.

Do I look like I am shitting dude? "Bet me then. Twenty bucks for each of us. We will kick ass around this entire trailer park."

He smiled and shaking his head in bewilderment said, "you're on."

"I'll drive," David said from the trailer doorway.

Bring it! And ...we're off...going so fast...around the turns...to the right... to the left...spitting gravel...tasting exhaust fumes...Autumn's a rag doll...the ...rush.

"You girls are wild," the loser conceded when we rolled to a stop again in front of my trailer.

You have no idea. If you have the cash I'll show you just how wild I can be. "Pay up boys." I push past them. "If you have the dust I can promise you a wild ride."

"Hell yea," they hooted slipping the bills in my bra and following me back inside.

Don't bitch out on me now Autumn. "Tell Lauren to have them sit on the couch." I instructed her. *Black strobe lights on. Turn up the music. Time to powder my nose. I don't care. Right here in front of everyone. Man I miss that feeling. Fire to the brain. Eyes are on me. Don't fall climbing up on this coffee table. Steady. I knew they'd join in. Lauren...Autumn...you're not naked but just flash some skin. Good girls. Vicki's passed out. Stacy's watching, Lauren's drunk, Autumn's stoned, and I'm soaring. All the green bills are scattered around my feet.*

November 4, 2002

Adrian

She hasn't called me in weeks. I have to track her down. When I do, she acts like she doesn't want to see me. She said she'd come today. What has she been doing? She's forgotten about me. And I can see how she could. She was right. That bitch. The first day she came to see me, she said I won't change. I won't. Lying to her about it isn't an option anymore. She knows better. Knows me too well. I thought she'd always love me anyways. She says things change. It's not that easy. Maybe for her it's easy to be motivated. To do some much. To have so much. Spoiled brat. She's always had everything. She doesn't know what it's like to be on the outside looking in. Yet she complains that her life is so hard. She's got everything and I have nothing. It's always been that way. It will always be that way. It's easier to do nothing. No disappointments. No one's got expectations.

So what? I'm not perfect. Never said I was. Never tried to be. It's her fault. Her fault I'm the way I am. She doesn't love me. Never did. Selfish bitch. She's abandoned me in here. And when did I ever abandon her? She busts my balls over my grades, my lack of motivation, and my actions. Who is she to judge? Who am I kidding? She's perfect. Why is it that easy for her to be so damn great?

I can only be what I am. I can only have this style. It's not ever going to change. That's just me. It's just who I am. She says all my friends are wastes of life. Delinquents. That's what she thinks of me too I know. Thinks I'm lazy. Thinks I'm a loser. I am. But why does she make me admit it?

"So what is it that was so important that you had to talk to me?" Autumn asked settling into a folding chair and glaring at me through the bars that separated us.

November 4, 2002

Tony

"Why would you go see him today?"

"I don't know…guilt maybe," Autumn said.

What do you have to feel guilty over? Adrian is a loser. Everyone knows it. Why can't you see it? Every time you make real progress you always revert back to him. He's like a disease. You've caught it. You don't know how to really get rid of it…and even when it goes into remission…sooner or later it always bears its ugly face again. "Guilt over what?"

"I don't know Tony. Things between Adrian and I are complicated and things have been kind of crazy for all of us lately. I'm not going to pretend I'm not completely head over heels for David, but I can't just completely turn my back on Adrian. Even if I don't love him; I do care what happens to him. I can't just let that go. I'm too invested. It's like our lives have changed. My life has evolved so quickly over the past six months, but his life has remained just the same. He knows nothing of all this. Honestly, I'm afraid of what's going to happen when he gets out and this is all over."

You're right things have changed...and they have for the better. I can't believe you really give a damn about Adrian...or his feelings. I know you hate him. And David...at first I was happy that someone...anyone... could divert your attention from Adrian but I never wanted you to love him. You love him! I know it. He knows it. I hate it. He rubs it in my face every day. Everyone knows how you feel about him. Why can't you feel that for me? What has being your friend ever done for me? Why couldn't I capture your eye? I hate how perfectly selfish you are. How clueless. I hate how much of a coward I am. Instead of stepping up to the plate and telling you, the girl I've loved since the first time I saw you, how much you mean to me. "You piss me off," I shot back at her. "You shouldn't be worried about him. Let him go Autumn. He's no good for you. You know it and I know it." She was shocked that I had raised my voice at her. *I don't care. I finally need the truth to register with you.*

"Why are you so angry?" she wailed.

I'm glad this is happening over the phone and not in person. In person, I would cave. In person I would not be able to tell you what I've known since Cameron's party on Halloween night. "I'm angry because I want you to really listen to me Autumn. I want you to know that I care about you and want what's best for you. I won't always be here you know."

"What do you mean?" she interrupted.

"I'm moving away..."

"What?"

"In a week actually. I'm moving to Jackson, Missouri."

"With your dad?" she gasped in disbelief.

Unfortunately. I can't believe mom is dumb enough to fall for his lies again. Women are so weak. "He called my mom and begged her to move in with him down there."

"I thought they didn't get along? I thought they got a divorce?" she questioned.

I wish. Adrian's going to be just like him. Two amazing pieces of shit. "Separated." *I don't see why that is. They get together. They break up. They get together again. Leave each other again…and again…and again…and again…with no regard for me.*

"No, I don't want you to go," she cried out.

The heavy sobs. You have David now. You'll be alright without me. "I have to."

"When? When do you leave?"

The sooner the better. I can't take this anymore. You will make me explode. "A few days." *More tears. I will miss you and love you. I hate myself for loving you.*

November 5, 2002

Vicki

"He's leaving in a few days?" *How is that possible? How does she know? Why wouldn't he tell me about it?*

"That's what he told me last night," Autumn replied.

"Lucky him," Lauren said taking another bite of her salad.

How could Tony tell Autumn before me? She only cares about her precious David. Why should Tony even waste his time on her? He likes her. He deserves someone who appreciates his worth. Me. She could never feel the way I do about him. "What else did he say?"

"I don't know. He was pretty angry with me," she said looking down.

Good.

"Well, the day after Cameron's party, when he gave me a ride home, he kept going on and on about how concerned he was for you. He really cares about you Autumn," Stacy said placing a reassuring hand on her shoulder.

Blah blah blah. He gave you a ride home? He never offered to take me home. Why would he pick Stacy over me? He can't be attracted to her. She's too fat. But there has to be a reason he chose her over me. And Autumn. Autumn...Autumn...Autumn...Autumn! Has everyone lost their minds? It's like she's God's gift to the world. If only everyone knew what she's really like. I don't blame Adrian for putting her in her place. I wish I could get away with popping her in the mouth myself. Selfish...conceited...deceitful. Foreigner. She doesn't belong here. I wish she'd go back to France and never come back.

"Hey Vicki are you coming? The bell rang genius. Lunch is over," Cameron said snapping her fingers in my face.

Must be off the cocaine again. You look down. The Benzedrine doesn't do it for you anymore. Barely takes the edge off. Those drugs are going to kill you. "Right...sorry."

"We better hurry if we are going to make it to American Government on time," she said grabbing her things.

This is the longest three minutes of my life. Are we there yet? Are we there yet? You just don't shut up do you? Can't wait to get to class. At least then I won't have to listen to you anymore. I could care less about Lauren's birthday present. What? Her parents got her a new car? I hope she wrecks it. Wouldn't that be classic. Are her parent's stupid or what? Buying her a new Mustang for her birthday. I bet my Jetta's faster anyways. American made cars suck.

"Don't you just love this class?" the motor mouth asked shoving her book bag under her desk.

I'd love it more if you'd shut up! Why do people even like you? You're strung out constantly. It's torture being your friend. "My favorite subject."

Sister Mary Thomas Bernard's voice boomed over the loud speaker. "Good afternoon students. I'm pleased to announce that the votes have been tallied for this nine weeks Scholar Student award. I can't say enough positive things about this young lady. With a GPA of 4.372 please congratulate your Student Council President Miss Autumn Marseille!"

You've got to be kidding me! There is no way that she beat me. That was my award! I worked so hard. I deserved it! All Autumn cares about is David. She's a pretender. It's only about him. She talks constantly about sneaking out every night to stay at his house. When she's not at practice she's with him. She never studies. I can't believe this!

"And...I'm proud to announce Cameron Richmond as Athlete of the Month for the month of October. Cameron led the volleyball team to the National Christian High School Volleyball Tournament in Jacksonville Florida where we placed first overall. Congratulations Cameron!"

The only reason you got the award is because you're doped up all the time and for whatever reason everyone likes you. It's not fair that it is voted on by the students. I should have gotten Player of the Month! Everyone knows that the setter is the most important position on the volleyball court. At least our wonderful spiker, Autumn, didn't get that recognition too! "Great job Cam."

"Thanks," she exclaimed. "This has got to help my chances of getting that scholarship to Notre Dame."

You wish. I'm better than you. If anyone should go Division 1 it's me. "I'm sure it will help." *They'll choose me instead. You may have had a good month, but I've had a great four year career.*

Class was called to order, and just as we did every day-in every class, we stood and bowed our heads in prayer. Our instructor, Sister Mary Teresa, extended our humble thanks and asked God to forgive us for all our sins.

REDUNDANCY

Thanksgiving 2002

Nothing ever changes. No, that is a fallacy- things only change for the worse. I keep track of the dates now, my unwonted attempt to retain some bit of sanity. Time is the only thing that has remained consistent in my life and even time has had the pleasure of misleading me. Day trips have become day falls and nightmares last for days. It has all become a web, and trapped and confused, I am adhered to it. Wandering through the labyrinth of life, most times I know not if the painted day around me is palpable, or if it's just my minds creation.

Changes for the worse; but even those changes are convoluted and subtle, as if they have been there the entire time. I've found that sometimes it is necessary to force myself to acknowledge what is going on around me-whether it is real of fake- even a whale must surface from time to time for a breath of air. Changes: Stacy has lost ten pounds (bravo for her) pill by pill and line by line. Cameron's bad habits have influenced her. I've grown to miss Cameron over the past several weeks. She attends school less often, and when she is present, she's not really there. Her eyes and nose are cratered, she grinds her teeth and habitually licks her lips, and she twitches from time to time. She's changed; but her love of cocaine, older men, and dancing for money has not. Changes: Lauren's self-love certainly will never change, she's lost herself, and she is fully amerced in her own self-importance, but she always has been. Though now it seems, she rarely pretends interest in anyone but herself- except Ram- I've noticed that he is the new prize trophy she is after. Vicki grows more withdrawn by the day; with Tony in Missouri she has no need for any of us anymore. She has changed her entire demeanor toward us all- especially me- you would have thought that I was the one that drove him away. Doesn't she realize that I miss him too? She is hypocritical, judging, she is the Word of God trampling over all of our heads. Changes.

School holds little interest for me, and in fact, it is the portion of the mundane that I dread the most. St. George's is a lonely place for me now, the feeling that overcomes me as I enter it's door every morning is the same as what I felt when I was stationed in Brussels- confined- like a schizoid stuck in their weaker personality. Every aspect of my life I try to escape, being with David is the only exception. I wake up in the morning in the same bed, sweating and ensnared in the same moist sheets, wearing the same navy sweatpants and the same navy tank top. I wake up the same way: gasping and clawing, fighting against the plastic bag that is over my face, the same plastic bag that is pulled tighter and tighter. I am awake. Or am I, just then, falling asleep? The routine is the same every morning. Seven strides to the bathroom, shower, seven strides back, dress, and sit at my computer desk to read the messages that David has left me while I've been asleep. His words are the adrenaline I need every morning to propel myself down the winding staircase, through the dimly lit library, past my father's study, and into the kitchen for breakfast. Things change. I don't care to be belligerently disagreeable to my parents anymore. I just don't care...about them anymore.

I converse with David on the way to school...every minute of that drive...every day...and our love remains the same. St. George's is drab and dreaded- it's once inviting atmosphere has changed into a place I only vaguely remember. The shadows that creep along the block walls follow me, and I've noticed that the saints and apostles in the stained glass mosaics stare at me- there eyes cut at me, carve me, like a sharpened meat cleaver. The prayers at school never change- the rituals at mass never change- the sullen look of Sister Mary Thomas Bernard never changes- Father Ontari's message of penitence and chastity never changes. Our solemn plea never changes: 'O God, who did grant to Saint George strength and constancy in the various torments which he sustained for our holy faith; we beseech you to preserve, through his intercession, our faith from wavering and doubt, so that we may serve you with a sincere heart faithfully unto death. Through Christ our Lord'. My faith has changed. What once was important is only an afterthought. The same lessons, the same bible verses, the same message; and David takes precedence above all.

The monotony of my sporting practices are burdensome to me- volleyball, basketball, and track- most days I wish I could record the practice session from the day before and rewind it and then push play. Nothing changes. In the showers after practice a sense of anxiety washes over me; I am naked and vulnerable, most times I am not alone. I stand under the same shower head, allowing the cool water to cleanse me; but I'm always afraid it will turn to blood, a tainted abomination just like the Nile River. After practice, whether rain or shine, I rush to my car, strap on my seatbelt, put on my silver necklace, turn the car to drive, check my rearview mirror, and every day my reflection is jaded, my nose severed off to spite my face. Nothing changes. I yearn for David.

Every second of everyday I fast until I am in his arms again. Cerberus welcomes me now every evening; he has accepted me into the family David says. Every day David and I are alone- his parents work long unconventional hours- I've been told- leaving us to wander in each other's love and pure devotion. Nothing changes. We sit together in front of the fire drinking spiced red wine out of gold trimmed goblets, we hold each other and stare into one another's souls, and we talk about life- of the human condition. I never want our time together to change. David is an excellent chef, the quality of his meals never change, but the menu he prepares does. I love that he is old fashioned, and writes the daily menu on parchment paper, and later, just before the meal is served announces 'on what we are to dine'. The flatware, the stemware, the linen is always the same- always extravagant; as is the manner in which I am served, which is always very proper. You would not experience more civility and grandeur at Pemberley I assure you!

Things change. I do not abide by curfews anymore. If I were not afraid that my mother, tottering in a vodky-trance, would not mistakenly call the police and report me as a missing person, I would never go home. Every night, I quietly unlatch the back door of the east wing of the old Tudor and scale the steps leading to my own private corridor, every night…or morning…at five o'clock I climb into my bed. Things only change for the worse, for every night the horror is more intense, more unmistakably tangible. I am held down, and the voices in my head wage control over my mind. Each night I see horrible things, unforgettable havoc, and each night the anarchy grows. The hour that I am asleep seems like an eternity; and in my dreams I visit more places, and see more of the world than I ever knew existed. I never knew such darkness- a never ceasing pit of tantalizing torture and turmoil. Awake or asleep? Fact or fiction? Ignorance or truth? Sleeping while Awake. Fictionalized Facts. Ignorance is Truth. Ambiguity. Redundancy. My paradoxical life.

I needed a change, but Thanksgiving dinner with my parents, my mother's socialite friends and my father's political idealists, absent Tony Greggory and his horticultural gifted mother, was not what I had in mind. The gossip of the peacocks; with their heads held high and beaks turned up haughtily, was revolting- each one eager to delicately spread their feathers, their prized accomplishments, for all to see. I was seated next to the fairest of the entire bunch, Miss Kitty

Richter, whose hot pink wax mouth was habitually stuck in a toothy grin. "Egad," she exclaimed smoothly the silk, nectarine colored napkin in her lap. "Autumn, my little darling it's been incredibly too long since I've seen you last. And what a little beauty you've turned out to be. Hasn't she Priscilla? I tell you, I've never seen such a well-dressed table in my entire life. I always say that Denise has such marvelous taste and when no one was thinking of this old Tudor! Well, I declare, who would have thought anything would ever have become of it."

"Although, my award winning roses are something to be had, I must say that Denise has a real eye for overall design," Priscilla Lovewealth replied, daintily sipping on her claret. Her husband, Mr. Lovewealth rolled his eyes and motioned for Odette, our server, to bring him another Jim Beam on the rocks.

Miss Kitty fluttered her lashes and smiled at my mother. "Priscilla you are quite right indeed. You always speak precisely the truth, doesn't she Mr. Lovewealth? Everything is so lovely too, and in its proper place. Those centerpieces are to die for and I am certain cost quite a pound! Dear gracious there I am, showing my age again, and no proper British women should ever do such a thing. Dear me, dear me! And speaking of such, did you see Selena Richmond the other night at the Women's Club meeting? I declare she looked as trifling as that wicked daughter of hers."

I glared at her. I didn't like her- didn't like what she said about Cameron- didn't like the blue eye shadow that drifted in the air and settled on the rim of my plate every time she fluttered her lying eyes. She was on more drugs than Cameron if she thought my mother had any hand in decorating our home or putting together this, or any of the elegant parties that we host. My mother had been in pain all day. She had not had a drink in twenty-four hours- it was important for her to appear to be normal- not a drunk. Nothing changes. She is deceitful and only cares about what others think of her. Miss Priscilla was right on one thing- though I could barely keep up with the stream of consciousness that erupted from her

101

volcanic mouth- the house and dinner table was decorated magnificently. My mother's shaking hands could barely hold the tumbler of claret that Odette placed in her hands- her lips quivered in anticipation- she was breaking a sweat, trying to fight the urge to grab the bottle of liquor out of her hands and consume its contents in a single gulp. I fought the urge to laugh at her- and her delusional friends.

I reached around one of the large brass bowls which was filled with an assortment of fresh herbs and various white glitter painted gourds that were positioned on top of the espresso colored table cloth, and filled my own glass with a double shot of Jim Beam. No one noticed, besides Mr. Lovewealth who chuckled in his napkin. I downed my glass and poured another. I imagined picking one of the crystal bowls, which was filled with peach colored water and a floating burnt orange rose and that had been lovingly placed next to each setting, and bashing in the faces of all the little peacocks. They try, in vain, to be everything that they never can be. Things never change. Kitty Richter, Priscilla Lovewealth, and Denise Marseille were nothing more than cocks- fighting-ready to peck the other's eyes out the moment the opportunity presented itself.

The gaudy three foot high fruit topiary, which was constructed with dark purple plums, ripened nectarines, concord and red seedless grapes, and white cherries, made it next to impossible to see my father at the other side of the dinner table. I ate small bites of food that I could not taste. Things only change for the worse. Everything was nothing without David to share it with. Today would be the hardest day of my life; David would be out of town with his family until late tonight. *What am I going to do? I needed a change. I needed to be with David every second for the rest of my life.*

"You must be Autumn," a tall thin man in his late sixties with thinning grey hair and a wrinkled face said to me from across the table.

"Yes," I replied, "Mr. Duwright I presume?"

"Yours truly," he said. "I hear you are quite the scholar.

Your father told me that among other things, you headed the St. George's debate team to the Ohio State finals last year."

Stark County's newest and highly decorated council woman, Genie Fastalc, was seated to my left. She nudged me in the ribs and with her plump jaws chugged with roasted goose said, "Duwright has a mind to recruit you, young lady, to work at his law firm."

"Don't you trust that swindling shark Autumn," Petro Alztruth, the oldest State Representative in the State of Ohio said hooting. "Lawyers...believe me...you don't want to become one of them." His beer belly jiggled underneath the starched white dress shirt he wore which was two sizes too small and the dentures in his shriveled mouth chinked loudly as he said, "Duwright let the young lady enjoy her holiday and talk business another time."

Fastalc heavy handedly spread a layer of caviar over her toast and crunched into another bite. "Bellino, I want to hear your proposal for the County tax initiative that is being put on the ballot in May. I know you said something at the Chamber meeting last Tuesday that it should be pitched as a tax for the criminal justice system and for roadway drainage and ditches."

I didn't hear my father's reply.

"Just ignore them my dear," Alztruth said reaching for another helping of foie gras with mustard seeds and black truffles. "Fast talker and Do no right need to learn to enjoy the finer things in life. It's too short not to."

The old man was right- but things never change.

The wind ripped through my thin plaid zip up hoody, and I pulled my fur lined winter hat tighter over my ears. Snow twinkled down from gray clouds that hung, in sadness, above my head. The ground beneath my boots crunched as I hurried across the front lawn toward the street where my Audi was parked. My fingers, stiff from the cold, were clumsy and rigid making it difficult to brush the light dusting of snow off my windshield. I sat in my car, and smoked a cigarette while I waited for it to thaw. Things change- I could care less if my parents or any of their party guests saw me smoking in front of the house- David's opinion was the only one that mattered anymore. I envisioned David and I lying bare, each of us turned on our side facing one another, staring into each other's eyes beneath his thick blankets. David's face would beam with light, the inner light of something more beautiful than words could ever express, and he would comb through the waves of hair falling over my shoulder. He would tell me how his life has changed because of me and how I was the most important thing in it. David's warm body would...

Thump! Ka-Boom!

I jumped and let out squeal. Something heavy had landed squarely on the trunk. Straining to see out of the side and rear view mirrors; I finally turned around to peer out the back window, but the cold air and my rapid breathing had caused it to fog. "Dammit," I muttered wedging myself between the front seats and leaning my upper body weight onto the back seat cushions. Using my sleeve to wipe off the condensation, I was able to clear a small area in the center of the glass.

The raven was back! It stared at me with beady enflamed eyes; the core of his breast expanded and a tetrahedron of light shot forth blinding me. I slipped causing my weight to shift and me to lose my balance. I scrambled back into the front seat. *Oh shit...oh shit...oh shit! It's happening again.* I fumbled with my car keys, panicking; the raven was out to kill me. Things never change. *Just for the worse...just for the worse...just for the worse.* I slammed the car into drive as the shadows of the haunting silhouettes surrounded the back end of the vehicle and rushed forward overtaking me. "Get away from me!" I screamed punching the gas and blasting through the black figures that blew away like dust in the frigid biting wind.

I didn't know where to go- I just knew that I wanted to get away. I wandered aimlessly down the now glacial rural roads of Osnaburg. *What if I just drove the car off the side of the road and into a tree? That would change things...would that be for the worse?* I slid through the trailer park where Cameron lived and thought of stopping, until I noticed the slew of cars that wrapped around her tiny street and onto the next. I couldn't know if they were the cars of family, giving thanks, or rowdy college boys watching a good show. I drove on. Although something told me not to, I resolved to go to Adrian's dad's auto-body garage. His purple truck was parked out front, and timidly, I approached the first metal bay door and knocked. The door was lifted moments later and Mason Waters stood before me. He tightened the Confederate bandana on his head and stuffed his paint stained hands into his tight jean pockets. I hung my head with guilt- I had not come down to visit him since Adrian had been locked away.

"Come on in, you're letting my heat out," he said.

I knew I was forgiven.

"Who ya got there Mason?" a husky voice called from behind him.

"Stray cat," he said maneuvering around a broken down Chevy and making his way toward the tall red tool case that held, among other things: thousands of dollars of equipment, a sizable amount of porn, and a hidden stash of marijuana.

I followed him and took my usual place in the folding chair next to the wood burning fire oven. The chair was precisely where I had left it over six months earlier. Things never change. The regulars were at the garage that day- as they were every day. Austen, with his bottle thick eye glasses and Harley Davidson biker outfit; Therm, who at nearly eighty still walked to the garage every day to joke with and keep Mason company; and Dalton, Mason's fat cousin who didn't smoke pot or drink beer but liked to sit around the fire and tell old war stories about when he, like the rest of the West Virginia boys, did too.

"You remember that piece of shit Corvette that was layin' in two pieces over there in bay three?" Austen asked taking quick puffs off the pinner joint that he had rolled.

How could I forget that mound of junk? "Yes, of course," I replied.

"You should see it now. Mason's been working on that

damn thing for months, but yea buddy, when he's finished with it she will stand up and scream!"

"Ain't that the truth," Therm said lighting another non-filtered cigarette and coughing mucus into his squalid handkerchief. The cancer hadn't stopped him yet.

"Dalton, get the door for my pretty gal here. I wanna show her what Mason's done," Austen said motioning for me to follow him into the back paint room.

"That your way of tellin' me to get back to work?" Mason said laughing.

"Hell no. I would of just told you to get your lazy ass up," Austen joked back. "Ain't she a beaut?" he said pointing to the lemon zest colored Corvette.

The transformation was astounding- from a pile of rubble metal, to now, a completely redone finished product. "Beautiful," I agreed moving into the corner next to the large floor fan that buzzed at full force at my knees and circulated the poignant air up and out through the vent above our heads.

"Yea, to bad she's got a salvage title," Mason said settling on his stool and refilling the paint gun.

The fumes began to nauseate me. My stomach flipped and flopped like a dying fish out of water. I staggered toward the bay door seeing black circles and hearing 'wah wah wah' redundantly echoing in my ears. I pulled on the grimy rope, cracking the door, and rejoiced as the crisp, fresh air filled my tightened lungs. A rap on the door jolted me- every shadow and the tiniest peep- startled me now, but thankfully, it was only Eric and Steve, flush cheeked and cherry nosed.

"Long time no see," I said.

"You're tellin' me," Eric said leaning over the handle bars of his lime green four wheeled quad.

"Just cause Adrian ain't around don't mean you can't come round," Steve added.

"I guess so, but things change, I guess."

"Wanna go for a ride? It's freezing out, but it might be the last time we get to ride before the snow really sets in this winter," Eric said.

"Mason, you still have my Honda right?"

"Sold it. Had to pay the bills."

"Liar," I shot back.

He laughed and paused his spray painting long enough for me to walk by him out the paint room and back into the warmth of the garage. "Close the door!" I heard him holler to his son's friends.

I lit a cigarette and pulled the tarp from on top of the custom lavender and black 2002 Honda EX quad that had been my birthday present this past April. I had taken it out only once- with Adrian- before things had changed of the worse. Carefully, I pulled it around to the last bay door.

"Let's go," Steve shouted pulling on his gloves.

I flicked my half smoked Newport to the snow covered pavement and fastened on my skeleton airbrushed helmet.

"Tell Adrian I said hi next time you see him," Mason called from the front door.

We circled around, creating figure eight patterns in the snow, and stopping in front of Mason I cut the engine, hopped from my seat and threw my arms around him. Things never change- I had missed Mason- more than I had realized.

He wiped his hands on an old rag that he kept stuffed in his back pocket and shook his head. "I don't know what it's going to take for that knuckle-head to learn his lesson. No matter what though, I want you to know that you are always welcome here."

"I know," I whispered back. Before the tears began to swell; I turned from Mason, mounted the Honda, and left him, his garage, and all the painful memories behind me.

It had begun to flurry and the flakes, that are typically pleasing to watch from the coziness of the indoors, were hell to navigate through. I turned off Main Street- not five minutes into the ride- and onto Pekin, the narrow dirt lane that accessed the strip mines two miles west of St. George's, the flakes began to solidify and pelted my plastic visor like round bee-bee pellets. The Honda skid a few times, churning the thick snow and spitting it back at Eric and Steve who followed close behind me, but handled remarkably well on the now ice covered tracks. I shifted up a gear as I led the way up and around the steep dune, then throttled down as I ramped over our man made jump- still cruising at forty-five miles an hour. I passed into the woods, barely avoiding a fallen sycamore trunk, straightened the body of the quad, and accelerated down the bleak trail.

I had forgotten how much fun racing the four wheelers could be. Eric and Steve pushed ahead of me for a time and weaved in and out of one another playfully. I felt released- free- happy. The odometer climbed to fifty-eight- the ice lined tree branches whizzed by at lightning speed. *Nothing can stop me now!* The chugging voice of the engines behind me decreased causing me to release the throttle and slow. Eric and Steve puttered their quads up next to me and idled. Eric lifted his visor, "did you see that?" he asked pointing back, down the twisting trail.

"What? What did you see?"

"You didn't see it?" Eric stammered.

"See what?" I repeated the hairs on my body standing on end- and not because of the cold.

"That friggin' huge black bird sitting on the stump back there!"

My heart began to pump at triple its normal rate. *No…please…no…not again.* I didn't dare turn around to see the giant fowl. Things don't change. I already knew what was happening- the shadows were coming after me again. "Drive! Drive!" I cried slapping my visor down and kicking the Honda into gear.

The horror manifested again. The tiny spheres of sleet hung suspended in the air. Steve and Eric's eyes were locked in terror. The whistling wind stopped. The world paused and I was there to witness it. The raven's vast shadow closed in on the three of us until it loomed high above. *This is the end.* A sudden burst of frosty air exploded down the wintery path and shook the clear coated trees, and caused the drifting snow, which had accumulated along both sides of the deep ditch which separated us from the dense thicket, to shoot up and then come crashing down again. Then it began to roll. "Shit! Go! Go! Go!" the strained words finally were able to escape my cracked and wind blistered lips. The back end of the Honda fishtailed and lurched forward. The avalanche of tumbling snow barreled down the narrow trail after us, gaining speed and force.

The clearing and Silver Lake was just around the next bend. *You're going to make it. Going to make it. Get to the lake and the Jupiter Motel is just a quarter mile up the hill. Get to the motel. Get to safety.* The rolling pile of snow had now reached over seven feet high. *Keep your eyes on the clearing. You're almost there.* I dared to look back again. The snow had become flesh- cold, gray, and concrete. The mass of bodies exploded through the mountain of snow; there must have been hundreds of them, the same shadows that had surrounded my car only hours before, the same silhouettes that I had seen at David's, the same gloomy figures that hid in the dark hallways at St. George's. They were gaining ground on us, galloping on all fours, a viral torrent of irascible snarling steel.

An artic gust of air rolled through us; the raven above let out a blood curling screech and swooped down for the kill. Scalpel talons tore through my coat and ripped through the wool sweater that was underneath. As the claws penetrated my skin, I howled in excruciating pain and in reflex, jerked the handle bars hard to the right. The sudden change in trajectory knocked the raven from my shoulders. *This is our chance.* The Honda went air born as I crossed over the wooden bridge and landed down into Silver Lake Valley. A QUARTER MILE. A QUARTER MILE IS ALL MY LOVE. YOU CAN RUN THAT DISTANCE IN LESS THAN SIXTY SECONDS. I SAW YOU AT THE TRACK MEET. YOU CAN DO THIS. YOU ARE GOING TO MAKE IT. THIS...WILL...END! I kicked the gear down to neutral again- the raging stampede had disappeared. The raven was gone. All that could be heard was hum of our engines and the cracking of the frozen tree limbs.

The semi-frozen lake was situated in the middle of the

valley behind Jupiter Motel and a trail less than three hundred meters from St. George's new recreational facility- Garden Hall. Eric and Steve removed their helmets, pale and terror stricken, they idled their quads next to mine. My heart crashed against my chest and my ribs ached. Suddenly, the ground began to tremor and before our eyes the words 'love and hate' appeared in a crimson blood spatter pattern in the pure white snow and in redundant motions, spikes of solid, jagged ice sprang from the frozen tundra, one after another. The spits of ice poked out of the ground like sharpened javelins; crossing the length of one side of Silver Valley and continuing across the lake- a briar patch of sickle thorns. YOU WILL BE TRAPPED. YOU HAVE TO GO NOW LOVE. Eric and Steve reacted before I could; the spray of slushy snow from their tires covered my visor and clouded my ability to see, but I blindly followed David's voice and raced to catch up with them. I felt the tires begin to climb the gradual grade of the hill, and sensed the snow packing in around the tires- grasping onto the wheels and holding me there. Smoke from the tail pipe billowed and I choked on the fumes which crept under my helmet and tightened around my neck. I fought through the tension and forced the quad forward. The bottom of the Honda scrapped over the cement curb, and I knew that at last I had reached the parking lot. The tears that rolled down my face had frozen and my eye lashes were stuck together. Eric and Steve were gone- they had left me again. Some things never change. *Where was David?* I needed him. The day trips and nightmares were never going to stop. My redundant nightmare-of-a-life was never going to change.

"Are you okay?" a sweet, high pitched voice called out to me.

I looked up and saw David's handsome redheaded friend leaning on motel room door and his partner walking toward me. I shook my head no and collapsed onto the hard blacktop.

"I'm Lamia and that is my husband Mara," she said helping me to my feet and affectionately placing her arms around me. "I've seen you around a few times. You're David's little princess. We've heard a lot about you and have been meaning to get together with you. We are old friends of his you know. Actually we are on our way to his house right now. Come with us."

Mara pulled the Honda in the carport that was behind the motel, and Lamia and I warmed ourselves in the back seat of her classic Firebird. I chained smoked Lamia's Marlboro Red cigarettes and rested my head on her inviting shoulder. I caught Mara smiling at me a few times in the rear view mirror. I listened to Mara and Lamia chatter back and forth and wondered why David opposed me meeting them, who were so nice and comforting. All I wanted was to be with David again. Things never change. No that is a fallacy- things only change for the worse.

THE ROYAL PAIR

Thanksgiving 2002

"Where is David?" I asked anxiously pushing my way passed Mara and Lamia. My eyes darted around the dimly lit foyer, and adjusting to my surroundings, I noticed an alluring glow from somewhere beyond the dining hall. Intrigued, I threw off my coat and hat and wandered through the living and dining room toward it- reeled in on a fish hook.

"I don't think he's returned home yet," Mara called after me.

"But don't worry about that," Lamia added, "we'll take good care of you until he gets back."

I paused at the doorway to the sitting room- someone was home- I could see the top of their head from where I stood. They were seated, quiet and motionless, on the black leather couch facing the window which overlooked the small yard that was mostly comprised of an enclosed kennel and a few barren shade trees. Cold fingers grazed across the back of my neck causing my blood vessels to constrict and my muscles to flinch at the unexpected stimulation.

"Have you met Captain Murmur?" Mara asked as he and Lamia squeezed by me.

It must have been Mara who had touched me as he and Lamia entered the sitting room, and it made me uncomfortable. It was not a friendly tap on the back, but rather, a lingering suggestive advance. "Yes," I replied from the doorway still apprehensive about proceeding any further.

"Come sit next to me," Mara said referencing the empty spot next to him on the opal colored chaise lounge opposite the noble Captain. "I won't bite."

"He won't but I might," Lamia said winking at me.

I heard Captain Murmur snort under his breath as I inched by him and took my requested position next to Mara. "You'll have to forgive me Captain," I said exhaling deeply. "It's been a very tiring day for me."

"I can imagine."

Lamia pulled off the flimsy shrug that was covering her arms and threw it onto Mara's lap exposing a tightly bound corset and bulging pale breasts. Placing her hands on her curvy hips, she strutted over to Captain Murmur and draping her arms around his collared neck, straddled his legs and pulled herself on top of him. The Captain placed his hands underneath her short suede skirt, flashing her violet thong, and rubbed her bare bottom, while she giggled and whispered in his ear. I glanced at Mara and desperately tried to gauge his reaction. His wife was on top of another man and his supposed friend was caressing her right in front of him; but the expression on Mara's face was not that of indignation or disbelief, but rather pleasure and amusement at her promiscuity. *Weird. Things keep getting stranger and stranger!*

"You seem tense," Mara said running the palm of his hand across my back.

"You have no idea," I admitted. I wanted to leave. The sexing that was taking place between Lamia and the Captain made my skin crawl and Mara's continued flirting made me feel self-conscious. I was worried what David would think if he came home and seen us together in his sitting room- Mara massaging my back and a part of me loving it. I didn't want to like it, but there was an unexplainable connection between us every time I sensed his cold touch. I knew it was wrong, and I hated myself every second that I sat next to him, absorbing the chemistry between us, and becoming more sexually aroused.

"Murmur, where is the mutt?" Lamia asked finally untwisting her ivory arms from the Captain's neck and frisking her fingers through his messy brown hair which was molded into a mohawk.

"I made sure to put him out."

"You didn't have to do that on my account," I said concerned and looking out at the fluffy flakes that were still falling steadily. "It's cold outside."

"Not where he's at," Captain Murmur replied, and the pair laughed with him.

Mara drew his hand from my back and placed it lightly on my knee. Squeezing it he said, "Lamia why don't you get our little princess something to relax a bit?"

"David did say that she is wound a little too tight," she said hopping off the Captain and grabbing my hands, which were clamped tightly in my lap.

I blushed with embarrassment. I had never been more open with anyone than I had been with David- and yet he told his friends that I was too uptight? I only knew how to be me and it bothered me that David was not fully satisfied. What more did he want from me? Why did he feel the need to sell me out to his group of friends- ones that I had not even met- friends he didn't want me to meet? *At least he told them that I was his princess. It must be true that he cares for me at least. That is all that really matters.*

"No need to be shy around us," Mara said smacking me on the behind. "When you come back we can all get to know one another a little better."

Captain Murmur stood straightening his starched uniform and looking toward the window and the darkness that was beyond it said to Mara, "I will leave you to it."

Mara smiled and nodded to him as we left. "Hurry back my sex goddess," he called to Lamia (I presume) as she guided me toward the bathroom.

After securing the door and lighting several votive candles that decorated the sink counter top, Lamia asked, "How are things going between you and David?"

"I thought they were going well. I fell in love with him the first moment that I laid eyes on him. I had never met anyone so beautiful and sexy in my entire life. I feel so lucky, you know? Lucky that David sees anything in me."

"Hmm," she said reaching down the front of her extremely tight violet and taupe striped corset and producing a yarn, hand woven pouch the size of pack of gum. "Sounds very romantic."

"I guess, except for the fact that apparently he thinks I'm stuck up and boring." I watched her place a Marlboro Red between her lips and light the tip with the flickering flame of one of the small scented candles.

"Don't take it too hard princess or read too far into it. I didn't mean anything by bringing it up, and trust me; it doesn't bother David all too much. It's obvious to all of us that he really cares about you. I mean he gave you that silver necklace didn't he?" she asked pointing to the pendant that hung from my neck.

"He did," I said fingering it. "I just wish I knew how to truly make him happy. That's all that I want to do."

"Here take this," she said reaching into the tiny pouch and producing two pills.

My hands shook and a thick heaviness settled within my chest. I accepted the capsule but didn't take it.

"Look," she said ashing her cigarette and offering the last few hits to me. "David is by no means the easiest person in the world to please. He is very needy, demanding, and emotional; but you will never meet a more loyal companion. Whatever you give to him, you will get twice as much from him. Just take the pill Autumn," she said popping one in her mouth and swallowing it without the aid of water.

"You're in love with Mara right? You married him. You want to spend the rest of your life with him? He is your life…he is your world? That is how I feel with David. Is that wrong?" I slowly placed the pill in my mouth and taking a drink of water I forced it down.

"A life is a tragedy. All of our lives are tragic one way or another," she said stuffing the pouch back down the front of her undergarment. "Show him that he is more important than anyone. Show him that you are willing to sacrifice everything to be with him. Show him that your love is unwavering and that your loyalty is never ending. And, have a little fun," she said lunging forward and planting her lips onto mine. She grabbed me by the forceps pulling me in closer to her and forced her wet tongue into my parted mouth. Her strike was quick and as lethal as a rattle snake- she kissed me aggressively but it only lasted a few seconds- I wished it had lasted longer. I was light headed and dizzy, and wanted nothing more than to lock my lip on hers again and taste her bitter sweetness. "Follow me," she said blowing out the votives.

Upon entering the sitting room, in my dazed and confused state, I noted that Captain Murmur had left and a new face, one I had never seen before, had taken his place on the leather sofa. The particulars of his countenance escaped me, he was ordinary and nothing about his person initiated special notice. He was just as plain as Lamia was magnetic and as easily dismissed as Mara was memorable. The later was crouched at the brick fireplace, diligently working on the flames which jumped and danced in light blue and orange splendor and caused his fiery red hair to glow against his pale creased forehead.

The room began to spin as I attempted to make my way to the chaise next to the fireplace. The roasted goose and caviar that I had eaten earlier bubbled and gurgled in the pit of my stomach and caused a burning, gamey, fish taste to linger near the back of my throat. *Why is this happening? It's the pill. It must be the pill that Lamia gave me.* The spinning intensified as I reached the lounge, and feeling my way more than seeing, I collapsed down onto it and closed my eyes. *Please, let this stop! I don't know how much more I can take.* To my surprise it ceased- slowly- the decreasing rotations of a merry go round, something that starts off fun, until you realize that you're stuck on it and can't get off. I opened my eyes, hoping the effect of the drug had worn off for good. *Had it? Or had it not?* I was removed from my current situation. I was watching myself sleep. There I lie, beautiful and still on the lounge, my chest raising and falling peacefully, my mind cleared and resting. *How is this so? If I am there...how can I be here? At the doorway again? Watching myself?*

The terror had struck again! The forged color lens that taint the way the world is viewed had been removed; all that remained was this- the black, the white, and the gray. A sense of relief washed over me. I am not afraid. I'm curious, more than anything else. I want to see further. I want to see deeper. I want to experience what lies just beneath the conscious.

SO GO ON.

I move into the sitting room not releasing my eyes from my body which has begun to twitch sporadically. I take a seat next to the fire and reach out to touch the arm of Mara who is still fussing over the fire. I feel nothing, and my fingers slip straight through him. He doesn't know that I am here.

"Enough with that," Lamia scolds and lifts his tight graphic T-shirt up, digging her long polished fingernails into his bare back.

"Mmm, I like it," he said. "Give me some more of that."

"You can't control yourself with me," she said grabbing a fist full of his messy hair and yanking his head back.

Swatting her away, he pulls off his partially ripped tee and flings it to the floor near my feet. My head turned back and forth from side to side, and I can faintly detect the sound of my back molars grinding against one another. "You won't satisfy me?" he asks his wife while stroking my flinching cheek.

She laughs and begins untying the violet ribbon of her corset. Seductively, she pulls the ribbon through each loop hole, exposing more of her pallid round breasts- inch by inch- until at last, she wiggles the lacy fabric down around her hips and to the floor. The sight of her hardened pink nipples causes me to breathe more rapidly. She stands directly beside me, and no matter how hard I try to feel her firm calf muscles that scream to be touched- I can feel only air. "You always get what you want darling," she said unfastening the thin metal clasp of her skirt and slipping off her matching thong. My cheeks and neck burn hot with desire. *I want to rub my hands over every inch of her body.* She left me yearning, and unaware of my alter presence; she stood hovering over my trembling, sleeping body.

"I see what you want," Mara said turning from the fire pit and joined her in slowly pulling the clothes off my body. Mara rubs his lips over mine and runs his fingers through my wavy hair. Completely naked, my legs shake and my skin glistens with perspiration. Lamia climbs on me first, and grabbing my neck in her vice grip hands, sinks her fanged teeth into my neck. Blood drips from the open wound sending her into a frenzy. "You act as if you never tasted her before."

My body jerks and my arms flail as if I were fighting her off in my sleep. My unconscious resistance only intensifies her delight causing the plump veins in her neck to pop out beneath her skin. She latches onto my nipples, biting forcefully and tearing the flesh down to the sponge-like fat layer. "Go enjoy your incubus," she said raising her head from my breasts. Blood runs down the sides of my chest and trickles down my abdomen. She pierces her sharp teeth into me again and again- a wild animal tearing into a dead carcass. I watch her rub her naked body with my blood, I watch her enjoy me, and I am aroused by it.

"Come here slave," Mara says to the forgettable one who sits on the couch watching it all. Obeying, the incubus approaches in a half bent stance- humbled and submissive. "I'm very pleased with your efforts, bringing us all together, I won't deprive you of all the fun. In dreams you come on to her, get inside of her, you've seen them together at night and know that the Master has gone astray. It was right of you to alert us of this…what The Reign has feared for some months now- that she must be destroyed. Your hard work will be rewarded my slave," Mara says rubbing himself. The incubus's hand, too, disappears beneath Mara's form fitting pants. I barely dared to breathe- in fear of being found out- as I excitedly watch the slave thrust his tongue into Mara's mouth and rhythmically move his hand to the harmony of his moans. "You make me feel good," Mara said breathing heavily and pushing himself away from his lover. "But, in the midst of all this…there is work to be done."

Pausing her feeding, Lamia said, "You're right; it's time to get down to business. Come here my sex god." Wiping the blood from her bottom lip, she climbs off my limp body, which in all the savage vigor, had slid halfway onto the floor.

Mesmerized with sexual anticipation, I move closer to the chaise desperate to feel on the couple's body- or more desirable- to feel them as they felt me. I need to know what it is like. To be ravaged. To be used. *All I want is for David to be here.* My thighs tingle and beads of sweat roll down my armpits. To see Mara kiss David or to feel Lamia's supple skin on mine, it was more than I could handle. The adrenaline that pulsed through me was everything that I could imagine, but never acted upon.

"My turn," Mara said kneeling down beside me by the fire. Impulsively, I tried to throw my arms around him but instead of feeling his slippery skin against mine, I feel my face smash into the hard marble floor. I push myself up onto my elbows stunned, and wincing in pain I massage my throbbing jaw. Tasting the rusty flavor of blood, I spit and wipe my mouth with the sleeve of my woolen sweater. Mara drags my limp body from the lounge and onto the floor beside me. I stare into my face which is twisted into a disturbingly defeated grimace. The pain of it faded my hurt away. Mara climbs on top of me, clapping his hands over my mouth and nose and digging his shin bones into my forearms, he makes it impossible to fight, inhale, or escape. "You may fight my incubus bitch, but you won't fight me. I will get exactly what I want from you."

Lamia laughs and joins in holding down my arms while her husband unbuckles his belt and pushes himself inside of me. "I think she likes it," Lamia shrieks as my body ripples in convulsions.

"I'll give her something she'll like."

"I found the perfect thing for the little princess," she said snatching a piece of wood from the pile measuring nearly three inches in diameter. "Flip her over!"

"Yum," Mara said licking my face and rolling my body onto my stomach.

Rape me. Rape me. Rape me. I loved watching them fulfill my secret fantasies.

"AUTUMN…AUTUMN." I hear someone whisper my name. The small voice is distant and where it originates from I cannot tell, but the pitch and consistency is familiar and loved.

"David?"

"AUTUMN, YES MY LOVE, COME HERE."

I wander in the direction of his voice and pass the couch where Mara's lover and my eyes connect, as if he can see me after all. I don't care, I am unafraid of the sinister glare that he permeates toward me, and taking one last look over my shoulder at Lamia and Mara, who are still consuming my trembling body I wander after my morning star. The hallway was black as night and a sudden chill filled the air.

"COME HERE PRINCESS. I'M TIRED OF SHARING YOU. I WANT YOU ALL TO MYSELF," David said softly and much closer this time.

Placing my hand on the grainy wall for guidance, I continue to feel my way through the hallway. Dense, sticky cobwebs coat my arms and the silky strands cling to my face. Each step forward brings me further and further back. I lose my footing and fall ungracefully; the floor beneath me had changed into uneven cobblestone which was sooty, cold, and damp. Taking a moment to wipe my scrapped palms onto the thighs of my jeans and brush the webs from my face, I call out to David again. "Where are you?" I wait, hearing nothing in response except the scuffing sound of shoes on the stone floor. "David is that you?" I ask again struggling to my feet and shielding my sensitive eyes to the light that formed in front of me. It radiated from a decorative lantern that sat on the edge of the serving table in David's dining room and was deposited there by a clean shaven gentleman with a bushy mustache, wired spectacles, and black top hat. "David?" I call more urgently.

The gentleman adjusts his brown suspenders and retrieves a small parcel from the inner pocket of his waistcoat. With steady hands, he produces a glass bottle labeled with the skull and bones symbol and pours the contents of the slender vial into one of the gold trimmed goblets- the same goblets that David and I had toasted on countless occasions. Another goblet is placed beside it, and into both, a fragrant wine from David's favorite crystal decanter is poured. A devious smile spreads across the gentleman's face and checking the pocket watch on his belt, he says, "no need to bother cook with preparing a meal this evening my dear for I will be dining out- far too many important matters to attend to tonight."

He watches the seconds tick by; until an elegant woman, with a pink frilled dress breezes past me and accepts the goblet of wine he readily offers. "Honestly darling, you work entirely too hard," the fine young woman says sipping properly from her glass. "You are a gentleman, and bred as such, from a gentlemen's family…" The goblet slides from her delicate hand first. She babbles stupidly for a moment, which is all her patriarchal husband ever heard from her anyway, and then collapses onto the floor grabbing her neck and wheezing away her last breath. "Free at last," the gentlemen says, kicking around the broken fragments of glass with his shiny walking shoes, standing over her lifeless body. The flame in the lantern is extinguished too, as quickly as the life of the young lady.

"She deserved it," David said, now close enough that I could feel him behind me.

Reaching out for him, I hoped to feel him reaching for me just the same. "I've missed you."

"I've missed the way that you miss me."

We embrace and the void and the want float away. "I need to talk to you David."

"I need to show you something," he said more importantly. His tone is almost joking, but it wasn't until the moment he knew that I was more concerned about his feeling than my own, did he grab me and look down on me and kiss my sweating forehead. "We can do this…what we do…your way, you know that."

"Do you see this…do you see everything that I am seeing right now? I know that some of this has to be real, but everywhere I turn I'm reminded how I have no one to turn to. I'm always afraid of what will be said if I ask…I'm afraid to know what will happen. So much of what goes on around me I can't keep straight, but now, things have gotten so bad that I have to tell someone about it. Right here, right now, you are the only one that knows that I'm here. Why is that? It's a nightmare, but it never ends," I stammer.

"A nightmare? Come wander in lust with me."

I hear the sound of running water. My feet slosh on the absorbed carpet. Sink, toilet, bathtub, and her cold dead body.

"I told you that you had to see this! She managed to slice them in the right direction," he said pointing to her wrists and forearms. "This is a nightmare, a tragedy, she was so young, so worthless; and think, the last thing that she witnessed in her sad pitiful life was a dirty razorblade splitting her skin and veins and her bath water turning pepto pink. This is no way to go love. This is what I see, and it's ugly, but it's reality- same as you. As for her, she didn't suffer much, but her misery is over- she left it to the ones she left behind."

"Good Lord," I said turning my head away.

"He had nothing to do with this," David said dragging me out the bathroom and into the darkness. "Or this either for that matter."

A rancid smell of burnt flesh lingers in the stagnant air. Sour and fermented, the smell attacked me, oppressing my senses further with each nauseating step.

"I admire her cowardice," David said snickering at me. "Sometimes you have to admit when the world would be better off without you; but really," he laughed. "She asphyxiates herself first as her head slow bakes in the oven? Coward. Just set yourself up in flames. Be a true purist. Be a true martyr."

We are in the kitchen, huddled around a 1950's Wedgewood double oven which had been used in a way it had never been intended. There were at least a dozen men standing on either side of David and I, some snapping photographs with the latest Calvo bulb flash cameras, others writing gingerly in steno notepads, and a few grouped together and pretending to investigate, but really they tried not to throw up on their spit shined penny loafers. I was desensitized- I felt nothing staring at the lower back, buttocks, and stumpy legs of the housewife who had stuffed her upper quadrant into the oven and turned it on. Her floral print dress was smoldering and burned mid-back as were the undersides of her flabby arms which were charred too and oozing a clear slimy substance- fat that had cooked and partially solidified.

"What a goddamn shame," one of the men said removing his hat as a sign of respect.

"She was a good Southern woman, a God fearing woman," another replied.

"A lot of good that did her," David said.

"I've known her husband Jim my whole life…Oh Christ…Jim…it's going to break him when he sees what she's done," the first mumbled. The two men shook their heads sadly. "In all my years on the police force, I've never seen anything like this."

"This is what I see love," David said leading me away.

I can't say no, staring into the blue eyes that I love, I can't say no. I don't want to say no. I want to follow in his footsteps until the end of time.

"And the worst of all," he says leading me through wasp clouds of smoke.

Where am I? The walls are sea green; the steps are clay colored cement. My back is facing the stairs- not my eyes. My feet are wobbling, teetering back and forth. I try to take a step forward, but I can't move. I look around. The stairwell is narrower than I remembered it. Very narrow. I look behind me and a single tear drops from my eye. I watch it fall…slowly…slowly. The steps seem to descend forever; a never ending fall. Panic. He's in front of me. His face is red. His eyes are red. He's screaming and swearing, but no sound comes out, he's a mute. *I've been here before. This is familiar.* I bite down on my lip and draw blood. *Shit!* I look down and can't see my feet, only the round belly that I had been hiding for months. *Shit!* I scream for help but no one hears me. YOU SERVIVED THIS ONCE…WHAT'S THE CHANCE YOU WILL SURVIVE IT AGAIN? *Shit!* His hands are on my shoulders. I'm falling…falling…falling and on the way down I see only Adrian's unrelenting, hateful face. My body meets the floor. I'm wrecked- gored- empty. Mara and Lamia emerge from the knotty pine paneling that covers the walls of Adrian's living room. They creep on top of me. My pants are wet-soaked with blood. Lamia's eyes bulge out of her head. She licks her lips. Mara climbs on top of my chest compressing my ribs. Petrified, I watch as Lamia devours my miscarried son.

THE REIGN

Thanksgiving 2002

"I've seen your reality my love," David says crouching beside me. "There are things, my reality, which you only read about in books and only experience in your worst nightmare. You think you know how terrible a nightmare can be, but trust me, you haven't seen it yet."

Still sprawled on the hard floor, I reach out to David. "Please don't leave me," I plead.

"I will stay with you for as long as you will have me princess." He strokes my cheek with the back of his hand. "You can never escape yourself," he says accepting my hand, "and you will always be your own worst enemy."

With my hand secured tightly in his, everything seemed right in my world again. We are traveling, David leading as he always does- leading my emotions- and I willingly following. I was unable to see where we were, where we were going- it mattered not- we moved faster, racing into the abyss. Warm air strung my face, the desert like winds sharp as the task master's whip, lashes out in a snapping vengeful fury. We weren't in David's home anymore that I was certain, but the mirage that floated around me only stayed for a moment, and then was gone. This happened several times; and instead of grounding me and providing me with a sense of my current locale, it only added to my disorientation. My surroundings spun around me, and images whirled around in my head.

"The feeling is similar to vertigo," David said as we began to slow.

"I wouldn't know," I manage to choke out, clutching my daedal head and finding it difficult to speak.

"Come...sit over here princess, we've reached our final stop."

I was alone in the dark. David had instructed me to sit on a hard chair of sorts and had left. I had heard the tap of his shoes grow fainter and fainter until I heard them no more. "David! David...David...David," I call out, my frightened words echo off the walls and bounce back to me. Running my fingers along the base of the chair, I find it to be porous, splintered, and uneven. The arm rests feel the same except for the very ends which are rounded, broad, and smooth. A thumping noise causes me to jump and grasp hold of the chair. Louder the thumping drones, growing more pronounced in my head. "Stop it!" I scream. It is hell within my hell.

"Give me the necklace," a voice whispers. It is a familiar voice, the same voice that I hear every night in my sleep.

"David!" I belt out panicking.

"The necklace. Give it to me." It crawls on top of me in the darkness, I can feel it- the prickly, itching sensation that molests my legs, arms, and chest- settling over me and crushing my ribs. "He will abandon you once he's used you up. Once his need is met. You are nothing. Soon you will see your own insignificance. My masters have you now- at this very moment. Thanks to me. They will get inside you. They will weaken you. You won't last long. Then it will be over. And the necklace. It is not yours to have. The Reign fears that things are different this time. The Dark Prince has never parted with it before. It is his statement to my masters' and the others as well. You are his. You are not to be harmed. How it enrages them. He commands you. He commands us all."

The silver necklace is ripped from my neck and the monster is gone. I wheeze heavily, trying to clear my airways, triggering a couching fit. I bend over, like any good track coach will advise against, and struggle to catch my breath. The sounds of approaching footsteps and muddled conversation quiet me as I strain to hear.

"I rule The Reign. I command and you all do as you are told."

A creak of a door and shuffling feet mark his arrival. As he enters, the room is illuminated from the sparks of fire that glow beneath each of his angelic footsteps. The fire climbs the walls, which I can now discern are constructed entirely of glass, and billow and crackle above my head. David had brought me to an enclosure with limited egress, a vault, and I am trapped in it. My sweaty palms clamp the arms of the chair, and looking down I screamed at the sight of the dried human bones that had been fitted together and the skulls that were fashioned as the base and the hand rests.

"Don't fret my love," David said calmly. "It is merely my throne- perhaps one of suffrage- but is mine none-the-less.

I gasp at the change in his face, a face I had seen before, scarred and weathered and pitted with the slivering vessels- purple and engorged with blood, and the empty eye sockets that leaked, the scaly skin that chaffed and peeled around his hair line- the death and destruction that owned him. I tried to run.

"Stay awhile," he smirks. "There really is no place for you to go, not in this place- not yet. Raising his arms, he sets fire to all that surrounds us, serpents of fire that coil and slither on every surface of ground, wall, and ceiling.

At first I had been ignorant to the breadth of space- infinity- that we hovered, suspended in guarded air- an all seeing cage, high above the pit of fire. I am cemented in place. I am a helpless observer.

"Now," David said pacing around the perimeter of the glass dungeon. "Madam Therriot, dear oracle, I want to know what you see. What has changed? Something must have

129

changed."

"Yes my Prince," the old gypsy said stepping forward. "I see your little girl is here. I'm amazed that she has made it this far. When I first met her at the festival, I underestimated her strength and mental stamina. It is not my place to judge, dear Prince, only to tell what is and what will be."

"So you maintain your assertion then Madam? She will die...too soon?"

"Before her time, my Prince."

"And to what end?"

"One that can't be altered."

"You dare to toy with me?" David said slamming his fist against the glass wall. "Speak it."

The old women's head sags and she drops to her knees. "My abilities only reach so far, my Prince, far inferior to what your eminence deserves. Forgive me."

"Fool, forgiveness is not within my abilities!" David said looking out at the swells of fire beneath and the multitudes of tortured bodies that wallowed in it. "As for The Reign," he said turning and facing me, "I believe you've met them all before."

I swallow nervously as he approaches me. Again, I try to bolt. He snickers, showing me his mouth which is laden with thick black tar which coats his teeth and snake-like tongue. He strokes the back of my hair and slowly circles around me eyeing me deviously. "Why am I here?" I cry out in defeat.

"This is where you belong princess, seated right there on my throne, with me always."

"Please David you are scaring me," I sob as the reality of the matter settles in. I'm forever trapped.

He laughs, feeding my fear, "and now the introductions." A wave of his mighty hand sends flames shooting into the scalding air. "Princess, may I present The Reign- my oldest and most trusted companions who work for me and restore the order above and manage the tyranny below. Stolas you know, or perhaps not in his human form, my keen night stalker- my fierce raven of death. "Tell me Stolas, how are you and your Legion managing to mold and influence the masses?"

"It is a simple task, eminence, as you always say. The jinn are weak minded and easily swayed."

"Feeble and mindless," David said squeezing the sleeves of Stolas's leather jacket. "It is your duty to instruct the Legion to draw them to me, for you must be the one to look over my flock. You…all of you… have been preoccupied with that pretty thorn sitting over there- and why? You have lost sight of the goal. She is already a part of me. Forget her! Be fishers of men- the jinn- I want them all Stolas, every last one of them. I won't be satisfied! Murmur, what have you to say?" he asks shooting the Captain a glare that cripples him and causes him to fall onto the glass floor.

"As always. Dark Prince, I strive to do your will."

"And your three slaves, the Erinyes?" David asks walking behind the Captain and placing his foot forcefully on his back.

"The Kindly Ones ask no questions, eminence, they do as I instruct. They obediently collect the souls of the fallen jinn, or what's left of their souls I should say. Neverending…she is a good soldier…dragging down all the habitual deceivers; Voice of Revenge…my sweet little school girl…captures those who never can let go; and my favorite warrior… Envious Anger…she is diligent in having those who lack contentment surrender. My innocent wretches, together they will bring in more debtors and transgressors than you could ever hope for."

David drove his foot further into the back of the vulnerable Captain, "I'm relying on it Murmur."

"Yes, my Lord."

"I need you down here, all of my Reign, there is work to be done. Murmur, the Kindly Ones must handle the outside while you focus on the core. The time has come for the Eninyes to take control. Ensure that is being done- that they don't disappoint me."

"Yes, Great One."

"Where is Mara and Lamia? Where is my Royal Pair?"

"When they are not preoccupied with themselves you can be assured that they are with someone else," the oracle said with a toothless grin.

"They have no self-control," David spat angrily. "Disobedient, gluttonous, slaves! Cerberus, seek them out," he demanded. The loyal bas rouge, which I had not seen lurking behind the massive throne, emerged and stopping to flash his pointed teeth at The Reign trotted to the doorway and awaited his chance to follow the Master's orders. "He is the only one that is truly loyal to me. The rest of you have turned against me," David said lovingly stroking the regal canine.

"No Great One," Stolas stammers. "What you fail to see is that we are trying to protect you...but your will is always what we strive to achieve."

"Silence slave," David hissed. "You have no opinions. You have no thoughts. You have no abilities to make decisions. That goes for all of you. All this time you have turned a deaf ear to my will. I've told you to follow the plan, to wander along beside me, but every last one of you has taken it upon yourself to meddle in affairs far above you. I told you to leave the princess to me, but you won't and you will damn it, damn us all. We are already in it," he screamed, fire shooting from his mouth. The Reign quivered in fear as David's thunderous voice cracked the glass walls and quaked the floor beneath us. "Do what I command. I reign above all!" Madame Therriot shook and kept her eyes to the ground; Murmur and Stolas, on their knees, reached to kiss their Master's hand as he passed. "Besides Cerberus, she is the only one that I can depend on and you all seek to destroy it- to take it away from me."

He posed his last statement in an awkward sort of rhetorical question and no one dared speak another word. "Don't you fear my princess," he said kissing my cheek. "You have nothing to fear when I'm with you...and that is always."

My lips are stitched together and I too, like the sullen others under David's control, were unable to respond. I sit frozen and wide-eyed upon his throne of death and mutiny and watch him pace incestuously from one side of me to the other. I longed for the David that I knew and loved, the blonde beautiful boy with skin as smooth and white as porcelain and eyes that I could wander in for days. This hell was more than I could bear, a twisted and deranged place where nothing was as it should be, where beauty was pissed upon and happiness was nothing more than an empty synapse. The fire consumed the glass cube we were trapped in- it ate its way across the floor in a torrent of swirling orange. The heat was suffocating, a blistering plague that welted my skin and slowly began to break down my flesh. David's disease was rampant, inflicting pain and misery on us all- and he laughed.

"Brace yourself my love we are to descend down. Nothing can prepare you for what you are about to see." The transparent vault began to lower, and I, an unwilling participant in his evil game, closed my eyes and prayed for the nightmare to be over. "No one is listening princess," David smirked. "There's no one there."

The sound of wailing startles me and I rock back and forth and shake my head violently to quiet the screams. They won't be suppressed. The cube settles at last on the solid ground, rattling the walls that separate us from- what I dare not open my eyes to see.

"Bring them to me Cerberus."

I squint my eyes and see the three headed beast walk from David's side out the heavy glass doors and into the blazing pit. The stench that filtered in from the open door attacked my intestines first, wringing them like a wet towel, then crushed down on my larynx- the foul odor of human feces mixed with sweat and ministration blood that had accumulated and sat rotting in a dry, one thousand degree heat for an eternity.

"Don't turn away my love," David said placing his scarred hands on my scabbed and boiled shoulders. "With the right direction we can reign over this together- you and I."

I shook my head no. I wanted to die. If I were dead this

would all be over.

THAT'S MY GIRL. His words grinded thorough my brain. "Get out," he hissed abruptly turning from me and directing his wrath toward his kneeling subjects. "You are my executives, fashioned after my own image. Murmur: go collect my faithful fallen ones; Stolas: influence and herd my flock; and Madam: we shall consort together soon. If you adhere to my commandments, the pieces will all fall into place. If you, my servants, do not fail me, the order will be restored as it has been foreshadowed. Now leave me."

The horrific screams ring in my ears, tortured outburst of his victims who were too foolish to repent of their Earthly sins. David stepped to the edge of the door and patting Cerberus on his flank said, "no need to bring the Royal Pair in...you know what to do." Cerberus wags his tail in agreement. "They must pay for their disobedience. They shall not surface again until I command it." The doors slam shut but do not muffle the savage barking and snapping, or the inhuman cries of Mara and Lamia that follow. I jerk forward unexpectedly- I had been struggling against an unseen advisory, to no avail, for what seemed like an eternity- hell's hold upon me- and was finally freed.

"Autumn! Autumn! Wake up my love. Come on dammit. Come back to me. Oh princess...what have you done?" David's naloxone voice stabbed my heart and my heavy eye lids slowly opened. I was cradled in his arms, and on seeing me stir, David buried his face into my stomach and sobbed.

"David?" I said weakly. "David what's the matter?" I rubbed my clammy hands through his shining hair and breathed in, to my delight, his comforting scent. Sitting up groggily, I scraped my elbow on the cider block fire place in his sitting room. He lifted his flushed, tear streaked face, which was lovelier than I had ever remembered, close to mine and delicately placed the silver necklace rightfully around my neck.

"I thought I lost you princess," he said wiping his face with his shirt sleeve. Pulling me to my feet, he assisted me to the black leather couch. "Leave it Cerberus," he called to his loyal one who sniffed and pawed at a red stain on the carpet. "Autumn, are you alright?" he asked tucking a blanket around my legs.

"A little dizzy," I admitted shivering. "I had another bad dream David. I had a bad day actually," I said recalling the terrifying chase through the woods that occurred earlier. "Things keep getting worse. The nightmares come more regularly and are more intense. The day trips are so real...they have to be real...but at the same time...I don't know. Nothing is real anymore. You think I'm crazy don't you?"

Two figures flinched in the corner shadows. I had not seen Mara and Lamia until now, cowering and holding one another in the darkness. Cerberus's low rumbling growl sent another shiver through me- chilling me to the bone. The hair on his strong back was raised like the quills of a porcupine, and inching closer to the pair; he snarled and snapped his powerful jaws in a rage. The sound of their inhuman squealing followed, and the predator-Cerberus- and his undutiful prey disappeared before me.

"No princess, I don't think you're crazy, I told you before...it's a false reality."

Part II

Thoughts of Reverie

"It is in our idleness, that the submerged truth sometimes comes to the top." Virginia Woolf

SUBLIMINAL SEMTEX

Email and Letters from November 30 - December 19, 2002

> **From:** autumnallstar@aol.com
> **Sent:** November 30, 2002
> **To:** T.Greggorydb7@aol.com
> **Subject:** Missing You

Tony:

You never know how much you miss someone until they are gone. Boy do I miss you. Things just aren't the same here without you. I haven't been the same. Is that being selfish you think? Sorry to always draw things back to me. Me Me Me. I know that is what you are thinking, but you were always that anchor for me. The calm consistence that always lacked in my life. Now you're gone and I'm falling apart without you.

I hope you had a good Thanksgiving. You were sorely missed this year at the Marseille dinner table. I had to fend for myself for the first time in what...a decade? Remember the first Thanksgiving you came to my house? My mother was trying so hard to impress your mother. We hit it off immediately...laughing at my father's snooty business partners and hiding the bottle of vodka from my mother. I'll never forget that spider you slipped into Mrs. Lovewealth's plate. Ha!

I knew at the precise moment that we would be friends.

I could have used your slyness this year that's for sure. I resorted to drinking myself...and guess what...no one even noticed. The peacocks were just as snobbish as ever and the sleazy politians the same. You know...always working their angles. My parents absorbing it all in glory and pretending that we have such a wonderful happy family. I am so sick of them. I can't wait to graduate and move out. When the time comes I won't hesitate and maybe I can rid them of my life forever.

There are some things that I wanted to talk to you about. It's too hard, too embarrassing really to talk about it over the phone and you know me...it's always been easier for me to write to you about these difficult things. You are the only person who I don't think will judge me. It helps that you are so far away and that I don't have to look you in the eyes after spilling my guts and telling you how totally twisted my life has gotten. I think I'm going insane.

I skipped out on Thanksgiving early. I couldn't bear to be there another second. I feel like that a lot you know? Like I can't breathe and I'm being suffocated. Anyways, I was sitting in my car and I swear to you a huge bird fell out of the sky on the trunk of my car. I've seen this bird before too! I saw it the night of your party, I've seen it hiding in the shadows of St. George's, and I see it in my dreams. The bird is evil Tony. It might sound completely crazy but the bird opens its chest and hundreds of zombie creatures float out of it. They are after me Tony. They surrounded my car and when I drove away I blew through them like they weren't even there.

I went to the garage too that night. I'm sure that you're not happy about it. I know that you think I should let Adrian and everything associated with him go by the wayside but it's hard to just cut people lose. Mason and I always had a good relationship even when I was on the outs with his son. I went four wheeling in the snow. Yes, I forgot to tell you that it snowed on Thanksgiving too. I was out in the woods and the strip mines by St. George's with Eric and Steve Wise and the damn bird was back! It and all its crazy monsters chased the three of us. It's hard to describe what happened Tony. It was like everything had a mind of its own and the bird and the monsters and the wind and the snow and even the Silver Lake was against me.

It was unreal but at the same time I was living and breathing every moment of the madness. When it was finally over I ran into two of David's friends who took me back to his house. The girl drugged me…and being naïve or maybe it was the urge to fit in, I willing went along with it all. I must have passed out from the drug because the next thing I remember was David holding me and crying. While I was out of it, I had the worst nightmare. I have nightmares every night now…for the past several months…even before you moved away. The nightmares are so bad Tony and they feel so real.

I dream that I'm being raped. I dream of death and blood and torture. I even dream about my dead dog Hero sometimes. The dreams are so vivid. I can see the evil in everyone and I can see the evil in myself. Yesterday, I dreamt about these people I had never met before, all of them from a different time and a different place, and all of them dead. I saw myself in my dream. I was being raped by David's two friends while a third sat on the couch and watched it. The sick part was in my dream I liked it.

The worse part of all was last night I relived the worst day of my life. I was at the top of a flight of stairs and…. oh never mind. I can't even stomach writing about that. I'm so scared Tony. I'm afraid to go to sleep. Actually I hardly ever sleep, but when I do, I have the worst nightmares. I'm paranoid all the time now. It's gotten so bad that now, I don't so much fear things on the outside anymore. The things I see on a day to day basis frighten me, don't get me wrong, but I'm more afraid of myself.

I wish you were here Tony. I wish you were here to tell me that I'm going to be just fine and I'm worrying over nothing. Maybe I really am going insane. Write me back when you have time.

Autumn

November 30th

Autumn,

It's been a long time since you've come to see me. I know how easy I am to forget about. Even my dad made it up here to see me. He told me that you came down to the garage on Thanksgiving. What's that all about? You miss him but don't miss your boyfriend? Pulled the Honda out and went four wheeling with my friends huh? Lucky you don't come up here cause I'd slap you in your mouth. You think you can just hang out with my friends without me? You have balls Autumn but you always did do whatever it was that you felt like you wanted to do. Eric and Steve told me about what happened out there in the woods. A giant bird attacked you and Silver Lake froze over with ice picks trapping you guys? No shit. They left out the part where you guys were doing acid until I really pressed them. Yea the last time I did it my mom turned into a queen angel fish and was talking to me. Dumb fucks. I might not be as smart as you and you're stuck up little prep school friends but I'm no idiot. You should leave the drugs alone they'll rot your brain and you can't handle them. Plus that's trampy and I thought you were above all that? I've heard that's all that you do now. You and your slutty friends stay strung out and party all the time. You don't think I hear shit just cause I'm locked up? I hear everything. I also know that you've been hanging around some new guy too. You want to play me and have your little fun while I'm in here. Try it. Just remember that you belong to me and when I get out of here I'm going to beat both of your asses.

Adrian

From: cammyrun21@aol.com
Sent: December 2, 2002
To: autumnallstar@aol.com
CC: vanderbiltrulz@aol.com, lacystacy@aol.com
Subject: Christmas VayKay

So what's the deal skank? By this time every year you are

going on and on about where we are going for winter break. I've not heard one peep from you this year about where we are going. Or what…don't tell me you haven't gotten around to planning it? Holla back girl.

Cameron

From: vanderbiltrulz@aol.com
Sent: December 2, 2002
To: autumnallstar@aol.com
CC: lacystacy@aol.com, cammyrun21@aol.com
Subject: Christmas VayKay

I've been wondering the same thing….what's up Autumn? You too busy for us now that you found true love? Haha! I say we head overseas. Screw the west coast beaches and screw New York. Although I wouldn't mind a day in Bloomingdale's.

Lauren

From: autumnallstar@aol.com
Sent: December 4, 2002
To: vanderbiltrulz@aol.com
CC: lacystacy@aol.com, cammyrun21@aol.com
Subject: Christmas VayKay

Sorry girls…and no Lauren I'm not too love struck to remember my own winter vacation plans. Jeez…it's like I told you at school. Things are kind of messed up for me right now. My parents are being complete assholes and are saying that my holiday might get cancelled. I know that I didn't have a lot of details about it today…but I came home and had to listen to both of them…the hypocrites sit there and lecture me about how my attitude has changed and the fact that they know I've been sneaking out of the house at night. I guess Sister Mary Thomas Bernard called my house and told them that I'm failing two classes. The trip is in jeopardy of being cancelled. No money from the rents means no trip.

Autumn

From: lacystacy@aol.com
Sent: December 4, 2002
To: autumnallstar@aol.com
CC: cammyrun21@aol.com, vanderbiltrulz@aol.com
Subject: Christmas VayKay

There must be some way to talk your parents into letting you go. I know we are all sounding like little brats, but you've spoiled us the past three years in taking us with you for Christmas. It's a tradition…we have to go. Puh-leeze!!!!!

Stacy

From: autumnallstar@aol.com
Sent: December 5, 2002
To: cammyrun21@aol.com, vanderbiltrulz@aol.com, lacystacy@aol.com
Subject: Christmas VayKay

Okay girls…so I talked things over with my parents again tonight and they agreed to let me…us…go on holiday after all. Thank God because boy do I need a vacation. They are "concerned" about me and said that I have to go to some shrink for a few weeks of talk therapy. They are the ones that need therapy. But…I took one for the team and agreed to do it. An hour two days a week for the next couple of weeks will be worth it…I guess. How does London sound?!?!

Autumn

From: T.Greggorydb7@aol.com
Sent: December 9, 2002
To: autumnallstar@aol.com
Subject: Missing You

Autumn:

I'm sorry that it's taken so long for me to get back to you. We've spoken on the phone a dozen times since you wrote me that email and you never brought any of this up to me. I don't understand. If I had known things were this bad for you I would be there to talk, and help in any way that I can. You know that I never check my email. Is that why you chose to write to me with all your secret confessions? The only reason I even got into my email was because I got on here tonight to play an online game and I had to go to my email to retrieve my password. I'm so sorry Autumn.

I was really hurt when I read all the things that you are going through right now. I wish I was still in Osnaburg so we could go through it all together. I hate being away from you and I miss you too. More than you can imagine truthfully. I've never been judgmental with you and I'm glad that you feel that you can trust me and talk to me about whatever it is that you are feeling. I'm here for you. I don't think that you are crazy. I think you're confused and that over the course of the past few months there have been some big changes that have happened in your life that you are trying to sort out. That is normal.

You always take things a little hard Autumn and you are very sensitive. I know that even though you hate Adrian that it has been stressful for you with him being arrested and sent away. I know that my moving has been difficult and that your feelings for David Huntsman have been overwhelming and out of this world. Sounds like you're not sleeping. Sleep deprivation does weird things to you. You need to get some good rest. The nightmares are probably caused by all the stress and pressure that you are feeling. Honestly it doesn't matter that the hallucinations that you have during the day are not real. I know that they feel real enough to you.

Try to take a deep breath and relax a little bit. I think…and I can't believe that I'm saying this but…I think for once your parents might be right. Going to talk to someone about what is going on might be the best thing for you. Sounds like you all are still partying pretty hard on the weekends…maybe you should calm down with that a little bit. Lay off the alcohol and everything for a while. Purge your system of all the toxins that are weighing you down. I'm not saying that it is causing the problems but there is no way that it is helping it.

I'm glad to hear that things are going so well between you and David by the way. You sound so happy when you talk to me about him. You deserve to be happy. You deserve the world. I talk to him too, quite a bit, and he feels the same way you do. I'd rather see you with David any day than that waste of life Adrian Waters. Stick with David he won't steer you wrong. That is unless you want to come to Jackson Missouri and be with me... kidding! (Not really). I will know now to check my email.

Tony

December 11th

Dear Adrian,

In all of what you said, I'm glad that Mason came to visit you. Things have been tough for me lately; not that I expect you to care or understand. I've wanted to come see you for some time but there is something that is holding me back. Your anger and you displacement of it...on me is hard to swallow, but it's always been that way so why I hope it will change is beyond me. Things never change...or when they do it is only for the worse. The worst as in our relationship. I know that in your heart you believe that everything is my fault and that I never cared about you. That isn't the case. I did love you...a long time ago. Sometimes I wish that it could be like it was years ago before so much jaded our lives and molded us into the monsters that we've become. We can't undo the past Adrian and all I can do is suppress all the pain and try to move forward.

It's sad really...I feel we never gave each other a fair chance. Just as we were beginning to mature and learn how to love and care for one another it all went to hell. I think once we learned I was pregnant. We were so scared. We were so alone. At that time all we had to lean on was one another and instead of doing that and holding onto each other tight, I let my own precious and insignificant ambitions and you let your jealousy and rage take control. Looking back I think that we could have gotten through it...together we could have prevailed. When the world was crumbling around us instead of picking up the pieces and building our own world we let it crush our hopes, our dreams, our future- our conscious. For my part, I'm sorry. Sorry that it all has come to this.

I've told you before that I was faithful to you and that I was not having a relationship with Tony Greggory as you so adamantly believe. That is the truth and whether you can embrace that as the truth or not is on you, but I want to reaffirm it as the truth. You were so angry…and even now you hate him and are bitter…you hate me. I never would have believed that your envy over our friendship would have driven you to the actions you took that night…at your mom's house…on the stairs. The moment I fell was the moment that sealed our fate. I have forgiven you but I can never forget the reality that you killed our son and you ruined my life forever. Although I said, after the dust settled, that I would stay with you and give you the opportunity to make this all up to me I can no longer honor that promise. There is nothing left for us. There is only horrible vivid memories that I only want to put behind me. I lied- I can never forgive you for what you did.

I'm glad that my misfortunes on Thanksgiving brought you some joy. Unfortunately, I was not doing drugs as you suggested- as for Steve and Eric- I can't speak to what they did before they came to your dad's garage, but I can say that I did not see them do anything. Maybe they said that to you so you wouldn't think that they were crazy…like you think I am. I don't care what you think anymore. I am free of your hatred and your judgments. What they told you is true. We were attacked and chased by a black raven through the strip mines and the woods. Everything around us was alive and had turned against us…the snow…the air…even Silver Lake. It is hard to describe-how time stood still and my worst nightmare unfolded right before my eyes. My life is a nightmare now Adrian. I see things when I'm awake that you only see in your most terrible dreams, and my dreams are of things that no one should ever have to experience. My parents think I'm insane apparently and have decided to send me off to a shrink so they can "help me". My Christmas holiday was even on the verge of being cancelled this year. Almost…so don't get too happy.

I am set to go to London this year with Cameron, Lauren, and Stacy. I know that you hate them…but guess what? They hate you even more. For once I am going on holiday without fighting with you and without feeling guilty about leaving you in Osnaburg. I feel no more guilt Adrian. That is the only thing in my life that is freeing. I know that you will not be happy or even satisfied with this but I want to let you know that even though I hate you on many levels, I still do care about you and want the best for you. Because of that…and all our history…I am willing to try to be friends with you. I can't be with you Adrian. I can never be your girl again. And yes what you alluded to is correct- there is someone else. I will not abandon you. If you want to work on a friendship with me, I am willing to work on it with you. I will await your reply when I return from London after the New Year. Take care of yourself.

Autumn

From: autumnallstar@aol.com
Sent: December14, 2002
To: T.Greggorydb7@aol.com
Subject: Missing You

Tony:

Thanks for writing me back and for all your kind words of understanding and encouragement. I truly believe that empathy is the greatest quality that a person can have and you, my dear friend, always have enough for me. You are good to me Tony and I can't thank you enough.

I took your advice and went into my first therapy appointment with an open mind. There was so much paperwork to fill out! I couldn't believe all the questionnaires and tests that they put you through before you are even able to go back and speak to a real live human being. It all felt very impersonal and I have to admit that I was afraid of the outcome of the first meeting.

The shrink, Dr. Helpnaught, was very nice and it was a relief to be able to open up and talk with someone about everything that has been going on. I know…I know…I have you to talk to but maybe I do need a mental healthcare professional on my side too. She asked me a lot of personal questions, many I was too uncomfortable to discuss on our first meeting, but I do feel that she could be someone that I could discuss my deepest secrets and fears.

I did tell her about the night terrors and about the things that I see and the voices that I hear in my head. She took a lot of notes and seemed puzzled by some of my recent accounts like the night of the big wrestling party and the events that took place on Thanksgiving. The only thing that bothered me was that she didn't say much. She didn't offer any real solution. She only asked me to start writing in a journal. The journal is supposed to be a place for me to jot down my feelings and the things that I see and dream of. I guess I'm to keep this journal for two weeks and then we will go over it and discuss my treatment plan at that point.

The task seems daunting to me. I really don't want to write about those things. The bad things. She also said that I am to write about my feelings…I honestly feel little beside the love I have for David. I am forever in your debt for introducing me to him. He is so perfect. We are perfect together. You would be proud of me I think. Even with all this shit going on…I am happy when I am with him. He is my crutch. I told you yesterday that Cameron, Lauren, Stacy, and I are heading to London for a Christmas holiday. I can't wait. I need a break from the mundane. I need some time away from it all I think.

I wish you were here Tony. I miss you. What is on your agenda for Spring Break? You know that I'm always looking for an opportunity to get away from my parents over the long vacations.

Autumn

December18th
Princess:
I snuck over to your house after you left me tonight. 5

o'clock comes too early and I've grown to loathe daybreak because it means parting with you. Holding you in my arms and feeling your innocent heart beating strong against mine is something that I will never tire of. I will give you the world if you let me Autumn. I will give you everything and in return I request only your heart and devotion. I need only your love and loyalty. If I am the morning star…then you are the world orbiting around me.

I trust that you're day will be filled with smiles and happiness and I look forward to seeing you this evening. I can't say that I am happy that you are going to London, whilst I will be stuck visiting my distant relations in Florida this holiday. A tropical Christmas away from you is will not me "Merry" I assure you.

I hope you find this note before your parents do…after reading this where would they recommend to send you? A shrink certainly won't do.

Are you smiling? I bet you are because I am- when I think of you. Until tonight…Miss me

Your Love—David

December 19th
Dear David,

I'm not sure when you will find this note or the present that I've left for you. I hope it is sooner rather than later after the intimate dinner and discussion we had last night regarding our feelings for one another and the hopes for the future that we both share.

I meant it last night when I told you that I love you and want to spend the rest of my life with you. Although I am not certain about a lot of things regarding my life and my future, I do know that no one in the world could make me happy and complete me the way that you do. You are an angel and the light of my life. I just hope that you meant everything that you said to me. I don't know if I could bear you leaving me…if we couldn't be together.

I'm sorry…I'm rambling. By the time you read this I will

be on a plane heading to London. I will be thinking of you…as I think of you always. My mind is forever filled with terrors, my eyes constantly deceiving me, my ears bombarded with voices. I know that they are after me…but when I think of you they all are silenced. My therapist and I discussed my journal today…the one that I have been keeping and writing down my thoughts, feelings, and fears. I've made a copy of it for you. It and everything that I do is for you- From the Heart.

My love and loyalty--Autumn

CHRISTMASTIDE

Email and Letters from December 22 - 26, 2002

From: autumnallstar@aol.com
Sent: December 22, 2002
To: T.Greggorydb7@aol.com
Subject: Abroad

Tony:

I'm in London can you believe it? You were right...as you always are...it was the right decision to give into the wishes of parents, as selfish as they are, to make this trip possible. Cameron, Lauren, Stacy and I will be in England for two whole weeks. I know, I know, it certainly would not be your first choice for a winter vacation, but I am so psyched! We arrived yesterday and already, I have completely fallen in love with city life. Yes, I the lonely French, country girl am soaking up the bustling Christmas spirit here in the biggest city in the UK. We are staying at the prestigious Park Inn, London at Russell Square. You would definitely appreciate the beautiful buildings that line the square and the park that surrounds it- not to mention we are just ten minutes from the west end of London. There is so much to do here, and as I sit on the private terrace in this ridiculously lavish hotel suite I can't help but to wish you were here with me. I miss you Tony and I hope that you are well. Write me back and miss me more.

Autumn.

From: autumnallstar@aol.com
Sent: December 23, 2002
To: T.Greggorydb7@aol.com
Subject: New Friends

Tony:

I was eager to open my email today and I'm disappointed that you haven't written me back yet. I realize its Christmas and you are probably busy spending time with your parents and settling into a whole new life in Jackson. How are things between your mom and dad? For your sake, I hope it works out this time. What's the news with you? When we talk, you tell me very little about your friends…are you feeling as alone as I do sometimes?

I was glad to hear that things are going well with wrestling and that you like your new coach. I talked to Ram today and he worked my ear over about the love hate relationship he has with Coach Fin. Seems like you are not missing much with skipping out on wrestling season at Local. From what you guys always say Couch Fin seems to be a real douche. He made Ram run bleachers until he puked- what an ass.

Speaking of which, I'm exhausted already! What was the point of running all those miles in the summer? I could just smack you and Ram! You promised me that all the running would pay off…yet here I am sore and completely beat after walking the city all day. Last night we decided to head down to the small café in the hotel lobby. We ordered lattes from a plain and homely waitress who smiled at us a lot and commented that we were awfully young to be out all by ourselves in London. I was shocked! Was it that we looked that young or did she know we were not English? Of course, Cameron mumbled some obnoxious comment under her breath. The old hag then proceeded to loiter by our table and comment on how lovely we all were. It was so weird Tony; at that moment, I think we were all a little uncomfortable.

I thought that Lauren was going to go off on one of her tirades so I decided to engage the waitress in conversation to diffuse the situation. Earlier we had tried to decide where to go out for the night, but of course we couldn't agree on a suitable place. Stacy said she didn't care as long as we could get a decent bite to eat. Of course to her that is all that mattered. I asked the waitress if she had any suggestions and her beady grey eyes lit up. She recommended that we take a cab to the west end, at Oxford and Regent Street, which offered the finest shops and wonderful eateries. She also said that the lights were really spectacular during this Christmastide. I was sold!

The only thing that I dislike so far in London is the traffic. I think if we ran everywhere we would get there so much faster! Don't think that you are off the hook without telling me all about the 3 mile race at the Monument. What was your time? I know you went to Quaker Steak and Lube for your yearly atomic wing challenge right? They do have Quaker Steaks in Missouri don't they? Did you earn a wall of fame photo? How you can eat 10 of those things is beyond me

I'm so pleased with myself, but my father isn't going to be when the American Express credit card bill comes in the mail because we shopped for hours and didn't stop until after 9:00 PM for dinner. Stacy picked the restaurant; an artsy establishment called The Firecracker. You would have been impressed with the place- the black sofas, the quiet corner tables, the sophisticated décor scheme. The lighting was kept low and the small tea lights and vases of flowers that enriched every table added ambience to the already romantic feel of the restaurant. They must have thought we were famous or something Tony! We were served alcohol on the house the whole time we were there! Just as we were finishing up our second round of wine spritzers someone from behind me asked if they could join us.

You would have just fallen in love with our new friends: the twins Stinne and Axel Rhys and his co-worker Silas

Stonemoor. Stinne is totally European chic. She models for a prominent designer here in London and is an actress to top it off. She is so lively and exotic too. Her tanned skinned and blue eyes...you get the picture. Lauren was so jealous of her at first but I think she is warming up to her. Anyways, Stinne and her twin brother Axel are originally from Sweden and moved to England when they graduated high school. Axel and Silas work for "The Old Lady of Threadneedle Street" as they call it or properly, the Bank of England. That may not sound impressive but it was founded in 1694 and is the central bank of the entire United Kingdom. I guess he modeled too when they first moved to London but gave it up after finding his footing in the financial industry- or so he said.

We felt like celebrities sitting there with such beautiful company and drinking champagne and later aged warm brandy. We listened to Stinne talk mostly. She rambled on about the night life, the culture, the arts, and the history of London. Her twin meanwhile sat silent most of the night smoking his sinful Benzedrine laced cigarillos and ensuring that none at the table ever had an empty glass. Neither one of the young men would fit into your circle- dear friend. Axel was too passive, too tanned, too pretty and Silas was too willing to please, too animated, too loquacious for your taste.

I have not had such a wonderful time in my entire life Tony. We closed the bar at 3:00 AM promising to spend much more time with our new friends while we were in London.

Ps. Have you heard any word from David? I've tried to reach him since we left Ohio and I haven't heard anything back from him. I left him a note and a copy of the journal that I have been keeping...a journal filled with my deepest professed love and my darkest secrets. I'm sure he's read it and now he won't talk to me. I haven't heard a word. I'm freaking out...I think it was a mistake to give him the journal- a mistake to tell him my true feelings. Do me favor and try to reach him. Tell him I've been trying to talk to him please. Take care and write!

Autumn

From: T.Greggorydb7@aol.com
Sent: December 24, 2002
To: autumnallstar@aol.com
Subject: New Friends
Autumn:

I got your emails. It's nice to hear from you. I see that the most interesting point in your letters came in your post script. You haven't heard from David huh? Well, I talked to him today. He called to wish me a Merry Christmas. I guess his family went on vacation too- he said that things were not the same without you. Unfortunately, I don't think you have anything to worry about. He didn't mention the journal to me at all so I don't know what to say about that.

The Firecracker sounds like a cool place to eat, but maybe a little too stuck up for me. I'd rather eat my wings at the Lube. Your new friends sound interesting but be careful- remember you just met them dear! Did I do the race you ask? They called the outcome a tie but you know who won it and to celebrate my greatness I did add my picture to the Jackson, Missouri wall of atomic wing fame. Aren't you proud?

Tony

From: autumnallstar@aol.com
Sent: December 26, 2002
To: T.Greggorydb7@aol.com
Subject: New Friends
Tony:

Merry Christmas! I can't believe that it has come and gone. I hope that you had a great holiday because I sure did! There is so much to tell you. I talked to David yesterday!!! He called me and we spoke for about an hour. He is visiting with his family in some swampy, hell of a town in Southern Florida and by the sounds of things is as miserable as any of us would be vacationing with our parents. He said that he appreciated the note I wrote him and that he has been cherishing every word that fills my journal- apparently he hasn't had a way to contact me and the day he called you, he tried to call me too but my phone was off. He said that he wants to talk to me more about our future...I think this sounds promising!! With my mind at ease about David, I was free to really enjoy myself this Christmastide.

We started the day with late brunch, with our new friends, at Knightsbridge at a fashionable spot called Marcus Wareing at the Berkeley where we enjoyed a seven course luncheon. As we were leaving the restaurant Stinne said that she would meet up with us for a late dinner because she had a photo shoot that afternoon. Stacy and Cameron decided to tag along with her and Lauren readily asked Silas, who Stinne said was in rapture with her, to take her to a few boutiques she had looked into last night and was dying to visit. I could sense that she wanted to be with him alone, so Axel and I spent the afternoon together. When it was just the two of us he was less shy and more personable than I thought ever to be possible. After a little coaxing I learned that he is twenty-four years old and has worked for the bank about 3 years. He is an outside banking consultant who travels to prominent banks all over the world training bank employees and government municipalities on fraud detection. He graduated from Cambridge (early) with a Masters in Finance and is rich from what I can tell.

We first went to Trafalger Square and walked the frozen walkways and once blooming gardens underneath the sixty foot decorated Christmas tree. Axel asked if I ever ice skated as we circled back and left Trafalger Tree. I admitted that I had, only a few times, and that I wasn't very good. He was gentleman enough to hold out his arm for me to brace as we slid across the icy pavement and hailed a cab.

Cameron and Stacy really hit it off with Stinne who invited them to a runway show and after party the day after tomorrow. Our Christmas night dinner plans were rescheduled until later thanks to Silas and Lauren who wouldn't quite say what they did all day because of course the boutiques were closed. Axel and I went to Hampton Court (the infamous palace of King Henry VIII). Axel claimed that he was a great man; I on the other hand believe he was irrational and dangerous, to which Axel responded, "there are many ways to measure greatness." His intelligence intrigues me Tony…it is a different sort than we are accustomed to see in and around Osnaburg Township. I'm sure now more than ever that no matter how much I enjoy London and our new friends, not a hundred seven course meals, or a thousand hundred dollar bottles of brandy, or a hundred thousand fleeting trips to Hampton Court will change the fact that David is my true Beloved.

    Best Friends Forever,
    Autumn.

WITHDRAWAL SYMPTOMS

Email and Letters from December 28 - 30, 2002

From: T.Greggorydb7@aol.com
Sent: December 28, 2002
To: autumnallstar@aol.com
Subject: New Friends
Autumn:
Sounds like you have been a busy girl. I just hope that you have been a good girl and have not disappointed me. I'm only saying this because I am your friend, but you are a total rollercoaster ride right now. I really don't understand you, but maybe that is part of the fun. On one hand, you claim that you always loved Adrian. I know that in your heart you hate Adrian. Now, you say that time has made you love to hate Adrian. I think in regards to Adrian, that asshole, you hate that you love him. To me, there is too many loves and too many hates wrapped up in the whole situation. Maybe that should be a clue to just kick his lame ass to the curb? I can hear you inwardly sighing and for some reason that makes me laugh. Adrian really doesn't bother me anymore...I know that it is going nowhere but south.

I have new worries. I am hundreds of miles away from you...when you are in Ohio...but now you are across seas in

England and it is really killing me inside. I knew that you had a crush on David, but he is your Beloved now? Really Autumn? I can see why you like him. I like him too…everyone does actually. I'm almost glad to hear about this Axel character. Good for me that the bloke lives in London and after you leave your little holiday it is the last that you will hear from the creep. Is the stick stuck up his ass permanent?

Wish you were here in Missouri. Bad news! Mom and dad have been fighting…a lot…over the holidays. I don't know if it is just stress or what but I want to tell both of them to go F off most of the time. One more year and I'm out of here. Anyways, enjoy yourself. What plans do you have for the New Year? I honestly can't think of anyone that I'd rather be ringing in 2003 with than you.

PS. (Since we are being formal now I guess??) I'm kind of mad that you let David read your journal and didn't share any of it with me.

Tony

December 28, 2002
Dear David,

I'm so glad that we were able to talk, just now, but I miss you already. Journal writing has become a bit of a habit for me…it just seems easier to write my thoughts than talk about them. Especially to you. I don't mean that in a negative way Morning Star I'm just being honest. There is so much that I want to say to you, but every time that I have the opportunity I back down…I back away from you. The position that I'm in is a delicate one. You are so perfect and wonderful, and most times I feel guarded and afraid. I'm afraid that I am going to lose you. You are the best thing that has ever wandered into my life, and the thought that I could possibly say something to drive you away is unbearable.

I'm sure that you don't understand. Your superiority is saturating, you bathe me in it and I know that you don't mean to. Being away from you has been really hard these past days in London. I try to keep myself occupied so that I don't obsess over you as much…but the truth is that I'm only appeased for brief moments throughout the day and all too often thoughts of you wander redundantly in my head. What are you doing? Are you thinking about me? When will I talk to you again? What will you say to me? How can I possibly respond? How do I keep up with you?

I've thought for a while that I have some serious issues…not just with you…in general. I'm not certain anymore when or where it started or what triggers these awful day trips but I still encounter them…even here in London. The shadows are still there, they follow me not interacting with me the way they did before, but they are here none the else. I've seen the raven perched on the building across from our hotel a few times when I come out to the terrace to smoke. There are things…other things…I can feel their presence around me. I'm paranoid and I need to sleep. Insomnia is a real bitch. I want to sleep but my racing pulse and the tension migraines that I've developed over the past week won't give me any relief.

I'm sick in love with you David. Just how sick you never will understand. To say that I miss you is a gross understatement- it feels like I can't breathe without you. I've been depressed before…when I was a kid…when Hero died and we moved to Osnaburg. I thought that I had beaten the depression and anxiety…but now it is much worse…now it's mania. It's not that I want you Morning Star, it's that I need you. I need to be able to touch you, to kiss you, to run my hands through your silky hair, to taste your sweet ruby lips. I want to crawl inside of you and flourish. I'm dead without you. Sometimes I want to die…is that wrong? Can you possibly understand?

I cry without you and curse the day that I met you…that I used you…that I tried you on for size. I get angry with myself that we can't be together always…it's not fair…because life is drained when you are not a part of it. I worry about when I will see you again…when I will feel you rush through my body. My hands are sweating; shaking in anticipation, all that matters to me is when I will get ahold of you again. My beloved…I don't know why I couldn't just tell you this when I had you on the phone a moment ago. I think that knowing how you dominate my thoughts and influence my actions would really turn you on. I can't help myself. I fight the symptoms...the withdrawal...of being without you...but I'm a junkie, an addict, I can't give you up. I can't live without you.

Autumn

From: autumnallstar@aol.com
Sent: December 30, 2002
To: T.Greggorydb7@aol.com
Subject: New Friends

Tony:

I'm so sorry to hear that your parents aren't getting along. Damn them...like you said...soon enough you will be able to wash your hands of them and the whole situation if you so choose. Parents...I think that most times God gave us the fuck ups just to make our lives miserable so he can laugh.

I am being careful. You have no need to worry at all, and stop being jealous of David! So what I gave him a copy of the journal? Most of it was about him anyways. It is so hard for me to tell him my true thoughts and feelings. My therapist is right...it is better to write them down, capture them in the moment, and share them with a special confidant. That is not to say that you are not a dear friend! Of course you are...probably my closest actually...it just seems that you have feelings about all this and I don't want to hurt you. I never want to hurt you.

All this talk has me down, and trust me I am down enough already. I was just writing to David the other day telling him how screwed up I've been without him...I'm sinking into the depression rut again Tony...the same one that you rescued me out of. You remember that? When I first moved to Osnaburg and my life was such a mess? I'm starting to realize that some people never are able to escape. People like me...we were never meant to escape our demons...the ones that latch ahold of us and never let us forget.

I have a confession to make dear friend. The reason it is so hard for you to understand is because you don't know the whole story...between Adrian and I. I don't talk about it Tony...not to anyone...not even my therapist- so far. Every time I think I have the courage to tell you, I don't. I'm a coward and I'm afraid that you wouldn't understand...that you couldn't forgive me. Let's just say some skeletons are meant to be buried and never exhumed....the type that haunt us from the grave and never let go. The kind that steal happiness and change your life forever...I didn't know what happiness was...until I met David, but even with that secured (at least that is what he tells me) I can't be happy because I'm terrified of losing it. It sucks living in pain and fear all the time.

I was hoping that this Christmas would change things....change my outlook on life. I'm a fool; although, I did make, what I believe to be, lasting friendships out of it in Stinne, Axel, and Silas. I'm starting to believe that you could even like them too- even if they are a bit pretentious. I'm jonesing for a fix Tony...I'm going mad missing David. I didn't know how strongly my addiction was until he was taken away from me and it feels like a piece of me was stolen. Can you relate to that? I'm crazy, I'm crazy, I'm crazy. I'm in lust...I'm in love...I'm in withdrawal.

There is New Year's Eve party at Stinne and Axel's apartment and we all have been invited. So, for the next few days I plan on doing some serious shopping and sightseeing to help take my mind off of David and his beauteousness. I need to keep my mind busy...run it through a meat grinder maybe... that was a joke. I told you...don't be worried.

Your Autumn

From: DeniseMarsaille@aol.com
Sent: December 30, 2002
To: autumnallstar@aol.com
Subject: Adrian
My Dearest Daughter,
I'm sure this letter finds you enjoying yourself in

Europe…where did you say that you were going again? You kids, so flighty and free, you make your poor ma' ma envious. I don't want to disturb you dear, but I'm writing to tell you that Adrian has been calling daily for you. I never knew that such privileges were granted at a facility of that sort, but what do I know of such things? The poor darling sounds fitful. Do contact him dear. I'm afraid that soon I will resort to unplugging the phone for the sound of it ringing has my temples thumping. It must be the weather.

Take care my sweet. My love, my thoughts, my fair wishes.

Dire Au Revoir,
Your Doting Ma' Ma

From: autumnallstar@aol.com
Sent: December 30, 2002
To: DeniseMarsaille@aol.com
Subject: Adrian
Mother:

Things are fine here in London. I've been shopping and touring. Met some new friends since we've been here and we are going to their New Year's party tomorrow night. You would like them. They are beautiful, wealthy, and established. Right down your alley mother. I talked with Adrian before I left. He knows where we stand which is probably why he continues to call. Do what you like- unplug the phone. And it's not the weather dear, doting ma' ma. It's the vodka. You know what the doctor said about your kidneys and liver. You're addicted. You need to stop.

Autumn

December 30, 2002
Princess:

I sent this same day express mail to reach you before the New Year. I enjoyed your letter just about as much as I enjoy you. There is no need to be guarded with me love, I want you to open up to me. I've tried it all and none of it is as pleasurable and fulfilling as you. You make me better and I can't give that up. What can I say love? Selfishness is my way, but you love it, and you love me so I know you can understand. I take a lot of pride in reading your darkest thoughts and desires which you eloquently penned in your journal; they will resonate for eternity with me. You are too right for me princess; and though you claim to be addicted to me, I am so far beyond that. I am you and you are me. We are one in the same. You say that you want to crawl inside of me and live? What you don't realize love is that you have and I've welcomed you in. Stay there...stay with me forever. This love is something I never thought I would feel. It is sick...but you make me that way. I'm content with wandering in your lust forever. Can you say the same?

Your Morning Star

AN APPEALING PROPOSITION

Email and Letters December 31, 2002

From: T.Greggorydb7@aol.com
Sent: December 31, 2002
To: autumnallstar@aol.com
Subject: New Years

Autumn:

So how is my little shopaholic doing? I guess being a shopaholic is better than an alcoholic right...wouldn't want you turning into your mother. Sorry, now it is my turn to be a jokester. So today is the big day, New Year's Eve, and it sounds like you have a very interesting night laid out before you. I can just imagine how excited you girls are to be invited to a high end party with models, designers, and artists. You are certainly right; we would never see the likes of that in Osnaburg. I miss it there so much Autumn. I wish I could move back...to be closer to you...and everything that is familiar. I'm out of place here and it doesn't help that my mom moved us out of my dad's house and we are staying in this run down flea-bag motel. How long will this last...probably until the revelation slaps her in the face- my father is never going to change. He is a selfish ass and she was stupid enough to fall for his lies again. I'm kind of bummed that we are stuck here, half way living out of our car and trying not to catch a disease from these nasty sheets that we've been sleeping on. I give this a week; we will be back at my dad's again.

I hope that you have a chance to read this today before you go to your party, but I'm sure you are busy and have much more on your mind. At this point, I'm crossing my fingers that we can talk when the ball drops tonight…2003…can you believe it?

Tony

AOL Instant Messenger

December 31, 2002 11:42 AM

cammyrun21: I've been calling your phone what's up??

Autumnallstar: I know sorry…on the phone with Adrian

cammyrun21: haha knew it was only a matter a time before he hunted you down

Autumnallstar: don't remind me was trying to just hop on the computer real quick to check my email and write Tony back

cammyrun21: how is he doing?

Autumnallstar: not good he is staying at a shitty motel with his mom and wishing his dad was dead I think

cammyrun21: wow really slumming huh? Bet he wishes he was here in London with us

Autumnallstar: you must have left the hotel early this morning I didn't hear you leave

Autumnallstar: it wouldn't hurt for you to leave a note and say where you are going or answer your phone was worried about you

cammyrun21: don't be worried about me I'm a big girl

cammyrun21: I came over to Stinne and Axel's to help with the last minute details for the party. Stinne is going mad over here obsessing over the little things

Autumnallstar: I can't wait it's going to be so much fun

cammyrun21: I know right…are you even going to be able to come…or are you still going to be on the phone with your boyfriend

Autumnallstar: he isn't my boyfriend and no I'm about to get off the phone with him now

cammyrun21: what is he talking about?

Autumnallstar: at first he was playing hardball like you better be with me and you better not ever be with anyone else

Autumnallstar: then I was like well it's a little late for that because I already am with someone else…I told you this already and it's not going to change

Autumnallstar: and for the past 10 minutes he has been crying and cussing me…it's hilarious

cammyrun21: i would love to hear him sob like a little pathetic baby hahaha

cammyrun21: I love it

Autumnallstar: I don't love it

Autumnallstar: just hung up on him

Autumnallstar: thought that would make you happy…where did you go??

Autumnallstar: HELLO

cammyrun21: Autumn hi…this is Axel

Autumnallstar: where did Cameron run off to?

cammyrun21: she is helping Stinne decide what type of ice sculpture we are going to have set up in the grand room…something about a focal point…I don't know

171

Autumnallstar: figures…

Autumnallstar: so how are you doing?

cammyrun21: looking for an escape out of here I like the finer things but I'm not much of a designer myself

Autumnallstar: understandable…most guys aren't

cammyrun21: yea but I think girls appreciate a guy who is

Autumnallstar: I do…my David back home is that way

cammyrun21: David…again…you told me a lot about him when we hung out last…he is a Renaissance Man huh?

Autumnallstar: the perfect all around gentleman

cammyrun21: I can be a gentleman too…let me take you to lunch

Autumnallstar: okay I guess…seems like Cameron is busy, Stacy said she is sleeping all afternoon, and Lauren spent the night with your friend and won't be back…oops I shouldn't have told you that

cammyrun21: no worries Silas already did

cammyrun21: did you forget that guys are typically more gossip queens than females?? Ha-ha

Autumnallstar: Whores you mean?

cammyrun21: maybe that too but that is harsh coming from an American…we just view things a little different here in Europe

Autumnallstar: sure!!

Autumnallstar: should I catch a cab? Where are we going to eat?

cammyrun21: I told you that I'm a gentleman

cammyrun21: i'll send one of my cars

cammyrun21: Cameron is shoving me out of my chair…I will see you in an hour

Autumnallstar: okay see you then

cammyrun21: it's me bitch…jeez I leave the computer for a few minutes and you are agreeing to a date with Axel?? Nice!

Autumnallstar: it's not a date I'm just going to get some food…I'm bored here at the hotel

cammyrun21: whatever you don't have to get defensive with me…I think you should have a little fun

cammyrun21: so I hear Axel telling the driver to get the Jaguar ready…hmm sounds like a date to me…wait until you see their place!! They have stupid money Autumn…I think it would even impress you

Autumnallstar: money isn't everything Cam…look at my parents

cammyrun21: yea but you have admit it's pretty hot to have that type of money when you're twenty something

Autumnallstar: if I had to pick money or love I'd pick love

cammyrun21: i tried to love once but I've never really been capable of it

cammyrun21: especially not myself

Autumnallstar: I know what you mean

cammyrun21: we are all thorns

Autumnallstar: oh stop it you are a rose don't forget that you are as beautiful as one and I know that those agents and designers who will be at the party tonight will think that exact same

cammyrun21: hope you're right

Autumnallstar: of course I am. You are great and you will be great tonight

cammyrun21: thanks have fun on your non-date

Autumnallstar: you can't help yourself can you??

cammyrun21: nope

cammyrun21: see you tonight skank

Autumnallstar: learned from the best ha-ha see ya

> **From:** autumnallstar@aol.com
> **Sent:** December 31, 2002
> **To:** vanderbiltrulz@aol.com
> **Subject:** Tonight
> Lauren:
> Hey girlfriend. I just got off the phone with Adrian like a half hour ago. I'm so emotionally drained from talking to him. Why do I even take his calls anymore? I wish you would have been here to convince me to hang up on him...sooner than I did. Yes, I hung up on him. I know that you are proud. Was AIMing Cameron for a while and then Axel got on her screen name and started talking to me. He asked me to lunch and I agreed. Cameron said that he is coming to pick me up in a Jaguar and that he and Stinne live in a ridiculous flat. I can only imagine. You told me how nice of a place your boy-toy has...and think about adding her actress, model, designer money to it too. Holy crap...at least I know that the lunch will be paid for ha-ha. Anyways, I've been trying to call you to get advice about what to wear to lunch...I don't want to be too dressy but I don't want to underdress. Of course you're not picking up because you are busy...doing??? Too much probably. Call me when you get this...and it better be before the party tonight when I really will need wardrobe advice.
> Autumn

> **From:** autumnallstar@aol.com
> **Sent:** December 31, 2002
> **To:** T.Greggorydb7@aol.com
> **Subject:** New Years

Tony:

I am sitting on the terrace at the hotel, chain smoking cigarettes and staring down the awful raven that has been stalking me all day- that is not quite true-it's been stalking me for months. It won't leave me alone Tony, and the shadows, they lurk about every corner. I should be getting ready now for the New Year's party that Stinne is throwing, but I can't concentrate. I don't know if it is the anxiety that is building inside of me…the fear of the intense nightmares flaring up again…praying that tonight doesn't end the way things did the night of your party; or if I am seriously contemplating the appealing proposition that Axel presented to me over lunch.

I'm sorry…I've gotten ahead of myself…or maybe my brain is just lagging that far behind. Adrian called me this morning just as I was sitting down to the computer to write you. The conversation started off angry as usual. He threatened me as usual…said that if he couldn't have me than no one could. He ranted and raved about you and the secret (non-existent) affair that we've been carrying on for years. I didn't even bother to negate his accusations anymore. I am taking your advice and refusing to feed his wrath. Apparently someone is talking to him…probably Eric and Steve Wise and disclosed to him that I have been seeing David since he has been locked up. Those assholes! Ever since we rode the four-wheelers through the strip mines on Thanksgiving and all hell broke loose, they won't even take my phone calls. The good news is that I'm not even worried about it. Of course Adrian says he is going to kick David's ass…I will have to be sure to warn him of that.

I've resolved to not take any more of his phone calls. I know you don't believe me Tony but all this fighting is going to cause an aneurysm I'm sure of it. So anyways, I hung up on Adrian and was too flustered to even write you…I'm sorry but I'm writing now so don't be too mad with me. Cameron messaged me which was kind of relieving because I woke up this morning and she wasn't here. I figured she was with Stinne, but it made me mad that she couldn't at least leave me a note tell me where she went. She is so independent- I don't think she realizes it when she does stuff like that- that people actually care about her and worry about her. So, we are talking and then the next thing I know she is not responding my messages. Can you believe I sat there and idled out? Next thing I know Axel is on her screen name and before I know what is happening I am agreeing to go to lunch with him.

An hour later I was escorted by his driver into a brand new 2003 Jaguar S. I'm not shitting you Tony! I sat next to Axel, and sizing up his black on black Versace outfit and sipping champagne at a hundred dollars a glass, and I came to the realization that he was attractive in his way. I could get used to these non-dates! He is only a few years older than us and he already has made a fortune for himself. I have to admit that even though I was a little in shock by it all, I was jealous of it too. Axel was on the phone with clients nearly the entire drive; I suppose that is the price that one has to pay to reap the big paychecks. Somehow it has to be worth it. We drove to north London…the Kilburn area to be exact. Axel said that he was taking me to his favorite restaurant and while he quietly conducted business on his mobile, I found myself mentally calculating. His designer outfit was easily two grand; Rolex ten grand at least; rings, sunglasses, aviator hat four thousand; and on and on and on.

The restaurant, Blois Dijon, is the most fabulous little French establishment in London. Tony if ever you are to visit France away from France this is the place to go. I instantly felt at home and I'm not sure if this was Axel's favorite or if he was just being cunningly polite in bringing me. Either way, the food and the atmosphere is the best that England has to offer. We sat at a corner table next to one of the windows and shared a bottle of Bordeaux and a delectable appetizer course of escargot, beef tar-tar, and chariot de fromage which was served authentically- cheese from a trolley of course. Axel was quiet through most of the meal which was fine with me…he is such the melancholy sort…and seemed content to smoke his thin Cohiba cigar and watch me out of the corner of his eye. When the main course came, duck with black truffles, Axel seemed to loosen up a bit and started talking to me about the history of Kilburn and some of the landmarks and sights in the area. I barely heard him though because my attention was diverted to a small shop wedged in the back alley behind North London Tower.

Axel followed my gaze and proceeded to tell me that "The Tower" was once a snazzy hotel and had been converted into a modern restaurant. What he didn't know was that it wasn't "The Tower" that had caught my attention but "Topps Furniture". It was the weirdest thing Tony! The first time I ever went to David's house, he told me about someone named Old Topps from Kilburn who was the best furniture craftsman in the world. I know …I know it sounds nuts Tony, but you should see the beautiful Victorian collection of furniture that David has. He claimed that it had been in his family for years. It was so weird the way he spoke of Topps…personally almost…but correct me if I'm wrong…the Victorian period was over two hundred years ago. Was it just a coincidence that I was dining (possibly) across the street from the very place- or was this another day trip? I was so confused.

My head was swimming as I sat stiff in my seat, sucking down a Newport and then lighting another one from the hissing butt. I was thinking of how to present my intentions, to cut our lunch short and investigate Topp's, but Axel's words careened me back down to reality…or not. You will never guess in a million years the words that came out of his mouth. He told me that as I could see, he admired the finer things in life. He was a model in his own right and made his first million before his twentieth birthday. He matter-of-factly informed me that his employment with the bank of England was quite lucrative and that his clients and his business affairs made modeling seem like chump change. He had a proposal for me, he said. He asked me to stay with him in London. He promised me a flat, a car, and ten thousand dollars a month to be his "personal assistant". Can you believe that?! I wanted to know what he meant by an assistant and he actually laughed (I guess there is a first time for everything). He lit his cigar again and told me to get my head out of the gutter. He did admit that he was attracted to me, but he was looking for no commitment, no girlfriend, and no he was not driven to this proposition by sexual motivations. He said that this was about business- he had it all- except the perfect trophy accessory.

At first I didn't know what to think about being called an accessory...and a trophy accessory at that, but after two more cigarettes, let me tell you something dear friend- his offer sounded pretty damn good. The only thing that is stopping me is David -and I told Axel this too. It wasn't until we were back in the Jag on the way to the hotel did I remember I hadn't gone to Topp's Furniture Store. I decided that before I left London I would come back and check it out...and in regards to staying in London...I don't know Tony...what could I possibly do back home to make that kind of money straight out of high school?? Be a dope dealer...kidding...don't you go having an aneurysm! Ha-ha.

Oh my gosh it's nearly five o'clock and I need to start getting ready for the party. I'm a little nervous about seeing Axel again tonight, although he said that of course he wouldn't expect me to come back to London until after I graduated. He said that this was a once in a lifetime opportunity and if I was willing, he would bring me on as a consultant for the bank, but I would have all the added perks of being his employee, and that it would behoove me to seriously think it over. Tell me what you think I should do Tony...you always give me the best advice. I will have to talk to David too of course...there is no reason he couldn't come with me to London...we could live well together of ten thousand a month that I am sure. I will call you when the ball drops tonight. Another 365 nearly down...is it wrong to want to make the most of the next? Don't answer that. If only that raven would leave...............

Autumn

SELF-RIGHTEOUS

Letters January 1, 2003

From: THERAM@aol.com
Sent: January 1, 2003
To: autumnallstar@aol.com
Subject: Tony
Hey Girl:
Tony was pretty bummed about last night. He said that you didn't answer when he tried to call you last night? What's up with that?? Call him Autumn. He is worried about you.
  Ramsey

From: DeniseMarsaille@aol.com
Sent: January 1, 2003
To: autumnallstar@aol.com
Subject: Happy 2003
My Darling:
I was so heartbroken to not have you here near me for the New Year- my lovely child. Your father and I attended a splendid little party last night (though it was sponsored by someone quiet beneath us) and had a delightful time. I kept saying to Bellino, it just isn't the same without our rose here to share it with us. Of course he was thinking the same thing

darling. Your new friends seem to be just the sort of people that I could be proud to say that you are acquainted with. Well done! You know that you won't be a child forever and soon enough you will have to put aside the childish things and think about how you will make your way in this world. An intelligent wealthy man is just want you need and I can't believe there is a shortage of those in London (though it has been some time since I've visited the continent.)

I must run, my pearl, for we are headed out of town again for another Earth saving mission of mine. There is nothing more important than these societal events my daughter, we all talk a good talk but it takes a true crusader (like your dear ma 'ma) to put these good practices to work.

Until we are together again,
Your Dearest Ma' Ma

From: autumnallstar@aol.com
Sent: January 1, 2003
To: DeniseMarsaille@aol.com
Subject: Happy 2003
Mother:

I'm glad to hear that you had such a delightful New Year. I did as well. Sorry I cut you short this morning but I'm trying to recover from a hangover. You know all about those. I will be with you and father soon enough- no worries. Also, you would be interested to know that those people you referred to that I met here in London are wealthy- a brother and sister duo- isn't that just darling? They have the kind of money that would put the entire town of Osnaburg to shame…yes even you mother.

Autumn

From: autumnallstar@aol.com
Sent: January 1, 2003
To: THERAM@aol.com
Subject: Tony
Ram:

I know I know…it's a long story. I would have called him earlier but I just woke up and had to reply to my mother. He just signed on Instant Messenger. Thanks for the heads up. It was good to hear from you. Call me huh??

AOL Instant Messenger

January 1, 2003- 1:29 PM

Autumnallstar: Tony hi…I'm so sorry about last night

T.Greggorydb7: I bet you are, what where you doing that you wouldn't take my call?

Autumnallstar: you sound like Adrian…it wasn't like that. You have no idea

T.Greggorydb7: so stop bullshitting and tell me

Autumnallstar: don't be angry with me please, it all started off great until Cameron got out of control

T.Greggorydb7: what else is new? She is always out of control

Autumnallstar: not like this…you should have been there…to help

T.Greggorydb7: so what happened?

Autumnallstar: well got to the party about 9. Stinne and Axel live on Prince Consort Rd in Knightsbridge which is an extremely wealthy area in London. I told you before that this past week Cameron has been spending a lot of time there with Stinne, but I had never been there. Their flat has to be valued in double digits (in the millions of course)…five bedroom total- 3 suites, reception hall, loft, a double height atrium, drawing room, sitting room, terrace, media room, bar and dance floor, two pools…you get the idea

T.Greggorydb7: sounds nice…I'm waiting to hear how something this good turned all wrong…

Autumnallstar: well the flat was chugged pack with more metrosexual men and anorexic female models than I ever knew existed. That is where it started to go wrong. The moment we walked in the door! Stacy embarrassed us all by stuffing her face with more food than everyone else at the party combined.

T.Greggorydb7: ha poor girl…I take it her "diet" isn't going over so well huh?

Autumnallstar: no she has all but abandoned the cocaine but at that moment …when she continued to take the same soiled buffet plate back and forth up to the table…I wanted to ram an eighth of powder down her fat nostrils

T.Greggorydb7: you're cruel

Autumnallstar: so I had that to deal with and of course Lauren…Jesus Christ- every pretty girl that walked passed her…which was all of them mind you…hundreds…she shredded. I have never heard so many negative things come out of her insecure mouth. She had something negative to say about all of them and as the night progressed and her alcohol limit increased she became belligerent. She actually slapped Silas (I mentioned him to you before- Axel's co-worker at the bank that she has hooked) because she swore that he was looking at another girl.

T.Greggorydb7: wow and he chased after her right??

Autumnallstar: how did you guess? What a freaking nightmare she was…pounding Cosmopolitan's and commenting that whoever designed the garments that the models were wearing (which let me remind you was a part of Stinne's sponsored event) was a complete "fucking moron". Of jeez, I hoped that that comment didn't get back to Stinne …or worse the designer.

T.Greggorydb7: did you really expect anything less from Lauren? She might have the lowest self-esteem of anyone I've ever met. That hard outer shell is just a cover up for the fact that she is not confident in herself.

Autumnallstar: Well let me tell you who were confident…all the beautiful guys working the party…and yes they were working it!! Strutting around the party with more makeup, glamour, and style than any girl could ever hope to achieve. The male designers had frayed flowing scarves, perfectly tilted top hats, pastel pinstripe suits, and patterned collared shirts with matching cuffs. The models sparkled in the dimmed lights of the flat with their thick eyeliner and rainbow colored eye shadow. Most had their nails manicured and polished, several wore varying shades of lip gloss, and a few wore lipstick. Needless to say Tony, you have never seen anything like it in your entire life.

T.Greggorydb7: Did I miss the Halloween memo?? What?

Autumnallstar: We've been sheltered apparently because this was the hottest group of young trendsetters in London…and I felt very out of place…but apparently not as much as Cameron did. This was her big chance you know…Stinne was making it a point of promoting her at the party to all the big name designers, recruiters, photographers, and artists. She had told us all that she believed that Cameron had potential and that she was going to make it her mission to introduce her to all the right people and take her under her arm in her new modeling endeavors.

T.Greggorydb7: Cameron is like 5 feet nothing…how the hell is she going to model?

Autumnallstar: Well certainly not on the runway like Stinne, but there is other modeling she could get started with. Stinne kept saying that it is all about knowing the right people…and being connected with her and Axel would be enough to at least get her foot in the door.

T.Greggorydb7: I thought you said that Axel doesn't model anymore

Autumnallstar: No he focuses all his time on consulting for the bank because that is where the money is he says….but it seemed like everyone really respects him in the modeling field

T.Greggorydb7: you never really made a big deal about him... was he in makeup as well?

Autumnallstar: He was by far the most sharp there. I had never seen him with his hair done, only slicked back, but last night he wore it kind of choppy and messy...and yes he always has serious raccoon eyes

T.Greggorydb7: is that what we are calling it these days? And that is supposed to be attractive?

Autumnallstar: Attractive...I don't know how to answer that really...about Axel. He is strange and quiet and different...but they say (they being the posh young designers and photographers) most times beauty is not what sells...but uniqueness.

T.Greggorydb7: too bad for Cameron...she might have more luck if it were about being pretty...cause she is all but unique.

Autumnallstar: I know...that was the beginning of the slippery slope. I think that was their polite way of telling her and Stinne that as far as high fashion goes...she didn't have much of a future.

T.Greggorydb7: So that was it?

Autumnallstar: I mean it wasn't all bad... okay Stinne's agent Lux didn't express any interest in representing her. The German bunch: Florian, Lukas, and the legendary designer Marina-Jana passed; the Brits: top style recruiter Aberle and her entourage were not interested; and neither were top emerging photographers Rowen Reeves and Val Trace who work extensively with Stinne. But there were several agents who specialize in print photography that were. Unfortunately their names escape me... but a modeling career is a modeling career right??

T.Greggorydb7: I wouldn't think so. It doesn't seem as promising as Stinne hoped for...and she is successful and knows what it takes to be successful. How did Cameron take the news?

Autumnallstar: How do you think? Not well. She locked herself in Stinne's suite and wouldn't come out. I sat outside the bedroom door and pleaded with her to come out for over an hour.

T.Greggorydb7: Damn…did you get her to?

Autumnallstar: No it wasn't until Stinne bribed her with coke that she opened the door. Two lines later she was on top of the world again, swearing at me and trying to fight me…like it was my fault. One of her crazy ass haymakers actually connected…and yes I have a black eye this morning.

T.Greggorydb7: Holy shit…are you serious?

Autumnallstar: Yes I'm serious. She was crying and throwing punches. At first she was sobbing that she wasn't good enough…wasn't pretty enough…wasn't important enough to be a model, to be Stinne's friend, to be anybody. She worked herself up into a panting sweat- jumping and twisting around in a rage. Then things completely fell apart- she was railing on and on that she knew she wasn't good enough…she knew…this was going to happen…everyone was out to get her…jealous of her…they were wrong…and she was right. Somewhere in there is when I got hit.

T.Greggorydb7: Cameron and her Hemanitis huh? She is famous for that…that cocaine is going to kill her. Her heart is going to explode doing that stuff.

Autumnallstar: If the coke doesn't her self-righteousness will

T.Greggorydb7: She has always been that too.

Autumnallstar: I know

T.Greggorydb7: I'm sorry to say it Autumn…but none of this surprises me. Stacy has always been greedy and uncouth, Lauren is an attention whore, and Cameron is a raging junkie.

185

What do you expect?

Autumnallstar: What do you say about me??

T.Greggorydb7: I will keep my private thoughts of you to myself...

Autumnallstar: hmmm

T.Greggorydb7: so what happened to cammyrun?

Autumnallstar: I went to nurse my swollen eye and Stinne promised that she would calm Cameron down and bring her home later. This was all happening right as the ball was dropping. By the time I was fussed over by every one of Stinne and Axel's guests and was driven home...it was passed 3:00 AM and I didn't want to wake you.

T.Greggorydb7: You can call me anytime Autumn

Autumnallstar: I was just so tired Tony...and drunk I came in and passed out. Cameron woke me at 9 this morning saying she was sorry and appearing to be much calmer...but less composed. I was too tired and hung over to talk to her so I said okay and went back to bed. And here I am...just waking up.

T.Greggorydb7: Lazy bum... hahaha

Autumnallstar: You're right about that...I'm sad our holiday is about over...but so excited to get back to see David.

T.Greggorydb7: Don't remind me...

Autumnallstar: Hold on a second ....

T.Greggorydb7: Autumn...what's going on??

Autumnallstar: Lauren is banging loud as hell on Cameron's door...and I'm yelling at her to stop. Which she won't...gosh if this is what my mother lives through on a daily basis I might have a new found sympathy for her...hold on again...

T.Greggorydb7: waiting...

T.Greggorydb7: waiting…

Autumnallstar: Sorry… damn her…she won't quit beating on the door. I guess she left some of her stuff in Cameron's room and she is trying to leave so she can spend our last day with Silas…figures huh?

T.Greggorydb7: like I said none of this surprises me

Autumnallstar: I told her to go get another key…jeez

T.Greggorydb7: ha-ha so what are your plans for your last day in London??

Autumnallstar: I'm going back to Kilburn to check out that furniture store I told you about-Topps. I've been curious about it since I saw it yesterday.

T.Greggorydb7: For some reason the British are able to maintain and pass things like estates and businesses down through generations better than we Americans can. It very well may be the same family that still owns the business after all those years.

Autumnallstar: You wouldn't be surprised huh?

T.Greggorydb7: Not at all

Autumnallstar: Shit…hold on again

T.Greggorydb7: hello…

T.Greggorydb7: hello…

T.Greggorydb7: hello…

T.Greggorydb7: hello…

T.Greggorydb7: Autumn…

T.Greggorydb7: hello…

T.Greggorydb7: Are you okay?? I've been timed out twice now…

T.Greggorydb7: Autumn…

T.Greggorydb7: I'm calling you now...

T.Greggorydb7: Pick up...

Autumnallstar: I can't talk right now...I can't...to anyone...I have to go

T.Greggorydb7: Tell me what is going on?

T.Greggorydb7: Autumn....

Autumnallstar: Lauren was screaming...still screaming...

Autumnallstar: this can't be real...can't be real...this is all just a nightmare...can't be real...this can't be happening

T.Greggorydb7: what is going on Autumn? Please talk to me!!!

Autumnallstar: All the vomit the blood. She is dead...Cameron is dead!

T.Greggorydb7: Oh my god what??

Autumnallstar signed off at 3:46pm

THORNS

January 1, 2003

Dear Tony:

This letter comes to you in a rush for I must dispose of this evidence. Everything is a blur right now and the police, the wasps, have swarmed upon us ever since the call to 911 was placed. I've barricaded myself off in my room. I can't bear to think of Cameron just a room way, yet never coming back. She's never coming back Tony...and I'm sick. I'm sick over this loss. She was too young to die...how could she do this? She took her own life- that we can be certain of. Those bastard cops in the next room are investigating and trying to piece everything together. Those dumb fucks...she was unhappy and killed herself. Why is that so hard to understand? There are vomit piles surrounding the bed and even by the window. It looks like she sat near the window for a while- there was a spilled bottle of Jameson on the floor there.

Lauren found her first that you know, and she is still in a state of shock. The cocky detective that responded first to the call said she was in a state of post-traumatic stress. She is whimpering and still shaking in a corner. It was a horrific sight- Cameron's body- limp and cold hanging over the foot of the bed. A pill bottle of Promethazine was on the nightstand and all that is left of the bottle are a few stray pills lying on the table. Also, next to the pills is a mirror and a razor and the faint residue of cocaine. The most disturbing is the needle that was lying beside her… I'm scared Tony…I didn't know that Cameron was doing that stuff. The coke, we all knew about that, but how could she have resorted to speed balling and us not know about it? Or did she get the smack at the party? Maybe someone there gave it to her. While those pigs stare on her lifeless body, and will I'm sure, dissect and pry into her life; I already know what happened.

I have a dark secret dear friend…one that is only to be shared with a few select people. I've enclosed it in this envelope to you. I need you to hold onto it and keep it safe until the time is right and I will share it with the rest. Don't speak a word of it to anyone. Even if you think this is wrong…please do this for me. I will not allow Cameron's memory to be further desecrated…she was troubled, but she deserves better. She deserved so much. I swear I didn't know her intentions. I didn't know things could have gone this far. I would have tried to reel her back in. I would have told her I loved her and that she was worth it. She was worth everything. She lost herself, but I will conceal, with all my heart, the truth of the matter and allow this to be ruled an accidental death.

No one has to know this was a suicide. We can keep this secret safe the way that Cameron would have wanted us to. If it is discovered that it was anything but accidental you know the aftermath that will follow. Cameron will forever be remembered in that light, she will not be granted a Catholic burial, her mother will be heartbroken and shunned, Cameron will forever be gossiped about and will never be able to rest in peace. I trust you now with this secret my dear friend. I know that even if you don't agree you will respect my wishes. Enclosed is her final testament. We depart for home in the morning. I will call you soon.

Autumn

My Thorns—

Wish I could have been the rose you believed me to be—Autumn share this last piece of me. I never understood why people get so overprotective and squeamish over these things. It's not until you're dead that people give a flying fuck. I want to be better but it's just not possible. I only can be what I am. Remember me in a better light. We can never be as wonderful as we think we are. My entire life is a visual disturbance and I'm so tired of it. Give me my six foot plot. Let me remain sick and unhappy. The truth my thorns—my fellow stabbing pains—is we were never meant to be happy. I try to pin point where it all went wrong. I'm met by a cloud of doubt. We are all just toys—his toys—and I'm sick of being played with. I want to be free from it. This is hell we live here on Earth. I'm ruined so I take these pills, and I'm a loser so I snort a line full, and I'm ashamed so I take a swig, and I just want to die so I tie this strap a little tighter on my arm and I hold this venom and take in a deep breath and get ready to shoot it up. It's not fair to live any longer. I'm robbing all of you---everyone—I'm squeezing you out. Not too many left behind to miss me. You will be better off without me---this crude world too. I do this for you.........................These drugs are my relief. Sharp as this needle Bad as this sting it's True. But I'm a thorn....and so are you. Hold onto your faults because like thorns they protect us--from ourselves. No escape. Can't do this do this anymore. Just want to float away. Realized today what I've known for some time—you spend time wishing the days away and it's not until they are passersby that you want them all back to hold onto tight and love and never let go. Let that ecstasy eat your mind. Thorns. Painful, sharp, and stinging. Things are going black. Raven. Hovering over me. No white light. No angels singing. I guess that means I won't be gracing heavens doors. I guess you all know where to find me. See you in hell. You're all coming too. But I love each and every one of you. Thorns. Autumn, Stacy, Lauren and your thorns--Your sins. Your pain. Your nevermind. Say goodbye to them for me. We are all damaged. We are all

191

damned. And in the end I am happy because I embrace it-------
------------------XXOO-------Cameron

REFLECTIONS OF THE SUN

January 1, 2003

Dear Journal:
I can't take this any longer. Coped up in this swanky
hotel room and having these pigs question me. They are
digging. Digging too deep and for what? The grave robbers! All
the digging in the world will never bring Cameron back to life.
They want to pry into my life and ask questions that they never
will get the real answer to. I will never let her down. I will
respect her, even if it was only a mask. It was her mask and
dammit no one can take that away from her...away from us.
Cameron of all people never claimed to be perfect; we can only
be ourselves. The cops try to psycho analyze her thoughts, her
intentions, her beliefs. All that talk made me know the
direction they were wandering down and I didn't like it- even if
it was true. The letter to Tony will be enough to bury this
along with Cameron- in peace. I just need the opportunity to
escape and mail it. Pigs, with their Freudian logic...they don't
have any idea, but I will allow them to blame it on the fact
that...I don't know...she secretively wanted to bang her
father. Pigs...if only it were that easy- to apply blame. The

truth of the matter is that we are all to blame. Cameron was right. Her words echo now in my mind redundantly. We are just thorns, and I don't blame her. I can never know the whole reason, maybe she had no reason, and maybe that was the point. She figured that it would be easier if she just took herself out of the picture. Damn you Cameron! I shouldn't have been your call, it was selfish and self-righteous and plainly just not fair. Perhaps I'm just jealous that she had balls to do it and the rest of us didn't. Why did you do this? I want to scream and slam my head through these walls. Cameron, you've left us all here to deal with this alone. The way they probed and prodded your body. Rummaging through your belongings, touching and talking over things that were meant to be private. Did you not think of us at all? That you were loved? You were loved! If by no one else you were loved by me. How could you do this? That room…that hell…with your vices exposed and left out in the open. Lauren was worthless after seeing you, bleeding and cold dangling off the foot of the bed. Stacy had her head in the toilet…where it perpetually is every other minute of the day. Were you looking down and laughing on us…on the scene you created…the horror you bred? Were you testing us? I tried to right your wrong the best I could…but I don't know if it will matter anyway. They are looking to uncover something…three American high school students vacationing in London alone, invited to a New Year's Eve party hosted by an A list barely legal model/actress and her equally wealthy, independent financial consultant brother, and one of us turns up dead. They are digging and all I can hope is that your secrets will rest six feet under with you my thorn. You didn't deserve this. I heard them talking…through these ridiculously thin walls. The preliminary cause of death is an accidental drug overdose. This looks bad for all of us, especially Stinne and Axel. I'm sure those rat bastards have already beaten down their door and interrogated them as they did the rest of us. I need to call them…but I'm afraid if that is found out it will only add suspicion and that I can't risk. I need to get out of here. I can't breathe. Maybe Cameron had it right all along. Escape the pain and the misery. The raven. She had seen the raven too. I can't even go outside and smoke and suck in some of the dirty London air. The black bird has been sitting outside my balcony door all day.

> **From:** autumnallstar@aol.com
> **Sent:** January 1, 2003
> **To:** T.Greggorydb7@aol.com
> **Subject:** Between you and me
> Tony:

I was so glad that I could talk to you tonight once the cops left. There is so much that I want to tell you, but I have to be sure that it remains just between you and me. I am sending something to you by express mail. It's the present that you were asking me about. I'm leaving now to send it to you. The shadows have come out and for some time they have been staring at me. Don't panic...don't worry...I'll be out for a while but I will call you. I need to escape.

> Autumn

January 2, 2003
My beloved Morning Star:

It's an hour before we are to leave for the airport, and as I wipe the tears from my swollen eyes I can't help counting down the seconds until I'm in your arms again. I keep praying that this is all a sick dream that I will wake up from- but I don't so it must be a reality. The awful day trips are back, and last night the nightmares returned. I thought maybe all that had gone away, but the hiatus is over and the demons are back in full force. My demons...Cameron's demon are...that which makes us thorns.

I'm packed and I'm ready, but a part of me will always remain here in London...the part that died right along with Cameron. There is so much for us to discuss when I return, and perhaps there is silver lining in all this. If I could only come to terms with fate the way that Cameron did, maybe I could see that everything- always- turns out just the way it is supposed to. I am afraid of what I have become, and angry at how far we have allowed things to go. Our holiday in London was supposed to be an escape, a place we could go and take a break and put your heads back on straight, but instead it has ended in tragedy. I want to deny the fact that Cameron took her life. Was I really that blind? We have all been so self-absorbed in our own lives, our own personal vices that we didn't even see her sinking. Why didn't she tell us that things had spun completely out of control? Was it because things are that out of control for all of us?

I pondered this today as I packed my duffel bag, haphazardly throwing articles of clothing inside, caring little about anything else but getting home and seeing you again. The blood stains are still fresh on the cappuccino carpet- drip patterns of an expressionist artist's brush. I lay down across the width of the bed, my feet dangling over the edge of one side, my head the other- just as Cameron had in her final moments. I choke back guilt tears as I remember the Cameron that I hoped everyone else will, the sweet and giving Cameron-the girl who in fourth grade was the first to welcome me to St. George's. I remember the girl who always saved me a seat on the bus and in the cafeteria and the teammate who always backed me- who fiercely admired me. I remember the friend who supported me when everyone else turned their back on me, and even when I was granted penance by my other friends, with Cameron I never needed to ask for forgiveness. I love her and I will miss her.

Your Princess

January 2, 2003

Dear Journal

I am standing in front of a liquid mirror; naked, scared, and ashamed. I look around and realize that I'm standing in the long hallway on the second floor of David's house. I call out to him but all is quiet, quiet as the blue ocean's lure.

"THE GLASS NEVER LIES, NEVER FEUDS

WITHIN OR CRIES. IT JUST REFLECTS, JUST DETECTS. ALL THE FAULTS- THE PAST. IT NEVER FORGETS THE FIRST OR THE LAST," David's voice whispers in my head.

Within the glass a face appears, diverts my eye and causes tears. It's so familiar and I say, "Captivate me if you may." Tentative- the face inches close, reminding me of what I've missed the most. One tear of fluid salt festers the sore that is my fault. "Open up to me mirror," I cry out. "Let me in and allow my rancid heart to be purged of sin." A moment freezes in time. David says it slithers within me like an oozing slime.

My neck swivels about, three hundred and sixty degrees. Cold shivers engulf my body dropping my temperature fifteen degrees to freeze. My blood once balmy but pumping to keep me alive, halts abruptly not wishing me to thrive. A wisp of purity touches my face having tranquil, amazing grace. Our fingertips are just about to connect, when again, the mirror forces me to detect. Cerberus breaks free and trots toward me majestically. I plead, "Pull me, pull me loyal one. There is little time until the mirror separates me from my Sun." Then, into the mirror Cerberus leads me, to my sun- into the sea.

With my sun now cradled in my arms I say, "Oh sun, how radiant you be. Turning away from you cost me an ungodly fee. Oh sun, polish my life I pray, listen to the words years have made me wait to say. Sun, let me orbit around your splendor; let me hold you oh so tender. Sun, blush the very essence of my soul; don't fade away into a distant glow. Pay attention sun or you will miss, duel time spent in a bliss. Sun, please hear me out; don't hide behind the clouds to pout. "

THE GUILT, THE GUILT, THE GUILT.

"Sun there are only precious seconds to shed light, and holding you now has my stomach tight."

IT WAS YOUR DESIRE.

"I weep when I sense your presence; you flutter my emotions like crazed demonic pheasants."

IT HAPPENED BECAUSE OF YOUR EMOTIONS.

"Sun, blanket me with your mercy; quench me when I'm parched and thirsty."

WHERE WAS THE POUNDING ORGAN THAT, NOW EXECUTES THIS TUNE? WHERE WAS IT THAT

MIRRORED MOURN IN JUNE?

I stare into the wide eyes of a confused and rejected child. "Yes sun, it was I that dampened your rays with rain. My beautiful sun, scorch this Earthly pain."

YOUR SON ALTERED YOU LIKE THE SEASONS, AND YET, YOU'VE FAILED TO REALIZE ALL TRUE REASONS. COWARDNESS. IT LEAVES YOU BITTER AND TREMBLING NONE-THE-LESS.

I see myself in the cruel mirror. I'm standing still, naked, and now alone. My sun is gone; as he always has been. Waves of past memories wash over my ashen reflection and I watch myself. I am lying in a white and empty room. White tiles, white paint, white ceiling, white reclining chair, and all the cold steel. I am motionless. I am a coward.

Lamia is on top of me holding me by the throat. Mara's spidery hands creep inside of me- my stomach cut wide open. He grins at his Incubus, who slinks from one corner of the room to the other capturing my dissection in his twisted mind for his master's eternal pleasure.

WONDER, WANDERING YOU SEE, FOR JUST A FRAGMENT OF NEEDED GLEE.

I curse the mirror that torments me. The mirror that dissolves me into my solidarity.

AND THE DEADLY SINS THAT COME OUT TO PLAY.

I watch the turbulent mirror splash and swell and one after another, images crash before me like an unforgiving tidal wave. Cameron dead in our hotel room, pills scattered around her pretty head and lava erupting from her pointed nose.

GREED THE ONE IN THE FLESH. WANTING . NEVER SATISFIED ENOUGH TO MESH.

I watch Stacy engorge herself; I watch her puke it up and eat her vomit all over again.

GLUTTONY THE ONE IN THE MIND. CONSUMING TOO MUCH- AFRAID TO FALL BEHIND.

I see Adrian sitting at Eric and Steve's house, day after day, doing nothing, and beating me.

SLOTH THE ONE IN THE SOUL. TAINTED WITH FILTH- BLACK AS COAL.

The mirror grows still and I see only my humbled face.

LUST THE ONE IN THE EYE. OBESSION OVER POSSESSIONS THAT MUST DIE.

The mirror gurgles and whirls and Tony, sitting and reading one of my letters, surfaces through the foaming waters.

ENVY THE ONE IN OUR EAR. LISTENING ONLY TO ONE'S SELF TRUE AND CLEAR.

Vicki emerges in the mirror next, standing in the middle of the crowded hallway at St. George's, withdrawn, clinching a binder with Tony's picture taped to the inside cover.

WRATH THE ONE IN THE HEART. PANICKY DISBELIEF. RESENTMENT RIGHT FROM THE START.

I shiver as the last of the deadly sins presents itself-Lauren standing in front of a mirror, lovingly hugging herself.

PRIDE THE ONE IN THE ARMS. DISTRURBING LOGIC; COERCING US TO HOLD ON TO HARMS.

Lauren's image fades to black and I silently pray that it is over-that the mirror too will dissipate. To my horror, the oil black raven steps through the glass with David riding on its greasy back. Cerberus, l'un loyal, prances dutifully around the long talons of the magnificent fowl. David dismounts the raven and affectionately stroking the bird's crushing and deadly beak, walks to me with his arms outstretched- and I can't resist him.

LIKE THE DEADLY SINS THAT CLENCH HOLD TO PLAY, I AFFECT YOU THE SAME COMPULSIVE WAY. A MESSAGE YOU'LL NEVER GET. ONLY THE MIRROR THAT YOU'VE MET. IT'S ABOUT DELUSIONS-ABOUT ILLUSIONS, RESULTING IN PERFECTION; YET, STILL FILLED WITH INCLUSIONS. THAT MIRROR PROVIDES FOR ME, A BRIEF GLIMPSE INTO YOUR MISERY.

The mirror disappears as does the giant raven and the loyal dog. It is just David and I. He holds my unclothed and scarred body in his arms, the way he has a hundred times before, and cups my chin in his worthy hands. He tilts his head to the right and then to the left forcing me to make eye contact with him.

"GLUTTONY, GREED, SLOTH, ENVY, PRIDE,

WRATH, AND LUST. MY TRAUMATIC LESSON IS INTENDED TO INSPIRE.

I gasp for air. I am awake. The nightmare has ceased, and Cameron and my sun are still dead.

Part III

Recompense

"Never forget that when we are dealing with any pleasure in its healthy and normal and satisfying form, we are, in a sense, on the enemy's ground." C.S. Lewis

LONDON FOG

February 10, 2003

I had taken up painting to cope with it all- the loss of a dear
friend and my now seemingly failing existence. Returning to
Osnaburg was reality, a reality like my head being beaten off a
brick wall. Once again, I was trapped within myself, a small
piece of dust in an insignificant, transparent bubble mattering
not if it were to pop sending me into yet another skeletal
existence. London was a distant memory, and all the beauty
and wonders of my time there had floated away in the winter's
wind just as Cameron's ashes had fluttered by, light and grey
air born doves from atop the steeple chase of St. George
Cathedral. The bells had tolled that night for mass and upon
hearing them, I dropped to my knees, in the biting cold, on the
outer lawn before the closed church doors and prayed for her
intercession. I hated what I had become.

Above all, I was a liar and the realization of that fact
made it harder each day to exist. The weeks that followed
Cameron's service, I metamorphosed from self-denial to self-
loathing. My main objective was to ensure the confidentiality
of the truth of her destruction. Tony had received the envelope

I had painstakingly mailed from Kilburn and after several phone conversations and coded emails; I was assured that the contents of her final testament were both forever safe and silent. The weight of Cameron's greed compressed my fragmented mind. Angered and spent, I latched onto the only piece of her that I had left- an unforgiving ocean of memories. I wandered down our trial of tears- it was mid-February now and I had barely noticed. I was blinded by the London fog, a numb and mindless ghost.

These thoughts stormed my head like a hurricane as I skid into the main parking lot of Local, nearly on two wheels, my heart pumped petrol, feeding the fire that raged inside of me. I had planned to play hooky and skip basketball practice afterschool- I needed to desperately slip into a state of unconsciousness, to sleep and possibly never wake up- but a voicemail message from Tony changed that. He had called to warn me, after reading a lengthy email from Ram, of the rumors that were circulating at Local about us, about Cameron, about our thorns. According to the email, the origin of the stories could be linked back to the individual who constantly perpetuated them- Vicki Tinsdale. During the last period, I had watched the second hand tick around the clock, counting the seconds until the final school bell notch by notch-one hundred times: what exact rumors were being spread? One hundred nighty-eight…one hundred nighty-nine…two hundred: how bad could they be? Three hundred: how true could they be? Four hundred: how could she do this? Four hundred ninety-nine…Five hundred: that stupid bitch-how could she! Six hundred…six hundred and one: as soon as this bell rings I'm coming after you. Seven hundred: I will not allow you to trample on her grave. Eight hundred thirty-four…thirty-five…thirty-six: I'm going to beat your ass I swear on Cameron's grave. Eight hundred seventy-two: my stiletto would look so nice smashing down on your larynx. Nine hundred….

I slammed on the brakes and tried to yank the key out of the ignition with the car still in drive. All logic and reason had escaped me, and replacing it was fear, resentment, and anger. I was wild, like a starved caged animal, and this was sensed by the isolated groups of students that loitered by their parked cars in the still half-filled lot. "Tell Vicki Tinsdale that Autumn Marseille is outside," I said to the first group of Local attendees who exited the building and were naïve enough to cross my path. "Tell her that I want to see her!" I knew she was there. I knew she had left St. George's and drove to the school to meet Ram. Bewildered, one of the students turned and re-entered the still partially opened front door of the school. The other two friends stepped aside and began whispering to one another. I heard hushed conversation behind me as well.

"Autumn Marseille? From St. George Prep?"

"Yea, that's her."

"Isn't that Adrian Waters girlfriend?"

"I heard they broke up."

"Really? When was this?"

I snorted inwardly and said, "that's right we broke up the moment I realized he was a loser and that I deserved better." My words hung in the air like thick London fog, and impatiently I waited for the messenger to return, for Vicki to emerge from the safety of her stronghold and confront me. I waited in vain. Tension began to form and settle on my crinkled brow, exciting a thunderous headache that throbbed against the sides of my head. My pulse quickened in anticipation and my hands shook more from anger than from the cold front that Jack Frost had sent our way. "Vicki!" I belted out, pacing from one side of the sidewalk to the next. Fuming, I stomped back to my car and retrieved the cellphone from the inner pocket of my purse. I dialed her phone number, and let it ring to voicemail before slamming it against the steering column in frustration.

A crowd had formed, the small clusters of Local student stood and stared, the expressions on their faces ranged from concern to utter shock. "Look...look, I see Ram peeking out of that window up there," one of the students exclaimed pointing up to one of the windows on the second floor. He was her lookout. He was protecting her! The sting of Ram's betrayal burned, and instead of allowing this display of insincerity to quench the fire within me, it manifested into a creature I no longer could control.

The pitch and hostility of my own voice startled me, "Vicki!" I screamed out again. It felt as if steel wool had been scrapped repeatedly across my vocal chords. I knew better than to engage her in a physical confrontation on school property- God forbid I land myself in juvenile hall with Adrian- but the alleyway running alongside the parking lot would do just fine. I dialed her phone again, but was greeted with the same fake and patronizing voicemail recording. Someone must have alerted her that I was here, and that I meant business. I envisioned grabbing her long ponytail and driving her freckled face into the pavement. I wanted her to choke down a mouth full of blood and spit out a few busted teeth. I wanted to teach the bitch a lesson. I could feel the lid beneath my right eye begin to twitch and my knees to shake as my soaring adrenaline begin to free fall. There was motion at the window again, this time it was Vicki- colorless, wide-eyed, and petrified. Slowly, the window was pushed open exposing her from the barrier of glass she had chosen to hide behind; but just like the mirror in my dreams, her reflection I could see through. "This ends now," I called up to her. Her non-responsive counter was the worst kind of attack. Was it fear? Was it regret? Was it a paradox? It was everything in nothing.

I itched for a reaction from her. I was no sense and all sensibility, I was all pride and too much prejudice, I was a fucking derailed Austen freight train. The proceeding moments passed in a state of disjointed fury. I held my keys in my hand- I was in front of a parked car- an extended scrapping sound- another sound…the sound my name- a familiar intoxicating smell.

"Autumn, stop my love," David pleaded.

The purity of his arms – this is not my car…its Vicki's and the graffiti down the side of it was my keyed violence. I glanced to the second floor window again and found it emptied. The loitering group of Local students had begun to disband from the parking lot. David shook his head disapprovingly at me and unlocked the weapon from my clenched fist. He placed the keys into the pocket of his army green jacket and held me close. "It's over now princess," he whispered. "Cameron can rest now in peace."

In the entire world, only David's light was able to penetrate the cloud of darkness that loamed over me, consuming my soul and muddying my objectivity. His presence was calming even though worry and displeasure were evident on his face.

"What were you thinking back there?" he asked lighting a cigarette and cranking down the window of his Camaro. The V8 glided effortlessly down Big Bend Road and as the snow flurries intensified and showered down on Osnaburg, I was relieved he had volunteered to take me home.

"I was thinking about Cameron. I was thinking about her smile, and that energy of hers that was like a glowing torch for us all. I was thinking about the first time I met her and the way she took me in and loved me when no one else could. I was thinking about all the moments we'd shared over the years and how I'd taken each one of them for granted. I can never get them back...I can never get her back," I sobbed into my coat sleeve.

An exasperated sigh was my reply. David flicked the butt into the winter wind and rolled the window back into place. He patted and stroked my knee as the tears and the grief escaped me. The warmth of his love embraced me, and I knew he could heal all wounds. I cursed the blackness that had infiltrated my life and had perpetuated the ruin and decay of everything around me; it had come to hunt me out, tracking me down and disabling my mental faculties. Even David, in all his beauty wasn't safe. On several occasions I had watched him transform into my inner monster; although it had been months, I didn't dare fool myself that if taken ahold of again, I would once more be faced with my darkest nightmare.

I pushed the hellish images from my scarred mind as David drove further from town and deeper into the back country of Osnaburg Township. "You really are quite lovely," I said reaching out to him and interlocking my fingers with his.

A small smile cracked around the corners of his naturally rogue lips and the weight of concern was lifted from his face. Squeezing my hand tight, he raised it his mouth and softly planted a kiss. "There will never be anyone more lovely than you princess." He paused, then removing the black winter skull cap from his head he said, "But your beauty is far down on the list of reasons that I love you."

"Tell me the reasons," I coaxed gripping his hand tighter. The mocking words of Mara and Lamia raced through my head- I desperately wanted David to share his feelings with me. Most times; any effort to that effect, revealing his deepest thoughts and emotions, were forced- though he often professed his love- he never could satisfy my innate wonder of its roots.

The roar of the engine increased as David dropped it into second gear and we cruised down Orchardview, a narrow gravel road, toward my Tudor homestead. "You are capable of so much my love," he said. "There are things I never imagined were possible which have transpired, and a rebirth that has occurred, spawning thoughts and feelings that in a million years I'd never perceived could be. You make everything possible now princess, and because of you I have the ability and desire to be so much more. I'm sorry to say, but the more fragmented your reality, the more defined mine becomes, and for that, I am able to give myself wholly to you." We pulled into my driveway moments later and listened to the hum of 290 Thoroughbreds idle under the hood.

"I've waited a long time to hear those words from you," I said wiping my face with a foundation smeared tissue I had found at the bottom of my purse.

"You make me brave," he said with a smirk, "but I do hate God for punishing me with you." David cut the engine and, in true gentleman fashion, walked to the passenger side and opened the door for me.

We walked arm and arm around the back and entered through the back stairwell and door at the east side of the house. Passing through the outer door and into the main access way, we immediately found ourselves in an open rectangular space of nearly four hundred square feet. The sun room had been abandoned for years, locked up and boarded, as what my mother had called unusable space. The floor was crumbling black slate, and in the areas of the worst wear, I had laid out several hand woven throw rugs which I had purchased at the flea market outside of town. Some of the old pieces that were shipped over from France were brought out of storage and provided comfortable seating and shabby chic style. In the summer, the solid glass ceiling afforded an overabundance of sunlight, and in the spring and winter months a perfect retreat to gaze out into the starry skies. Since returning from London, I had added several indoor plants and had fashioned a four by four raised dirt bed where rosemary, thyme, basil, dill, and tarragon seedlings had just began to sprout. The sun room was the ideal place for me to paint.

I took our jackets and tossed them on the couch. David smiled as he looked over my herb garden and then moved across the room to my writing desk. He leafed through a notebook positioned on top of the stack of chicken scratched scrap sheets and tri-folded posted notes. "More of your work?" he asked lifting the tablet for me to see.

"It is."

"Your writing is eloquent, yet at the same time it's contagious."

I returned the smile, "sometimes the words can't be silenced but sometimes they don't speak for days."

"And this is what they say?" he asked tapping the cover.

"I try to search for meaning, but as hard as I try I see only emptiness in this life," I said sitting on the stool in front of my art easel.

David placed the notebook back on the desk and came toward me. "Your life is like this canvas my love- blank and wonting. The colors you chose and the technique in which they are applied is strictly at your discretion. There is this," he said picking up the brush. "And there is this," he said holding the pallet, "our intentions and then our actions. That is all. The artistry of life is completely up to you."

"If only my life were as collected as my paintings."

"This life is only the beginning princess. The fruition of your labors is the finished masterpiece in the afterlife."

"You make it sound simplistic," I said taking the brush from his hand and dipping the tip into the black paint. With long sweeping motions the London skyline took form on the canvas.

"I never said it was simple…but it's true."

I ingested the poetry of his words as I used a sponge to apply the dimension of fog to my abstract scene.

"Don't concentrate so hard my love," David whispered in my ear.

"I must," I said blushing at his seductive gesture of wrapping his arms around my waist and nuzzling his face on the back of my neck. "How can I paint when you do these things to me?"

"Let your hands be free," he said rolling his tongue over my ear and nibbling on the lobe.

"I love how you think David," I said taking in his touch and smell. Thoughts of his naked body snaked through my mind and the urge to feel him inside and out was almost too much to bear. My hands continued to glide over the canvas- I watched myself create the emotions that were locked inside of me.

"I want you to be lost in me, in my mind's maze, a bewitched labyrinth that only I can survive."

"Take me there," I said longingly, placing the paint brush back into the water wash cup.

David released me and walked around to the other side of the easel to better observe my finished work. "It's reflective and visually layering to be sure."

"It's just a piece of baggage that I'm trying to rid myself

of," I replied.

"Let me help you clean up," he answered and began to put the caps back on the paint tubes.

"Thanks," I said slowly, noting the way in which his piercing eyes never left the painting. "You can have it- you can have them all," I motioned toward the side wall at my collection of water color and acrylic portraits.

"You would give them to me?"

"Of course," I said attacking him with my hands and lips. "I want you so bad. You're an addiction I just can't break."

"You're perfect," he said with a smirk. "If you want me so bad lead the way."

I knew what he wanted because I wanted the same thing from him- only David was brash enough to speak it.

"I want to own you," he breathed.

I grabbed his hand and pulled him into the hallway. His tone excited me and the realization of his words and the desire for them to become a reality caused me to quicken my pace as I navigated down one dark corridor and another. We reached the door at the end of the hall and after descending the winding metal staircase reached the entrance to the library.

"Here?" he laughed.

"Why not," I said with a shrug, working my hands over him like a sculptor molding a piece of clay.

"I love you," he said lifting me off the ground and carrying me to the back set of book shelves. He squeezed the back of my thighs and thrust his body into my midsection. With my legs wrapped tightly around his torso, I let go of his neck and began to unbutton his shirt. "You're such a tease. There is only so much of you that I can take." He dropped my legs and undid the button and zipper of my jeans.

"What are you going to do?" I asked playing along with his sensual game.

David's face instantly drew serious. "I'm going to show you that I'm not bullshitting."

"Really?"

"Yea, really. Turn around," he demanded spinning me toward the bookshelves and placing his forearm in my back.

My chest and rib cage were smashed against the wood, and the weight of David's body leaning on me pinched the skin under my arms causing a great deal of pain. I tried to push back against his force, but the more I attempted to leverage my upper body against him, the more excited he became and the harder he pushed himself inside of me.

"I'm going to make you mine," he hissed in my ear. "You talk about baggage...I'm the type that you can't get rid of."

The room began to spin around me; the books lifted themselves from the shelves and before my eyes the pages within them were ripped from their binding, old classic tales floated in the air like the white tops of aged fluffy dandelions. It was happening again- the dreaded chimera held me in its hungry grasp. Afraid to turn to face David's distorted image, I laid the side of my head on the cold, smooth case and waited for the nightmare to end. I heard distant giggling, it was high pitched, eerie, and crazed- and in the passing moments it drew closer and closer, bouncing around in my brain and leaking from my ears. I felt an icy touch on my shoulder-a ghastly and familiar sensation that I could never forget-I had experienced it repeatedly in my nightmares. Lamia's frigid hate. Where she was, the red-headed bi-sex crazed Mara was not far away, nor his Incubus play thing.

"It's so good to be needed," Mara said stroking the side of my face. "I always appreciate it when you think of me.

My head was yanked back, my neck strained in a hyperextended position. Out of the corner of my eye, I could see the Incubus hiding in the shadows behind one of the tall book racks.

"Tell me that you like this Autumn," Mara sarcastically spat, twisting my loose curls around his steel hands and pulling my head further back.

His forearm was wedged underneath my chin and pressed sharply against my windpipe. I tried to scream, but it

212

was hoarse and raspy and altogether useless.

"I think the little princess likes it," Lamia retorted and like the strike of an angry cobra sank her razor fangs into my flesh.

The pain was excruciating- the burn of liquid acid penetrating tissue and soaking into blood. She hovered over me naked, taunting me with vicious falsehoods, and licking her blood stained lips.

"Turn over," Mara demanded. "Trust me you're not going to want to miss this." With one hand clasped around my throat, compressing my airways and adding to the dizzying disorientation, he effortlessly lifted me from my feet. I kicked my legs wildly in protest and pried at his cold fingers, as Captain Murmur, the wounded soldier, appeared next to me. Lamia rubbed her bare skin over Murmur's uniform and reaching for his hands, placed them firmly on her pale breasts; her encouraging squeals prompting him to massage her body and all the while his listless eyes never deviated from mine.

"She's irresistible isn't she?" Mara sneered. "Just like you."

I closed my eyes and prayed for death or for David to come rescue me- whichever came first. The hollowed faces of the three vagabond girls-the Erinyes- flashed in my mind. Their botchy blue skin stretched over the protruding bones of their face like cling wrap, and the severed noses and butchered ears further added to the appearance of what they were- damned, scavenging beasts. The horror was all around and no matter what; I accepted the fact that there was no escape. David, my morning star, had said we paint our own lives; I didn't understand how this portrait was mine.

Eyes open: Mara is smiling up at me. Eyes closed: the black greased raven flaps its spanning wings as it shrieks and flies through the air. Eyes open: Lamia kneeling before the Captain, her face in his pantless lap as the Incubus intently observes over her shoulder. Eyes closed: the raven is perched on the sprawling corpses of the Erinyes plucking out and devouring- three pairs, six eyes.

THEY DON'T NEED EYES TO FOLLOW AND SERVE.

Eyes open: Mara releases me and I collapse on the library floor in a heap. I struggle to catch my breath and begin to claw my way across the room.

"You thought I was letting you go slave? No. Never. I can't ever let you go. You taste so sweet and though I've sucked away your innocence, I can't get your dirty taste out of my mind." Using the tip of his boot, Mara rolled me to my back and after undoing his belt and pants crawled on top of me. "I've got to feel it every night. I've got to taste it every night; and I do, even if you don't know it…even if you don't remember it…every night I'm doing this to you," he grunted pushing himself deeper and deeper inside of me. My legs were pushed up and bent at the knees, and Mara pressed his muscular chest against them pinning me down.

I hated that I loved how amazing he felt rocking violently on top of me. Using one hand to support his body weight, he reached with the other for the silver necklace that was fastened around my neck.

"The necklace, let me have the necklace slave!" he said grabbing onto it. "Shit!" he screamed withdrawing his hand.

Engulfed in painful pleasure and seeing Mara, for the first time, in a vulnerable state, I seized the opportunity and rolled him off of me. The smell of burnt flesh churned my stomach, and the sight of Mara's enflamed hand, skin peeling from the bones, caused me to roll to my side and hurl. The reaction to flee was non-existent. I closed my eyes to the pain and the sex and the violence- shutting out the sin and the darkness. Mara's helpless and unanswered wails drown in the vast waters of my conscious. I'm lost within myself, searching for my morning star, wandering in wanderlust through the unforgiving London Fog.

STELLAR

March 7, 2003

I won't allow them to destroy you. As much as you've seen and the pain that you've gone through, I can't allow this to go any further. I wanted you so bad, and like with everything else, I must have what I want. The first time I laid eyes on you, I longed to push you to your limit, to see just how far you would go. You've made me proud princess, but soon you're true love and devotion will be put to the test. **Autumn, my love, wake up.** "David," she said rousing from her fitful sleep. Fearful she clung to me, shaking and pitiful. "What happened?" *If I were to tell you, it would only frighten you more. Lust rules you and overtakes your emotions, I can't stifle that. You're puppy eyes, gazing up at me stirs my fire love. If you knew...if you could feel the burn that I feel...you'd turn away from me at once.* **What do you remember?** "All I know is that we came in here together to...you know...and that's it." **I don't know.** *Squirm for me baby underneath that soft skin. You blush at me and get embarrassed over these little conversational volleys and I don't understand it- but I like it. I've had you as naked as you can ever be, but I stab you with my eyes and play coy and you about lose your mind. Pretty little girl, lay it out there for me.* "To make love I meant," she whispered and pushed herself to a sitting position on the floor next to me. **Right, of course and I remember**

215

how interesting I thought it that you decided to do this in the library. "So we did then?" **Yes. Why are you asking me this princess? Am I that forgettable? I take it that I must be because you fell asleep right when we finished and you wake up and act like you don't remember any of it.** *You flinch and I'm certain I've struck a nerve inside of you. Your mouth will to try to deceive me, I'm sure, and you're so cute because you actually think that you can. How much do you trust me? You're a smart little girl Autumn but even your mind can't keep up with mine. I'm leading you right where I want you. My slave- tell me about the dream. You have a heart that is full of compassion, and toward me it has, thus far, endless depth. You love my smile...I'll smile for you baby. Will that that help persuade you to trust me enough, or will you bite that tongue of yours and let me feel used? You wring those delicate hands of yours and I know that you won't let me suffer at your expense. That's why I love you. Every time, you sacrifice yourself for me.* "No, David it's nothing like that I swear," she gushed reaching out for my hands. **Then tell me what is going on love. I told you a hundred times before that you can trust me, and whatever it is we can get through it together. I can't be in this with you if you don't fully let me in. What are you afraid of?** "I'm afraid that I will push you away. The nightmares had gone away for some time and I thought whatever it was... I had gotten over it. They are back though David, and they are worse than ever before I'm afraid." *I've seen worse than anything your fretful little mind can handle. Into my world you wandered, and in a matter of months you're so close to the edge that I feel compelled to reel you back in. A small taste of my world, like the succulent fruit from the forbidden tree. The temptation has always been there for you and you've fought it- perhaps dabbled in it a bit- but now you bathe yourself in sexual thoughts of me. I don't think that you are afraid of pushing me away. That is the scab that is covering the wound. You're afraid of yourself, but unfortunately all we have is ourselves. You have you and I have you...and if you will break, you will have me too.* **The nightmares are back? I'm sorry my love, but you know nightmares are nothing more than a false reality. They seem true and real at the time, but soon enough you wake up and they're over.** "I wish that were true David," she whispered. "They never go away. That is the false reality of it- I just think that they do." *Now we are getting somewhere.* "It's not just when I'm sleep, it's when I'm at school, at practice, at church, at home, and even when I'm driving in my car. Things go crazy. I see things...I see death and torture and pain. I just don't know how much more of it I can take," she cried. *I knew it was only a matter of time before the sweet nectar of your tears would begin to flow. Sometimes you shed them to suit yourself- to artificially comfort the hole that is inside of you, but not this time. This time your crying suits me. The virginity of your ways draws me into you, but I must be cautious not to go too fast, not to go too hard, not to have you climax before I'm ready.*

Let me hold you princess. I know that it's hard for you to talk about it, and I don't want you to feel like I am pushing you. I just want you to know that I'm here for you and I love you no matter what. You are the most important thing in my life, and I want you to know that and believe it. You've had a hard time of it lately. It's not abnormal what you are going through right now. You've broken up with Adrian, that worthless piece of shit, who abused you and drove you into a rut of depression that you didn't even know you were in. "This isn't about Adrian," she said pouting, but allowing me to stroke her kitten soft hair. *Of course it's about him Autumn. You are not even able to look at things subjectively anymore.* **You let go of the one person who had control over your life. Tony, one of your best childhood friends moved away, and even adjust- you lost Cameron. You are just weeks after dealing with his loss- before you could a strong girl Autumn, but that is a lot for anyone to deal with.** "So what are you saying? You think it's just stress?" **I'm saying that I think you've been through a lot and you shouldn't be so hard on yourself. I think that what you need right now is some time away to rest and heal. You're pushing yourself and it's only making these nightmares worse.** *Could I have grossly misjudged your current situation? I knew you were scared and wavering, but holding onto you- your thin fragile body trembling, I experience it all now, through you.* **I**

will save you princess. Come with me and let me take care of you for a while.

I followed Autumn from the dark and now defiled library. The narrow hallways of the old Tudor were little more than a maze, a place that I would love to lose myself with her. We took a short cut through the conservatory and after a swift climb of a flight of stairs we were inside her bedroom. *One time with you is not enough. I want to bind you to the bed and take you back to hell. You couldn't handle another go round with me. If only I could bind you up with rope. One around your slender wrists, one around your ankles, and one around that pretty little neck of yours. Ahh…I want to twist you around into a pretzel and get inside of you and make you sweat.* "David, do you think that my parents will miss me?" she asked snatching clothes from her dresser drawers. *They despise you.* **I think that they will understand that you need some time away from everything.** "They will probably be glad to be rid of me," she said with a tone of indifference. *Your mother will be too drunk to notice, and your father has no ability to empathize with the feelings of others- a man after my own heart- and will be happy to have the time to satisfy his own personal aspirations with no distraction from you.* **Their loss and my gain my love.** *Which is always precisely the way I like it!* "I suppose that I should at least write them a letter," she said as we descended down to the main level of the house and entered the kitchen. She sighed heavily as she stared out of the wide and frosted-over bay window overlooking the back garden with its high hedges, broad beds, sprawling lawns and gravel walkways- all hidden under a blanket of early March snow. "You're right," Autumn said grabbing her purse and flipping off the kitchen light. The farewell letter left for Bellino and Denise Marseille had little information and no feeling. The basis of it relayed the message that she was staying with a friend for a week and for them not to be alarmed, everything was fine and she would call them in a few days. *They will scarcely read the letter on their return home and will not miss you. I'm the only one that can love you now. I must not fail you- for now is your greatest time of need.* **I'll get your bag.** I pulled the heavy backpack over my shoulder and followed her back out into the frozen iceland called Osnaburg.

I watched her from the corner of my eye chain smoke cigarettes and warm her rose fingertips on the heat vents. "Are you sure that you want me to stay with you a whole week? You'll be ready to bring me back in a day or two," she said in a serious and melancholy tone. *I was hoping to keep you for an eternity.* **Don't be silly princess, and cheer up , I have a surprise for you.** I turned onto Main St. as she said, "really?" **You're going to love it.** "Of course I will love it if it is from you," she exclaimed excitedly clapping her hands and smiling wildly at me. *That smile of yours drenched in loving adoration could distinguish Hades and the fire that consumes me. The little things that you do are common place, but the uniqueness of your unwavering devotion is simply to die for. If only it were that easy. If only I could die and be with you, but it's only your death that can ultimately bring us together. I need that. Surrender. But, at the same time, it's enjoyable to watch you, when you are at your best, in an element of the worst- teetering on the edge of obliteration.* The Camaro sputtered as I pulled it into the safety of the garage and cut the engine. Looking through the rear view mirror at the snow that continued to fall from the skies reminded me of the glittering stars, the stellar realm from which I came- the heavens that I had for all these years forgotten.

"Where is Cerberus?" Autumn asked concerned as we entered the quiet blackness of my lair. **I'm not sure.** I lied to her face and smirked with inner enjoyment as I hung our coats in the main hall closet. *Cerberus come to me my un loyal, our mistress has come again.* "He is always here to greet me David," she said. "Do you think that he is alright? Let's look for him." The happiness that was just moments before written on her face had drained under the pressure of deep rooted concern. *You're thinking of your bas rouge Hero, but I have something to fill the void.* **I'm sure that he is fine, princess, but if it will put your mind at ease, yes let's find the little devil.** We wandered around the first floor, silently searching the living room, dining room, kitchen, and bathroom. With each room that we entered, finding him not, the more anxious she seemed to become. *I was not aware of your true affections to the monster. I know that over the past few months, he has taken a keen interest in you, spending hours discreetly watching you…watching us together, and even making his way by you, rubbing his long, strong body against your legs and nudging you from time to time for a second of physical contact. My un loyal, I'm most curious at his acceptance of you, the one creature in all the world who never glared at anyone but for an attack and never sought approval or attention from anyone.* I waited for the thud of bold footsteps, but all was silent and bleak. **Come with me to check upstairs.** I patted her reassuringly on the back. **Don't you worry about Cerberus, the big clod, he's probably just napping on my bed and hasn't heard us come in.** *As if anything could escape his notice.* She nodded and looked somewhat relieved, but about-turned and instantly headed for the grand staircase. Taking two steps at a time, she hit the landing and was almost in a jog by the time she reached my bedroom. Without hesitation she barged through the door and the sound of ecstatic squeals filled the air, and like a virus, infected feeling within me that had lain dormant for the eternity of my existence. I wandered through the door behind her, and smiled at the sight of her holding the only surviving bas rouge pup of a litter of six. "David he's perfect!" Autumn breathed cradling the black bundle of fur in her arms and kissing his tiny head. *A lone protector for you my love, a piece of me that you can have and hold…even when I'm gone.* **May I introduce Ancient Iago, the only surviving pup in the litter that Cerberus sired. The owners of the dam were so heartbroken over the loss of the other pups that they gave this one to me and now he is yours.** "Mine?" she asked in disbelief. **He will never be able to replace Hero, but I hoped that you could keep him for me and love him and care for him just the same.** "Oh, I will!" she exclaimed. "Ancient Iago?" she said laughing. **Named after the greatest character ever created.** "Well, that may be the case, but I think just plain Iago will do fine." *As you like it.* "And you say that he is the only surviving of the litter? What happened to the rest of the puppies?" *They were gobbled up.* I looked at Cerberus and snickered. **They barely**

survived birth and died rather quickly. "That's terrible," she said shaking her head and hugging Iago tighter. *Only the strong survive.*

"Did I tell you that I found Old Topp's furniture store when I was in Kilburn?" *No, indeed you didn't my devilish little minx.* **You are utterly amazing Autumn my love. How did you manage to find it? That store has been around for centuries-still producing the same quality of products they did back when Old Topps was there.** She ran her fingers along one of the straight back chairs that were positioned in front of the fire place. The glow from the fire and crackling of the logs set a tone of ambience, that was, until Autumn doused it with her London fog. She settled in front of the fire, curled in a ball, staring into the hypnotizing flames. She was thinking about that day, about everything that she had left behind, about Stinne and Axel. I grabbed an old quilt from the hall closet and wrapped it around her. "You talk about Topps like you knew him," she said finally dragging her eyes away from the fire. *I do don't I?* I smirked at her and lit a cigarette. **Do you ever get the feeling that you can connect with someone even if you've never met them before?** "I guess so," she said pulling the quilt up to her nose. "This quilt smells so good," she sighed dreamily. "It smells just like you." I laughed out loud. *She was so sweet, so loving, so lost in wanderlust.* **Well I've heard so much about Old Topps...you know stories passed down from generations in my family. I feel like I do know him personally. I guess it helps that I have all his shit lying around here.** "This house is like a museum," she said reaching out and lifting the filter from between my fingers. *You have no idea.* **All I have is old and dead memories. I like to be reminded what I come from...and of course my parents would never have it any other way.** "When do I get to meet them David? I know that they are busy, lecturing all around the world, but it's been ten months and I've not had the pleasure." *We continue to hit one detour after another. You ask too many questions and are concerned about things that really are of no consequence. I like you so much better when you sit there* *quietly and pathetic, or when your mouth is occupied in something more pleasurable.* **As soon as they get back you will be the first to meet them princess. It's unfortunate that the moment that we moved here and got settled in they were called away. Some special grant funded lecturing tour overseas is all I know. I'm used to it really- them being away for ten months out of twelve. It has been this way for as long as I can remember. I'm always alone...that is until I met you.** She flicked the cigarette butt into the fire. "Is that why you had your friends come to visit you?" *Again more of the bullshit questions. She is prying, like a grave digger, she is shoveling the dirt over my head.* I stood, uncomfortable and agitated. I stuff my hands into my pants pockets and tried to mask the contempt that was building. *She was trying to defy me.* **Yes, they are really the only family I have.** I stare at her and I see her break. *Poor doll, she lasted less than sixty seconds against me.*

I helped her settle in for the night. We had sat in front of the fire, talking, mostly of nonsense until two in the morning and now exhaustion and fatigue began to plague her. Those hours in front of the fire place had been nearly unbearable. The way she fingered the portraits that lined the mantle and inquired as to the history of each, not excluding the figurines and tapestries, each piece of furniture and hard bound book that was situated upon the tables. It made my skin crawl. I was most content when the conversation detoured and changed to her: to France, to Belgium, to what old Osnaburg was like. She would talk and laugh and merrily sip her cordial of warmed apple brandy, but after just a few short moments she was diverted again by some nothingness of mine. At first the brandy seemed to lift her spirits, but after a while, her giggles trailed off and she sat in awkward reflection. *Helpless. Hopeless. I have the soul for that.* I tucked the quilt around her as she shifted in the bed searching for comfort and warmth. The night was raw and I wanted nothing more than to climb in the sheets next to her and provide her with the only warmth that she would ever need, but I had other matters to attend to. I would leave Cerberus to guard her tonight and make sure that no harm became her. *I am depending on you my un loyal. The Reign is coming.*

I waited, impatiently for The Reign to arrive, sitting in front of the fireplace, sipping the sweet apple brandy and smoking the harsh menthol cigarettes I had grown to love. I hated the way my mind would wander back to the innocent creature, who tucked safely in my bed; I must admit, I had begun to already take for granted. Every thought of her was of the sexual kind, but I couldn't help myself- every inch of her smooth bronzed body was imprinted on my mind, and the satisfaction that was gained in owning her was call for erection enough. In my years, I had had the opportunity to be in the presence of the most glorified of beings, and in my own personal area of expertise I had experienced many different people, all with different amiable qualities- but none could ever be as loved as Autumn. These thoughts circulated in my mind, and as the anticipation of The Reign arrival and the anger at their tardiness began to stir, I perceived the already dim lighting in the living room began to flicker and die out. *It's about time slaves.* I threw the final Newport butt in the hearth, sparking an extraordinary burst of flame which cackled and hissed and then died out into a single thick puff of coal colored smoke. The cloud drifted from the fireplace, expanding and elongating until suddenly the outer rim of smoky blackness folded back into the center and out of the darkness emerged Stolas. **My bird of prey, it is nice to see you again…though you are late…but of course you are the first to arrive.** "Further complications eminence," he said moving to his post near the side window. *There are always complications. That is what we do. We complicate things.* He nodded and opened the window, sending a gust of frost chilled air through the room. **What sort of complications?** "You are aware that the sloth soon will be freed?" he asked turning once more to me. *And this is good thing is it not? Fitting so wonderfully into our plan.* **And what of it?** "I'm not sure how to properly say this to you, my lord, without being overly brash…" *Spit it out slave. It is your job to advise me in these matters.* **It is my job to determine if what you say and** the manner in which you present it is unsatisfactory. Stolas hung his head and fixed his white gleaming eyes to the floor somewhere to the distant side of me. **Look at me slave and speak.** "In the recent months eminence, you have distilled up us, your loyal Reign, to facilitate many matters that are out of our realm of familiarity. At times you are driven and focused, committed even to our good cause, leading us fearlessly through the fire; however, equally is true of the way in which that whore is able to turn you from our cause." *Enough!* **You have indeed spoken to carelessly raven. If you, and this pertains to the others as well, are too incompetent to follow my orders or think-in some ill construed fashion- that you are above complying with my wishes...well I need not tell you that you can easily be replaced.** "Yes eminence," Stolas said, and looking out of the window again, announced that Captain Murmur and his three beastly Erinyes were at the front porch. **Well, let them in.** I turned my back to the door and facing the mantle, scanned the old and yellowed black and white photographs that had intrigued Autumn's curiosity earlier that night. *If you had looked close enough you would have seen that The Reign always is and always will be.* "General," Captain Murmur said walking to the mantle next to me. **Captain it is good of you to join us, and the Erinyes too, what news have you?** "The same as always my prince, that I am happy to report- degradation of the heart and flesh inflicts many, and many have been herd up," he said lifting one of the oldest dated frames and staring at the photo. **Do you remember that day Murmur? Do you remember what it was like even before then?** "Yes, eminence I do," he said lowering his voice and deflating a bit. "And I must say that I was a pretty handsome young man back in those days." *Handsome? You are still handsome, my dear soldier, but now you are maimed.* **Do you remember what happened the last time you disobeyed me Captain? When you fell out of rank and did not follow the orders of your superior officer?** He flinched and shied away. "Yes, General." *You have best remember it! All of you keep in mind exactly what I am capable of.* I stared at the gaping hole in the back of Murmur's head and laughed. **Your disobedience fueled me Captain and now- you are a part of The Reign.** *It felt so good shooting you.* "How could we forget what you are capable of," Lamia said wrapping her arms around my neck and attempting to kiss me. *Away from me disease!* I could feel the veins in my face begin to surface and the blood within to begin to burn a pulsating, putrid purple. "David...David... is that anyway to think of my wife?" asked Mara appearing in front of me, a wicked smile on his face. *I would be very careful, the both of you, and that lowly Incubus of yours.* **I told you to leave Autumn be and you purposefully defied me. I condemned you once and I see that has made no difference at all.** "But that is what we have come for..." **That is what we did come for, but you were perfectly aware that things had changed and that she is no longer the subject of our wrath.** I said this, staring into his empty eyes and daring him to combat me. He said nothing more, but wandered to the corner where his Incubus slinked in the shadows.

We are waiting for one more- the oracle Madam Therroit, another jinn damned to wanderlust- I summoned her here as well, and where is she? "She won't be coming tonight," Lamia said reading my mind and seductively licking her lips at me. "But she did give me a message to pass along to you. **A message? Let's hear it then.** "She said that she regrets not being able to attend tonight, but she has matters with the sloth to attend to." *He is becoming too much trouble and delaying our ultimate goals.* **What of the sloth Murmur?** *Did you think that I stationed you with him for any other task than to ensure that he would serve his sentence and then be released, timely and unscathed?* "Strong willed I'm afraid General and thanks to the Erinyes, very set his ways," *God damn you!* "That has already been done," Murmur said under his breath. I paced around the room, and stopped in front of Stolas. **What do you recommend? What are we to do about the sloth?** "Well, we cannot fault the good Captain and his beasts for perfecting their trade can we?" replied Stolas. Lamia giggled moving toward Murmur and settling herself in-between his legs. *If there was any other place to cast you, adulterer, I would.* She giggled louder and began to work her vices on the willing Captain. *Or maybe I should leave you here?* She stopped and looked at me, "you wouldn't." I refused to think anything of the matter, but preferred to have her wonder just how unforgiving I could be. "My advice eminence," Stolas said, "is that we revert back to our initial goal." *That is not possible!* I hissed at him. **My time with her is not complete. Autumn Marseille is different and I will not let her go until I am sure that all the pieces are in place and that…in the end…we will be together forever.** The look of scorn was evident on all their faces, for they did not approve. This feeling came not from any evil inclination, but rather had originated at the first sign of my goodwill toward her. I was wrong they felt, I was weak, and I was allowing her to overwrite the past and change the future for us all. **The sloth… he is the key in all this as much as I would like to assume otherwise. We will use our skills to the best of our ability to ensure his release. In the meantime, I will admit that you have done wonders here and aboard, but the princess will be exempt from your efforts.** I gave this a moment to settle. **Let it be understood that any disobedience will result in…serious consequence. You have all pushed her too far- it is not her time** - *it is not our time.*

Satisfied at last to the compliance of The Reign, I lit another cigarette and commenced to allow them to play. Mara and the Incubus kissed and touched one another and themselves in the corner. *Nasty slaves.* Lamia continued in her oral pursuits of the Captain, who reclined on the couch and watched her swallow. The biting and the bleeding and soldiering role-play would certainly follow. Stolas stood alone, still next to the window, longing looking out to the cold open air. *You want to escape… to fly away.* **Go on raven.** I said this meeting him at the window once more. Spanning his arms out to the sides, the change was complete, and he flapped his oil black wings to signal to me that he indeed wanted to be on his way. Perched to take flight, Stolas looked at me with his beady eyes and bobbed his head in a sort of farewell. **Oh and Stolas,**

you need to be more careful. Her dead friend saw you. He cocked his head to the side, let out a blood churning screech and was gone. "David?" I heard a small voice say from behind me. It was Autumn, pale white and horror-stricken, standing on the stairs. She looked from me at the open window to Lamia and Captain Murmur on the couch to Mara and the Incubus in the corner. "Wwwhat is going on?" Before I could answer or reach her, she collapsed under the weight of, what to us, had always been all too familiar.

Italics indicate David's thoughts; Bold text indicates David's spoken words.

DERAILED

March 11, 2003

I couldn't bring it within myself to get out of bed. I felt safe in the solitude of David's room, and though he urged me on several occasions, I would not leave it. The constant state of confusion that I found myself in, all too often, tired me—draining every bit of mental and physical stability that I possessed. Cerberus was the only company that I could tolerate; even David's visits were better in short sporadic intervals. He would come and go from time to time, checking on Iago and parting the thick damask curtains that covered the windows. He insisted that the daylight was good for me. I must admit that several times when he entered the room, I pretended to be asleep; I just couldn't face him anymore. How weak he must think me! To have had another nightmare just days ago, and then I apparently fainted on top of it all.

He had said that I had awoken from my sleep, in a state of hysterics and had fainted as I tried to descend the steep stairs that led to the living room. I didn't remember anything...at least that is what I told him. The truth of the matter was that I recalled what had happened precisely. The only question upon my mind was whether or not the incident was real or if indeed it was just another false reality. I had tiptoed to the steps and heard talking and laughter, and in deciding to seek it out, I quietly made my way, one step at a time, to the first landing that overlooked the living room. The scene before my eyes could not have been anything closer to a most heinous and graphic horror fantasy.

David was by the window. His contorted face was flushed and bulging purple veins slithered beneath dead gray weathered skin. He was talking in a hushed voice with the midnight raven that seemed to stalk my every move. The fire had died out, or was distinguished and the air that drifted in from the fully open window was biting with cold. On the couch was the wounded soldier. I had seen him so many times, and the hyena like beasts that always crept about at his feet. The vampiress was present as well, sucking the Captain, blood running freely from the corner of her mouth and dripping from her chin onto his starched military uniform. The sight of her jolted my heart, and the way in which her eyes darted over to the dark corner beside me caused me to rapidly inhale. I held my breath and following her verde eyes, I spied her red-head and the one that they called the slave. Mara and the Incubus paused their frivolity and both glared back at me. That was the last thing that I could recall, another horrible trip…a demented adventure that I never wanted to be a part of. David had laughed at me saying that I had a wild imagination, but seeing that I was serious- it felt so real no matter if it were a dream or not- comforted me and cared for me as he had originally promised. After four days of not eating and drinking little, David finally came to my side and with a face carved from stone said, "Autumn we really must talk."

"I was thinking the same thing. I just didn't know how to go about starting the conversation."

"Is it really that difficult? You find it too cumbersome to speak to me now?"

The expression on his face portrayed the hurt that I was certain he felt at the lack of confidence that I bestowed upon him. It had never been my intention to shut him out; but most times, it was simply easier than explaining what was going on in my own head. I wished that he could understand what a predicament I was in. The more I reached out for help, the faster I drown. How was I to talk about these things when I did not fully understand them myself? "David, you always think that my intentions are bad and that I am purposefully blocking you out. The last thing that I ever wanted was to separate myself from you. You know that from the first moment that I saw you, I loved you. A lot of times it is just too complicated to really talk about."

"Thank you for your honesty princess, but I feel like you are fading away from me and it worries me. Since I've brought you home, you haven't left the bed but to use the restroom. You won't eat, you barely will drink anything, and you haven't showered in four days now. You are refusing to talk with anyone. I can't say that I blame you for putting your parents off, but Stacy and Lauren have both come by to see you and you've had me turn them away. I'm not the only person in this situation that is concerned about your health. You haven't taken any phone calls from Tony…he's called at least twice a day for four days straight now. I'm aware that you have looked at your emails, but you haven't responded to any of those as well. You've read numerous messages from Stinne and Axel, but when I checked your outbox, you haven't bothered to reply to either one of them."

"So you are checking my email now?" I asked surprised.

"I wasn't trying to pry my love; I'm just worried about you."

"I would think that you would be happy that I didn't return Axel's emails at least," I said blushing.

"Why would you assume that? Do I come off as the jealous type?"

"I really don't know," I replied.

"I'm not insecure like your ex Adrian. The only reason that people react negatively to differing sex relationships is if they are not confident in themselves. If you haven't realized already…I don't have a confidence problem," David said smirking.

"Well…if you are okay with it then I will write him back," I conceded.

"That would be nice. It sounded like you two really hit it off in London. Have you thought anymore about the proposition that he made you- to move to London and work independently for him?"

"I have a little bit."

"Maybe going back to London after this school year would the best thing you could do. It would allow you time away from Osnaburg, from Adrian, from your parents, and friends. It sounds as if you would be able to make a nice living, and even if you just decided to stay for a while, it would be a diversion for you."

"What about college?" I asked.

"They have the best colleges in the world in England," he said pulling me off the pillows and pressing his lips against mine.

"What would you do? There is no way that I would move to London and leave you here waiting for me."

"Are you afraid that I wouldn't be here when you got back?"

"I won't take that risk," I said adamantly.

"You will never have to princess because no matter what happens, I will always be with you."

"If you think it is best," I mumbled rubbing my open palm over his soft pale skin.

"I do," he said. "However, at this very moment I think the best thing that you can do is get out of this bed and come with me outside for some fresh air."

"Where do you want to take me?" I asked skeptical.

"I made an appointment for you this afternoon to go back for another therapy session."

"Oh David, why would you do that!" I cried. "The talk therapy didn't work last time. I only went to it to begin with because my parents made me. Why would you schedule me to go back? The only thing useful she suggested was writing-from the heart-in the journal and painting."

"It won't hurt you to go talk to the therapist again," he said, forever the voice of reason.

I sighed and swung my legs around to the side of the bed. Unsteadily, I stood, and using the side of the mattress as support, I walked around to window where beneath it Cerberus lay, curled in a ball around Iago, his two week old bas rouge. I smiled down on the pair, and thought about the first time that my father and I had gone to the Dutch trader's home to see Hero. It had been so many years ago, but I remembered seeing him curled, in the corner of the whelping box, a sleeping beauty- just like my tiny Iago. Cerberus raised his head as I approached, and I swear, he winked at me. I giggled softly and tapped him on the head a few times as I looked out of the window at the thawing street below.

David convinced me join him that morning and to my astonishment he served me a very bountiful brunch. I shook my head and admired the Belgium waffles with strawberry topping, crisp greasy bacon, fresh fruit and vegetables, and walnut and dried cranberry salad. Carefully, he poured me a cup of steaming Earl Grey tea and we sat down together at his dining room table and equally enjoyed the delicious meal and engaging conversation. After we had finished, David pulled out my chair-as a true gentleman should-and led me outside onto the porch where we huddled closely together with our second cup of tea and our morning smoke. The weather had turned fair and breathing in deeply the mid-fifty degree air, my mind wandered back to the breaking of spring that I had enjoyed when living in France.

David must have been reading my mind for he remarked, "it feels like spring may finally be here."

"I hope so," I replied longingly. I wanted to kick myself for squandering my precious time with him. Why had I been so silly and selfish? Of course it had all been a bad dream- every dream was real, but I had allowed it to affect me to the point of completely alienating myself. Frustrated with my own sensibility, I took a long drag off the cigarette and said, "As always you are correct David."

He shot me a sly, twisted smile and kissed me once more on the head. "That would not be the first time I've been told so."

The remainder of the morning was spent in the same leisurely fashion: David and I cuddling one another in front of the warm glow of the fireplace, playing a few hands of rummy in the black on white modern sitting room, and sharing cold cuts, cheese, crackers, and left over fruit and vegetables for lunch. Around two o'clock as we were clearing the lunch plates and loading the dishwasher, David suggested that I return upstairs to dress myself for the therapy appointment. Reluctantly, I obeyed and searched through my book bag for something appropriate to wear. I chose a black pair of slacks with grey pinstripes, a black long sleeve shirt, and a grey zip up sweater. I combed my knotted curls in the mirror above his dresser and hastily applied a bit of foundation, mascara, and lipstick. Bounding down the stairs, I nearly collided with David who whistled loudly at me.

"You are stunningly gorgeous princess," he said piercing me with his ocean eyes and hugging me close.

My face turned an embarrassed shade of pink. I must have looked practically medieval the past several days, wallowing in self-pity, and succumbing to the tiger hold of yet another bout in an unforgiving depression ravine. "Thank you," I said savoring the words, the touch, and the smell that I had always loved.

"What word would you use to describe the way that you have been feeling lately Autumn?"

I shifted uncomfortably on the tweed patterned couch. I looked at Dr. Helpnaught, remembering why I didn't like going to psycho-therapy sessions- they ask too many damn questions.

"Derailed," I said directing my answer to the brown rug covering the dotted tile floor.

"And why did you chose that word?" she asked. She didn't even notice that I was not maintaining eye contact with her. Her hazel eyes never left the legal tablet that she busily scribbled upon.

"Because I'm off track and I feel like at any moment I'm going to crash."

"Crash-what do you mean by that?"

I didn't answer right way because I was afraid that if I did too quickly, I would give a careless response. "Just...an emotional wreck I guess." I lied. LIAR! YOU WANT TO CHECK OUT EARLY LIKE CAMERON.

"Do you feel that your life is an emotional wreck right now?" she asked, still feverishly writing on her tablet.

"Sometimes."

ALWAYS.

"How do you cope with that?"

"I try to find an uplifting outlet," I said thinking of David.

"What type of outlet? In other words Autumn, what do you find uplifting?"

"My boyfriend David," I said smiling. "He always makes everything better."

Dr. Helpnaught raised her eyes over her small, designer spectacles. She placed her tablet and her pen on the table beside her and folded her hands in the lap. "I'm so glad to hear that you have someone that is supporting you in this challenging time. We spoke before at our last appointment that it is important for you to maintain the positive relationships that you have. It seems easier sometimes to go at things alone, but the fact of the matter is that having a strong support team is the best thing for you right now."

YOU HAVE EVERYTHING YOU NEED- IN ME.

I nodded.

"Have you been keeping up with your journal writing?" she asked lifting the tablet up again, poised and ready to begin taking notes.

"No I haven't," I lied

IT'S POINTLESS AND NOT HELPING.

"That's too bad Autumn, because it is my medical opinion that writing in the journal and working your way through the challenges in your everyday life will force you to face your fears and grow from each experience."

I nodded- though she didn't notice. "I will go back to writing if you think that it will help get rid of these nightmares."

"Let me speak frankly," she said. "I'm not saying that writing in the journal will stop the nightmares. What I am saying is that by writing them down, and writing about your feelings, you are opening yourself up for enlightenment. That is really what you are striving for- to understand what is going on in your life and why," she paused her pen a moment. "How is your painting going?" she continued.

BEAUTIFUL.

"I enjoy it very much! I have a whole room dedicated to my painting and my writing and to be honest; when I'm not with David I am happiest there."

"Why do you think that is?"

"I feel safe."

"Where don't you feel safe?" she asked, pen flying over paper.

Most times I don't feel safe in my own skin. "I don't know."

YOU MASK THE TRUTH SO WELL.

Dr. Helpnaught flipped a page in her tablet and continued writing. "We've made a lot of progress here today Autumn. My recommendation is that you continue your writing and painting regimen, and above all, I want you to reach out to your support team. The more you occupy your time with enjoyable and positive influences, the more physical and mental relief you will gain."

AFRAID NOT.

She placed the tablet and pen back on the table and stood, smoothly her suit jacket. She extended her hand, strictly out of professional decorum, and gingerly shook mine. She herded me from her office, handing me another business card- as if I didn't already have an enough of them- and pumping a palm full of rubbing alcohol on her hands, the germaphobe said, "take care of yourself Autumn, you don't look so good."

I turned to answer her, but she had already shut the door in my face.

TESSERACT

April 2, 2003

The words: Adrian's Release Date stared at me. Written in bold red ink, the letters seemed to jump off the calendar and strangle me. Over past month, I had taken Dr. Helpnaught's advice: I diligently painted, wrote in my journal every day, and reached out to my friends Lauren, Stacy, and of course David; but none of it seemed to help. All I could think about was the fact that Adrian would soon be released and everything would change...for the worse. Against David's protests, I had visited Mason and the West Virginia boys at the garage. It stirred up bad memories and the moment I had ducked through the open bay door, Eric and Steve made a hasty exit. I guess there was no hope for that friendship to ever continue. They hated me, and I was okay with that.

Mason was happy to see me, though he pretended to be agitated that I had stopped by and interrupted his work. That was the thing with Mason, if ever his sarcasm and sly jokes faded; I knew that something was truly the matter. He was in good spirits and offering me a beer, and of course cracking one for himself, proceeded to ask me how life was treating me- it was ten o'clock on a Saturday morning. Our conversation had then switched to Adrian, and he shook his head in disgust as he sanded down the fender of a 1998 Pontiac Trans Am and raised high hell about what a fuck up his son was. He concluded that the best thing that could happen to him was that he stayed locked up for a very long time. I couldn't have agreed more, but I acted indifferent to his commentary, I had heard it all before. I stayed at the garage until lunch time, and eased away as Dalton fired up the propane grill and tossed hamburger patties and hotdogs over the open flame.

Today was Tony's birthday. I had dropped a package in the mail to him earlier in the week and presently, I dialed his phone number, anxious to wish him a happy birthday and to make sure his gift had arrived on time. "I know what today is," I said when he picked up the phone.

"Oh yea? Let me see, today is April 2nd," he said.

"It is? I thought it was April Fool's Day."

He laughed, "the joke is on me then?"

"Never! Happy Birthday Tony!"

"Thanks and thank you for the new football cleats," he said. "They are so bright and light. When I first opened the box, I thought you had jumped the gun and sent me track spikes."

"Let's take it one sport at a time," I said. "Football comes first, and the last time we talked you said that you were looking for something that would help you be a little faster on the field this year."

"Absolutely, I have to be at my best when I'm going up against those receivers. They are all taller than me, but I can compensate with being quicker."

"I'm sure that you will be great," I said giving him the boost of confidence that he was looking for.

"How are you doing Autumn? All is going well for you I hope."

"Same old," I said trailing off. I didn't want to get into the particulars.

"Still going to therapy?"

"Yes, but it's a waste of time. David won't hear of me

not going at least twice a week. It's so pointless though. My shrink, Dr. Helpnaught sits there, like Bartleby Scrivener- the scribbling fool- and gives me advice that I think a two year could come up with."

This made Tony chuckle and after a moment he said, "well David thinks that it's helping, so do I."

"So you are taking his side in the matter?"

"I'm not taking sides Autumn. We both care about you and just want what is best," he said softly.

"That sounds like the words of someone else I know. Someone who is always telling me what to do, how to do it, and when to do it. Someone that I used to love and now I hate."

"Don't you ever compare me with him!" Tony said angrily. "Is this what this is all about? What day is he getting out again?"

"Twenty-one days."

"I'm not saying that it is going to be easy, but he will have to understand that you have moved on and that the two of you are not going to be together."

"Really?" I said dryly.

"Why are so negative? What is the worst possible thing that could happen?"

I recollected the day that he pushed me down the stairs...the day he killed our child. To say that Adrian lacked empathy was an understatement, and to think that his ability to let go of our relationship, one that defined him as a person, was ludacris. I pushed the painful memories from my mind, "I don't know."

"Nothing is going to happen," Tony said matter-of-factly. "He will be released and the two of you will finally be able to move on with your lives. I don't have to tell you that your relationship, as unhealthy as it was, has been over for a very long time."

It ended the day his anger overtook him and he nearly killed me. Sometimes, I still wished that I would have bled out right there at the bottom of the stairs. I would take the place of my child any day, but for whatever reason, or divine intervention, I am alive and my sun is dead. "You're right," I said, not out of conviction, but because I wanted to change the subject.

Satisfied, Tony inquired about the masquerade ball that was held at St. George's every year in commemoration and remembrance of the good Saint.

"I haven't given it much thought," I said.

"That doesn't sound like you. I talked to David on the phone yesterday and he seemed pretty excited about taking you."

"Planning has begun, but this year I've kind of taken a back seat and allowed some of the other committee members to take charge."

"You? The most anal person I know has given up control over the school's biggest event? Wow! As freakish as you are over these things, I could almost say that this is a...good thing."

We laughed together because we both knew his statements to be perfectly correct. A twinge of excitement sparked at his omission of David's anticipation to attend with me, and we spent the next hour talking about the dance and when we would be able to see one another again.

The remainder of the afternoon, I devoted myself to painting and writing. I was pleased with the outcome of my efforts: an abstract ocean scene done with watercolor on paper. I had mixed and re-mixed, added and taken away from the pallet of blue; until painstakingly, I had blended together the perfect hue- the color of David's eyes. Once completed, I hung it up on a string that ran from corner to corner, measuring not more than two feet in length which created an icicles triangle, adjacent to the two large windows above the raised flower bed. I was interrupted only once by my father who tapped on the door, and upon opening it, he stood with his arms full of mail.

"Can I come in?" he asked.

Reluctantly, I opened the door further and let him pass.

"I think it's great what you've done with it in here Autumn," he said looking around.

"Thanks," I mumbled. I just wanted him to leave.

He sifted through the pile of mail and laid a sole envelope on my desk. "This one is for you," he said.

Lifting up the envelope and turning it over in my hands, I noticed the postmark from England. "Great," I said looking from the letter to my father again.

He stared back at me, as if he had something to say, but instead turned and left.

Good riddance. I silently fumed and wished that I never had to see his face again. Sitting at my work desk, I opened the envelope and unfolded a single, sea green colored piece of stationary. It read:

March 29, 2003

Autumn,

I hope that you have given further thought to the proposition that I made to you over our lunch in Kilburn. Stinne has relayed to me excerpts of your conversations, and piecing it together with what you have told me, it seems that your time back home in Osnaburg is sore and unhappy. We would love to have you here with us in London. Your every comfort will be provided for and I am convinced that you will find peace in our renewed connection. My sister shares in my enthusiasm and we both hope to hear from you soon.

Regards,

Axel

In all my selfishness, since our return from England, I was grateful that Stinne and Axel still regarded me as a friend and still wished for me to join them at the end of the school year. I folded the letter and placed it back into the envelope. I carried it with me, pressed against my fluttering heart, to my bedroom where I sat at my computer desk and signed onto AOL instant messenger. David had told me the night before that he wouldn't be free until early evening, but I thought it best to at least post an away message in case he returned home ahead of schedule. It bothered me that he would not give me any particulars for absence, for I was accustomed to spending the entire weekend with him; and above all, I wanted to check up on Cerberus and little Iago. I typed the following and then hit enter:

Autumnallstar: Imprisoned within myself with nowhere to go. Caught in a three dimensional net- a tesseract with no hope of escape.

I left AOL running on my desktop, and grabbing my purse, I quietly made my way down the west hallway and exited through the back doorway and rusted scaffolding at the rear of the house. My mind was preoccupied with the thought of Adrian's pending release, Axel's letter and proposition to move to London, and Tony's reminder of the fast approaching St. George's masquerade ball- and where was David? I didn't know what to think, I didn't know what to do, so I did the only thing-in desperation- that I could do. I started the Audi and headed into town, in the general direction of St. George's Cathedral.

CONFESSIONS

April 2, 2003

Walking under the arched doorway of St. George's Cathedral, I dripped my fingers into the holy water and crossed myself. I entered at the south transept and walking along the crossing to the center, I turned facing the apse and knelt down on the stairs before the alter. As it was nearing evening, the candelabras flickered to both my right and left, and the small candles that were positioned on the railways and lined the stairs, apse, and alter illuminated the souls of any who stepped upon the holy ground to pray. The bronze chandelier that hung overhead was dark and the two thick, circular columns supporting the elaborate gold archway failed to shine but instead, stood stately and erect, hidden in the shadows of dusk which was quickly approaching. Silently, I recited a novena to Our Lady of Hope: *I am the mother of fair love, and fear and of knowledge, and of holy hope. In me is all grace of the way and to the truth; in me is all hope of life and of virtue. Come to me all that desire me and be filled with my fruits. O Blessed Virgin Mary, Mother of Grace, Hope of the World. Hear us, your children, who cry to you.* I felt a sense of calm wash over me, one I had not felt in, what seemed like, an eternity. Inwardly, I cursed myself for my selfish ways, for my sins, and for my lack of fortitude in asking for forgiveness.

Rising, I wandered down the nave of the church with only the globe-shaped hanging lanterns to light my path. To either side of me where rows of dark mahogany pews and beyond them, marble pillars that branched up to the high vaulted ceilings and expanded- one symmetrical archway after another. The rounded ceiling above was decorated in a pattern of stained glass and solid gold rectangular tiles. All of the intricate details of St. George's had previously escaped me, but tonight, my senses were heighted under the grace of God's loving forgiveness. About halfway down the nave, I ducked into one of the pews and reached into my purse for my rosary chain. Finding it, I reached around my neck to remove the silver necklace, but drew my hand away at once as my fingertips burned at the contact. The pendant burned against my flesh and the nightmare of Mara crying out in pain under the same pretenses flashed before me. As I thought of this, the heat began to subside and the pain in my fingers slowly vanished. I stroked the necklace and tucking the pendant, once again, safely under my shirt, held the rosary beads in my hands and began to recite my prayers that before held little to no meaning, but now were the only comfort that I had.

I heard the heavy doors open on the north transept behind me and the hushed tapping of footsteps of another crossing to center and then making their way up the nave to a pew directly behind me. It was not a sense of fear that engulfed me, but rather a peculiar, awkward helplessness. I ignored the shuffling sounds and the creak of the bench as they settled in and began to pray. I closed my eyes once more, allowing the feelings of guilt to be purged from my body. With every word, my convictions strengthened and a renewed sense of purity resonated in my heart. I would be forgiven. THAT IS SELF-RIGHTEOUSNESS. I heard David's angelic voice whisper in my head- and the baptismal feeling drew away from me like a churning tide. The hairs on my neck prickled and stood on end- the raspy female voice behind me muttered, "Your power brings us to birth, your providence guide our lives, and by your command we return to dust," in perfect French. In unison, the eyes of the patron saints glared down on me and the statues that stood, majestically, at the opening of each archway lining the nave turned their heads and stared down upon me. Even the images artistically detailed in the stained glass windows came to life, their lifeless bodies seemed to emerge from their rightful place and surround me. I was cast out. At that very moment I became fully aware of the serious nature of my situation, for even the holy apostles turned a judging eye at me.

"They see the dead walking amongst the living," the voice cackled.

Unable to control my impulses, I turned and was face to face with the aged French gypsy, Madam Therriot. She didn't flinch as I scanned her face and tried to block out the eyes that bore deep into my soul. "Do you mean that you are a ghost?" I asked.

She reached her hand out to me, palm open and said, "Is that what you really believe Autumn? Do you think that everything over the past year has been ghosts playing tricks on you?"

"I honestly don't know what to think."

"Ghosts present themselves in many ways my dear. The ghosts that haunt you are not the dead…but rather the ghosts that live inside of you."

"What does that mean?" I asked frustrated. Peripherally, I saw the saints hone in further on me.

Madam Therriot grabbed my wrist and applied enough pressure for the rosary beads to fall into her open palm. "Nearly a year ago, I met you at the festival and that day I told you that you would die too soon. The reason the ghosts follow you Autumn is because you are already dead."

Her words struck me like a spear under the ribs. I snatched my hands away and frantically grabbed my purse and tucked it under my arm. As if life had been breathed into them, like Adam lumps of clay, the statues closed in on Madam Therriot and me. She laughed at me as if welcoming the saints to orchestrate my demise. Fretful, I nearly tripped as I dashed down the nave and ran around the side of the apse and alter, to the rear of the cathedral. Though the hallway was dark, I continued on, past several side devotional rooms and the confessional booth, until I reached the back doors. Locked! Once again I found myself trapped in a holy hell with no escape- no escape from the ghosts which Madam Therriot said haunted me because I was dead. If I was dead, then why was I so afraid? Could it be possible that I was dead and I just didn't know it? I dismissed the thought as pure gypsy foolishness- those things only happened in movies- and at this moment, I was desperately trying to survive the real world- my own false reality.

"Miss Marseille," a voice called out to me.

Relieved, I wandered toward it, and stopped outside the confessional booth.

"Come my child," the voice urged, "your Father always knows when one of their flock is in need."

The voice belonged to Father Ontari, the Italian priest, and in my state of panic, I entered the confessional and listened.

Father Ontari began, "I sense your despair my child. Tell me what it is that you have to confess?"

I thought about this for a few moments. It would take days to confess all my sins. I contemplated bolting, but the thought of meeting Madam Therriot again or walking down the nave, past the breathing statues and pictures was more than I could fathom. Maybe it would be better to simply confess. Perhaps, if I cleaned my soul and asked for forgiveness the nightmares and day trips would subside. I had strayed from the path of righteousness a long time ago, and I had been too ignorant to realize it or to repent. Adrian would be out of jail in a matter of weeks and I felt as if I had little protection. *Had God turned away from me?* I shuddered at the thought, remembering that for the most part, I had blocked him out of my life all together. I had so many questions, and I needed guidance- the only way was to accept him back into my life and pray that God would forgive me and accept me back as well.

"It's been…too long since my last confession," I admitted.

"There is always a place for you my child," Father Ontari said softly.

"Father, I am so afraid," I began. "It has been longer than I can remember since I have been at peace with myself. So much has happened to me and it's all been negative. I broke up with my boyfriend and it was not because it was the right thing to do at the time. I was angry and vengeful with him, and honestly, I just wanted to rid myself of him all together. He has hurt me so deeply over the years, and instead of being there for him, instead of forgiving him, I turned my back to him. I think that God is punishing me for this."

"Why do you think that God would punish one of his flock? That is not how God works my child."

"Ever since the day that I told him that we couldn't be together anymore, bad things have happened to me," I said sniffling.

"What sort of bad things?"

"I have horrible dreams Father, and during the day my eyes deceive me and I see and hear things that I know cannot be real. I have visions where people change into monsters before my very eyes, and places that are familiar become something else…something evil. I feel angry a lot of the time and am confused by things that go on in my own life." The words began pouring out and I didn't try to stop them. "I hate my parents and wish that they were dead. I hate Adrian, my ex-boyfriend, and wish that he were dead too. My best friend, Tony, left me and I feel so abandoned Father," I sobbed. "I feel responsible for Cameron's death. It was …my fault."

"Confess my child, tell me how so."

"I knew she was unbalanced!" I cried. "I knew for a long time that she was miserable, but so many of us, myself included, am miserable in their own life. I saw her going down the wrong path- she only cared about money and drugs and her own self-importance, but I was too wrapped up in mine that I did nothing to help her. In fact, I contributed to her downfall. I should have been there to catch her when she fell-in London…at the party. She was wild and out of her mind on drugs, but I never tried to stop her. I should have known…" I trailed off.

"Her death was an accident my child," Father Ontari said.

"It wasn't. Cameron killed herself. She wrote a suicide letter and everything. I was the one who covered it up. I just couldn't let everyone know. I couldn't allow her to be buried without a proper funeral. It would have destroyed too many lives…so I protected her. That was the least I could do."

I heard Father Ontari sigh. "That was wrong, but God knows your heart my child and your intentions in the matter were pure."

"God had forsaken me!" I cried. "He has turned his back on me a long time ago."

"His love and mercy have no limits my child. Confess your sins and they shall be forgiven."

I swallowed hard and wiped my tears away. I took several deep breaths and tried to compose myself. "I've never confessed these things before Father," I said in a voice barely audible. I leaned in closer to the iron grate that separated me from the priest and said, "I'm a murderer."

There was no movement from the other side of the confessional booth. "Go on," Father Ontari said.

"Three years ago I found out that I was pregnant. That is when the lies began. I hid this truth from everyone besides my friend Cameron and I concealed the pregnancy by continuing in the everyday activities like I always had-the club and committee meetings, school, sports… everything. One day, Adrian's two closest friends Eric and Steve Wise saw me outside the home of my close friend Tony Greggory and they told him about it. That night, I went to see Adrian at his house and a physical altercation took place. It ended with him pushing me down a flight of stairs and me, bleeding out on his living room floor. I made the decision to stay at his house and let the consequences our actions unfold as God saw fit. It was a bastard child, and because of that, I am certain, the fetus died and I was left to deal with the horrible guilt and memories. You see Father...I had the choice to do the right thing, to go to the hospital, and if I had my child might still be alive. I was too selfish and cowardly to do the right thing, and because of that I will never be forgiven."

"Ask for forgiveness now my child. Do not bear the weight that is not yours to bear."

I cried freely and closing my eyes and crossing my hands, I begged for forgiveness. "I have lived with lust in my heart for nearly a year now," I confessed. "I've met someone Father, his name is David and he is the love of my life. From the day I meant him, only thoughts of lust and idolization have run my mind. As wrong as it is...I can't help it...and I'm not sorry for it."

"Purge your heart of him my child. The way you speak of him and your feelings toward him are not spiritually clean."

"I will not Father. I will love him and I will be loyal to him and I will feel this way until the day I die," I said absolutely. "If I have to burn in hell for it...the Devil himself can come claim my soul."

"I urge you to recant," Father Ontari warned, "but perhaps that is confession for another day."

"I confess to all of the sins Father. I have been a liar. Deceit has become my nature and hate has ruled my heart. I've destroyed my body with alcohol and drugs, and I confess to premarital sex with multiple individuals. I have been unforgiving, manipulative, and the worst kind of daughter. The worst of my sins are those of my mind. I want to die...just like Cameron." It was painful to admit these transgressions, but a sense of peace settled over me. This was something that I should have done long ago, but I had been to self-righteous.

"God will never give you more than you can handle my child," Father Ontari said. "You have confessed your sins and now you must cleanse your body by fasting for three days and ceasing communication with David- the one that your flesh so keenly desires. You do these things and you shall be forgiven."

"I will fast as long as it takes Father, but I will not leave

David," I said grabbing ahold of the grate.

"You must if these things are to be washed clean…and that is what you want isn't it?"

"More than anything in the world Father," I said sinking my head into my hands and sobbing uncontrollably. It was bullshit! There was always a catch…even to God's forgiveness. "But I told you before- David has my love and loyalty."

The iron grate was suddenly slid aside, and David stared at me through the half foot by half foot opening. I jumped back and hit my head on the wooden ledge behind me. "Does he truly?" David asked me smirking.

I rattled the handle that was on the inside of the confessional door. It was locked! The grate slid shut as quickly as it had been opened. I inched closer to the opening and peered through the detailed engraved iron. "David?" I asked.

There was no response, and unable to clearly see through the opening, I tried the door handle once more. The door swung open freely, and without hesitation I exited the confessional and quietly tip-toed through the dark hallway to one of the devotional rooms. I could still see the confessional booth from where I stood, hidden in the shadows. I waited for nearly ten minutes; afraid of returning to the main sanctuary of the church for fear that Madam Therriot was waiting for me. I gasped, as moments later the door of the confessional swung open and Father Ontari emerged. He unsnapped his gold colored robe and placed it on one of the outer hooks on the wall next to his office. I was directly across from him and as he turned on the light of this office and gathered his things, I sank further into the blackness to avoid being discovered.

I watched his every movement, and scolded myself allowing my imagination to run away with me again. The light to his office was flicked off, and the sound of keys jingling on a key ring could be heard at the rear entrance door. It took several moments for my eyes to adjust to the darkness. A cool breeze drifted through the air and the thud of the door shutting was my cue to leave. I checked over my shoulder, paranoid, but thankfully I was alone. Quietly, I slipped from the shadows and crept down the hallway. Surprisingly, the door was still open, and easing it ajar slowly as not draw any unwanted attention to myself, I snuck outside. I scanned the back parking lot for Father Ontari's old Lincoln Town Car, but the lot was completely empty. The sound of squealing tires fast approaching, and the smell of exhaust overwhelmed me. I ducked back through the rear church door, as David's Camaro barreled around the corner of the cathedral and disappeared from sight.

THE RED

April 24, 2003 St. George's Day

"Open the door! I know that you're in there!"
Sluggishly, I opened my eyes and directed them toward the clock hanging behind the couch. It was just before 7:00 AM. I had come in through the rear entrance not two hours ago after staying at David's, and must have fallen asleep at my writing desk. The beating on the rear door continued, the shouting amplified, and my blood pressure spiked as I stared down at my monthly calendar- Adrian's Release Date, written in red screamed out to me.

"Autumn! I will come through this door if you don't open it I swear to God!" he screamed.

I had no other choice. With shaky hands I unlatched the lock and twisted the handle, but before I could open it properly, the door was kicked, sending me staggering backward until my shoeless foot hit the outer rim of the raised flowerbed. "Ouch!" I cried instantly grabbing my throbbing heel.

Adrian charged into the room after me and dragging me by my hair, he pulled me, kicking and fighting, to the nearest couch. I swung my arms at him, but it was useless. "Sit there," he demanded looking from my writing desk to the wall which housed my collection of paintings. "What the hell is all of this?" he asked, not truly seeking a reply.

I trembled with fear, smelling the alcohol on his breath and noting the blood shot red eyes that glared angrily at me. "It's nothing," I mumbled, wondering what to do next. My wits usually offered me the advantage of out-thinking him in these situations- so many times before, like a skilled chess player, I defeated him by staying two steps ahead.

"It will be when I'm finished," he spat ripping the framed portraits off the wall. With two hands extended, he clawed at the wall, sending each portrait crashing to the floor. The glass cracked and busted, exposing each medium to his wrath.

"Please stop!" I sobbed as he ripped the water color pictures and snapped the canvas boards of the acrylic pieces I had labored so diligently on. I saw him reach for the last painting, the landscape of the London fog I had done the first day that I had brought David over to see my studio. "No!" I cried jumping off the couch and shoving him, with all my force, into the wall. He collided into it, and stunned, stood for a moment with his back to me, his thin shoulders rising up and down as his rage exploded. I took a few steps back; I was cornered with no way to escape.

"You stupid bitch," he growled turning around and dropping the portrait to the floor. "I told you when I was locked up that I was going to make you pay. Did you think I was bullshitting? Did you think that all this time you could leave me in jail, slut around with some other dude, and get away with it?" He started after me, the red of his eyes burned into me, and I knew that I was in trouble.

"Let's just talk about this," I said back peddling. My backside reached the writing desk- I had nowhere else to go.

"I asked you so many times to talk to me Autumn, and you just blew me off. You thought you were the shit then. How is it working out for you now?"

"Adrian...please don't do anything that you are going to

regret."

"Oh, I won't trust me. The only thing that I regret is not beating your ass more," he snarled.

He was in my face now, his gin tainted breath smelled disgusting, and desperately I tried to push him back. A power struggle ensued, and ended with him snatching the silver necklace from around my neck, breaking the clasp.

"Bastard!" I screamed as he held me at bay and examined the pedant under the light of my desk lamp.

"You are too funny," he said not laughing in the slightest. "What? Did your new boyfriend give this to you?"

"Yes, he did," I said, frantically trying to pry it from his fingers.

"You will never get this back…and wait until I run into him. He thinks he is going to steal my girl? Well, that prick has another thing coming."

"It's not up to you Adrian! That is what you don't get," I said growing rigid and still. I had decided to quit fighting. All we ever did was fight and I was so tired of it. "There is nothing you can do to me. There is nothing that you can say that will change the fact that I don't love you anymore. In fact, I fucking hate your guts! I am in love with someone else and we are going to be together and there is nothing that you can do about it."

Before I knew what happened, Adrian, with the thick necklace chain wrapped around his fist, cocked back and swung. The punch landed squarely on my left lower jaw, the impact of it knocked me off of my feet. I hit the floor, and a shooting spike of pain climbed the entire length from my hamstring- up my back- to the base of my neck. I winced in pain, unable to move for several seconds.

"Is that what you wanted…huh? You wanted me to do that to you?"

I shook my head. "You are insane." I rubbed my jaw, which was painful to the touch, and tasting blood, I spat onto the beige hand woven rug beneath me. I was shocked at the red, which spread and soaked into the fabric, a visual picture of the years of abuse I had withstood. I raised my eyes from the rug and looked at Adrian, who was unmoved, unremorseful, and unforgiving.

Just then, a spanning shadow formed behind him. The vast wingspan of Stolas, the raven, stretched from one corner of the wall to the other. He flapped his powerful wings, and presented himself in a way that I had never witnessed before. His body, black, muscular, and towering was both part man and part bird- his face and body were that of a man, but his arms were mighty feathered wings. I couldn't remove my eyes from the whiteness of his, and I watched as his chest cavity opened, spilling forth a thousand shadows of the Legion that he ruled. He stood behind Adrian like a deadly bird stalking his prey.

"Autumn, I heard a commotion up here from the study," my father called through the door. "Are you alright?"

Stiffly, I got to my feet, wiping the blood residue from around my mouth. Afraid to take my eyes off of Stolas, I reluctantly cracked the door- exposing only the right side of my face- and assured my father that it was nothing. I shut the door quietly, and spun around, bracing myself for another surprise attack from Adrian. I was relieved to find that he had left, back through the rear entrance, and that the raven hybrid also was gone. The only thing that remained was a single black feather and the red.

LOVE

April 24, 2003 St. George's Day

"These are for you," David said handing me two dozen bound red roses.

"They're gorgeous," I breathed, lowering my nose to the petals and taking in the sweet floral scent.

"Not as gorgeous as you are," David said smiling, "let me have a look at you." Taking my hand, he spun me around and delicately wrapping his arm around me, softly kissed my lips and neck. Pulling away he asked, "where is the silver necklace?"

I had not told him what had happened earlier that morning. I hoped that he would not notice that the necklace was missing, but as usual, nothing escaped him. I was grateful that the dance was a masquerade, though I had applied nearly a half a bottle of foundation and heavily caked on face powder to cover the deep purple bruise that covered the left side of my cheek and chin, I was concerned that as the night wore on, that secret too would be exposed. "I'm sorry that I didn't tell you earlier David…but Adrian stopped by this morning and we got into fight and he took the necklace." I nervously fingered the lace and beading of my dress and waited for his response.

"Audacious asshole," David said under his breath.

"Don't worry, I talked to him just before you got here and he apologized and said that he would meet me tonight at the masquerade and return it to me."

A sly smile surfaced on David's face. "Did he? Well… that is good news indeed."

Relieved, I kissed him again, and grabbed my handbag to leave.

"Don't forget this," he said reaching onto my vanity table and lifting up the mask. He turned it over in his hands, inquisitively staring at the black and white design and silver glitter accents. He ran his fingers over the speckled black, grey, and white feathers that outlined the top of the mask and the single black raven feather that I had added to the center. His eyes darted over to me, and all the while, he continued to stroke the long ebony feather.

"Thanks," I said taking the mask from him and placing it into my purse.

He nodded and silently followed me outside.

My gown; long, full, and white, was hell to manage. I struggled to lift the thick undergarment layers as I bent to climb into the Camaro; sweating and flustered, I smoothed the puffy, tulle outer layer and tried to recompose myself. It was going to be a long night. My parents stood at the doorway and waved as David backed out of the driveway- they had pretended so well. My mother had fussed over how beautiful I looked the entire time in which my father snapped pictures of David and me. In his graceful way, David bared it all very well, though I could tell he thought both Denise and Bellino were ridiculous. I was embarrassed for both of them- they had no idea how easy it was for outsiders to see through their forced, loving charade. They hated each other and I couldn't blame them.

David had arranged for us to meet Lauren and Stacy and their dates at Pacifica, a new seafood restaurant that recently opened in Meriton. We arrived early, and as David wandered to the hostess stand to check in for our reservation, I couldn't help but stare after him. He had decided upon a form fitting ocean blue tuxedo, a white vest, and a blue, pink, and white striped tie. The colors complimented him perfectly, and the bright lightening of the waiting area further added to the glow of his skin and golden hair. Everyone who laid eyes upon him stared, and several tables of patrons paused their forks mid-bite to turn and look at him. The love that I felt for him swelled and my heart raced- I was always racing after him.

"Princess, our table is ready now. Do you want to go back or should we wait for the others to arrive?"

"I don't mind waiting if that's okay with you."

"Perfect," he said taking my hand, and turning to the hostess he said, "we'll wait outside."

Opening the door for me, David and I walked down the wooden deck, whispering intimately to one another and looked at the tropical fish that played along the lily pads and glided on top of the corral colored rocks that lined the ponds bottom.

"Hey guys," Lauren called out to us.

"Who is that with her?" David asked.

"Oh my gosh…I can't believe it," I said shaking my head in disbelief. Standing next to Lauren, in an emerald green and cocoa striped suit, was Silas.

"Nice to see you again Autumn," he said taking my hand and kissing it.

"Same here. Silas this is my boyfriend David," I said making introductions. "David this is Silas. I believe I told you about him before. We met him over Christmas when we were in London."

"Of course," David said shaking his hand. "As I recall, you and Axel Rhys work for the Bank of England?"

"That's right, and let me tell you Autumn," Silas said, "you really made an impression on Axel and Stinne."

"She's great isn't she?" David said rubbing my shoulder.

I blushed with embarrassment.

"They both just rave about her, and Axel is really serious about you moving to England and joining our team at the bank. Have you decided if you are going to take him up on his offer?"

"I've thought about it, but I haven't decided anything yet."

"It's an opportunity of a lifetime."

"Come on guys let's not rain on St. George's parade with all this business talk," Lauren said guiding Silas toward the restaurant entrance.

"And Stacy?" David said looking around, "shouldn't we wait until she arrives before we go in?"

I began to answer in the affirmative, but Lauren shrugged her shoulders and continued walking.

"Unbelievable that she is late. God knows she's never missed a meal," she said crudely.

"That was cold," David whispered to me as he held the door open for us all.

"Why don't you take everyone back to our table and I will wait for her," I said.

As soon as the hostesses grabbed the menus, Lauren dressed in a glittery hot pink halter dress, took the liberty of leading Silas and David into the dining area and to our table. Stacy arrived a few moments later, flushed, sweaty, and out of breath.

"Autumn...I'm so sorry that I'm late," she wheezed, wrapping her arms around me for a hug.

"It's not a big deal at all," I said ripping the tag off of her turquoise floor length gown. "What happened?"

"You're not going to believe this," she said as we were escorted down the hall and to our table.

"Isn't this a different dress than the one you picked out at the boutique last month?" I asked noting that the color was the same but the cut and accessories were different.

"That is what I was going to tell you," she whispered. "I went to put it on and can you believe I ripped the seam trying to zip it up?" she giggled with embarrassment. "I guess I haven't lost as much weight as I thought I did."

Like Cameron said- our thorns "Well just forget about that. This one looks even better on you," I said taking my place next to David and accepting a menu from our server.

"You're too kind," she gushed, "Now, what's for dinner?"

After a four course meal consisting of raw oysters on the half shell, garden salad, baked red snapper and vegetables, and chocolate mousse, and driving twenty minutes from Meriton back to Osnaburg; I was stuffed and a little sleepy. All of that changed the moment we reached St. George's. A sense of anxiety and regret, at my lack of contribution to the overall planning and decorating of a ball held in honor of the Saint we so wholly loved, took hold. In previous years the dance had been held in the school auditorium, but this year, thanks to a sizable donation from the three peacocks- Kitty Ritcher, Priscilla Lovewealth, and Denise Marseille- a new hall was constructed on campus which was determined to be perfectly fitting.

"Well, here we are princess," David said flashing me a lovely smile. "I know that you are nervous but just take a deep breath…everything will be great.

I hope that you're right. "I just hope that the ball is a success that's all."

"We are here together. That's all that matters in my book. You have to appreciate the time that you have with the people that you love because you never know when it can all be taken away from you," David said helping me from the car.

"I know," I admitted, "and I hope you know that I cherish every minute of it."

The sly smirk was back, "of course my love…I know your heart."

"It belongs solely to you." I could feel myself beginning to choke up as he placed the beautiful fresh rose boutique in my outstretched hands.

"I told you before the only thing that matters is your love…and your loyalty."

Together we wandered hand and hand down the shrubbery lined walkway, and I couldn't help but inwardly scoff at the thickly plated bronze welcoming sign- 'Garden

Hall: Graciously donated by the Osnaburg Twp. Women's Garden Members (etc. etc.)'. I squeezed David's hand and prepared myself for the worst as he opened the door for me. "I hope that you know that you have both," I said. "My love is everlasting."

I was pleasantly surprised. Garden Hall was an expansive building, modern, simplistic, and open. The lobby area was painted a soft shade of lilac, and in the center, an oval shaped water fountain and a statue of St. George himself was there to greet us. Several rows of coat closets had been smartly disguised with a layer of sparkly iridescent fabric and honeydew colored spot lighting. If the main room was decorated as elegantly, I had done a lot of worrying for nothing. *Cameron would have been proud.*

"I told you love," David said as we passed under a seamlessly assembled archway that blossomed with pastel pink tiger lilies. "You should have a little more faith in people. If I can…than you certainly have no excuse. Look at what they've done with the place."

The Student Council Planning Committee was still busy finishing the final decorating touches and didn't even notice that we were there. Like trusty worker bees, they hummed by David and I completing a task here and quickly moving on to the next. I was almost sad to admit the fact that David was right. I should have had more faith in my fellow committee members, and whether I wanted to swallow the harsh reality of the fact- it was true- they didn't need my involvement at all to make the masquerade a success.

The newly polished cherry hardwood floors gleamed and the tall bistro like tables that were situated against the walls were set with floor length white table linens and stout octagon shaped crystal vases with colored stones, clear water, and floating candles. The hall was wide and deep, the ceilings vaulted, and the wallpaper, textured and sage afforded a sophisticated space that could easily be dressed to suit nearly any occasion.

An unexpected spurt of rap music caused me to jump,

and from the corner I heard the DJ call out that it was time to test the sound equipment. The next song that jolted from the speakers was a slow one, and seizing the opportunity before the dance floor became too crowded, and my time with David too public, I took his hand and led him to the dance floor.

"This is bold of you," he said looking around as we swayed together in each other's arms.

"Sorry," I said looking up to him and resting my face on his chest. "It just felt so right."

"What are you apologizing for? I just think that sometimes…however strange…I bring out the very best in you."

"That's always."

"I wish we could stay like this forever."

We were so perfect together, David and I, and brushing a tear from my eyes, I prayed that what we shared would never change. I heard clapping and whistling, David and I were still dancing and the song was over. "Yea, Autumn!" I heard from a few and "Isn't that sweet" from others. David stopped and spinning me around- full circle- he took a bow. "The love of my life," he proudly announced. Everyone clapped and a round of hoo rah's and whistling ensued. I blushed wildly and the Morning Star seemed to shine brighter than I'd ever seen before.

HATE

April 24, 2003 St. George's Day

I'm doing it again. I'm doing precisely what I shouldn't be doing. Why do I always bend? Why do I always give? He has what I want. The silver necklace. I must get it back. Where is he? I heard voices not far off, and standing at the back entrance of Garden Hall, cellphone in hand, I wandered toward it. *It must be Adrian.* He had called only moments before, I was standing with Lauren and Silas at one of the empty tables watching David and Stacy dance to one of her favorite songs. He had asked me to meet him on the trail that ran behind the hall, and as my stiletto heels sank further into the soft dirt and sparse grass, I began to hate him even more. The sound of voices grew more distinguishable as I stumbled down the dark path. The back door was no longer visible behind me, and clicking the end button on my phone, I attempted to use the small glow of the screen to light my way. *I hope nothing comes out of these woods to get me.* I walked another thirty paces downhill and could make out the outline of the dock at Silver Lake.

"There you are," Adrian said emerging from the dense wood that lined both sides of the trail.

I looked around expecting to see Eric and Steve, but he was alone. "Adrian...hi."

He stared at me, from head to toe, raping me with his cold red eyes. I rubbed my arms uncomfortably and tried to avoid his suggestive glare.

"White never suited you Autumn. I didn't think that they let whores where white."

"Coming from you Adrian, I will take that as a compliment."

"I see that you haven't changed your mind about us," he said taking another drink from a bottle he had tucked in the front of his tattered jeans.

"The only reason that I'm here is to get my necklace back."

"Selfish bitch," he spat. "It's always about you. You only ever gave a damn about yourself, but honestly, I can't even say that I know you anymore."

"Whose fault is that? You were the one who got sent away."

"Always the fuck up, am I?"

"You chose to fuck up," I said. *Where the hell are those voices coming from?* I stepped past Adrian and continued to walk down the path toward the clearing. Pulling a cigarette from my handbag, I lit it and stepping onto the dock, I carefully wandered down the creaking wooden planks toward the edge of the water.

"Where the hell are you going?"

"You don't hear that?" I called back to him. I stopped at the edge of the dock, frozen in horror at the sight of Mara and Lamia, naked and playing in the cold water below.

"Hear what?"

I turned to look back at Adrian who was drunkenly leaning on one of the posts just at the edge of the soggy embankment, and then redirected my attention to the silver rippling water. Mara and Lamia were gone. Shivering, I turned and calling out to Adrian said, "never mind."

"You're hearing things now?" he asked, jeeringly

amused.

More than you know… and seeing things too. "Never mind just give me the necklace."

"Ahh… right the necklace," he said taking another swig. "Yea, you're not getting that back."

"What do you mean I'm not getting it back? That was the whole reason that I agreed to meet you."

He laughed, "yea I know, but you're still not going to get it."

"I hate you Adrian…with every ounce of my being I fucking hate you," I snapped.

"I know that too," he said, squinting his eyes at me and toeing his cigarette butt into the ground. "And I bet you would hate me even more if I were to throw this piece of shit into the lake!" He pulled the sparkling chain from his pocket and swung the pendant in front of my face.

"No! Adrian, please stop!"

"You sound desperate Autumn. Would you jump into that cold water after it?"

"Yes. Yes." I sobbed.

"I was counting on that. Jump in with that smock on and you are going to sink for sure."

"Why are you doing this Adrian?" I cried. "What is it that you want from me?"

"I'm getting it right now. I want you to beg and plead. I want you to feel what I've been feeling for a year. I want you to hurt. I want you to strip out of that dress and I want you to go after this piece of shit that you love so much."

"It's not the necklace that I love…it's what it represents," I said softly.

"What it represents? What does it represent?"

"It's the love that we share Adrian. It's something that you will never understand."

"Oh, the new boyfriend of yours. What's his name again?" he said grabbing me by the wrists forcefully.

The snap of fallen twigs and rustling from the thicket at the edge of the clearing caused both of us to pause and look toward it. "David Huntsmen," a raspy voice said in reply, "and right now... I'm hunting you."

I gasped as David appeared before me stepping between Adrian and I. Behind him, I could make out Captain Murmur and the three creeping she-beasts.

"What the hell?" Adrian said shocked, glancing back and forth between David and I- he hadn't noticed the solider and the three prowling crocuta behind him.

"Now you're speaking my language," David smirked. "Hell is exactly what has come down upon you."

I staggered backward, groping for the dock post to support myself. *Holy shit! This can't be happening!* Instead of finding the post, I hit something thick and solid, and turning around I came face to face with Stolas. He pushed me aside and stood at the right hand of David. I clapped my hands over my mouth to silence my scream, and sank to ground in fear.

"No need to release the Legion, bird of prey. I intend on handling this one all by myself." He reached out, and with one arm grabbed Adrian at the shoulder, and spinning him around clamped him into choke hold. "Give me the necklace slave," he hissed. Adrian wedged his elbow behind him, using David's body as leverage, in an attempt to break free. "Do you think this is necessary to end you? I do it purely out of pleasure." David lessened the pressure around Adrian's throat, causing him to drop to his knees.

I didn't dare make a sound. I couldn't move. The silver necklace dropped from Adrian's hands as he struggled to catch his breath.

"I hate you Autumn," he said choking and glaring at me. "I'm going to kill you before this is over."

His words, sharp as a lashing whip, stung and in a traumatized daze, my eyes wandered from him to Stolas, and then to the Captain, and back to David. With the strike of a hungry snake, David ceased him from behind; the moon reflected the glimmer of the silver necklace that he held in both hands. I watched as David pulled the necklace tighter and tighter around Adrian's neck, and I was no longer afraid. The fighting and the kicking lasted only a few seconds, as David lifted him from his feet with brute strength. Adrian's body began to shake fiercely. He seized and his head snapped back and forth uncontrollably. His skin drained of color. Satisfied that his work was complete, the Morning Star dropped his arms and the necklace dangled innocently from his fingers. Adrian's body pummeled to the earth in a heap, and looking down upon it-like fresh road kill- David nodded to Murmur and Stolas. Mara and Lamia petted the three Erinyes who snapped their dripping jaws like the carnivores that they were-constantly feeding on the flesh and souls of men. Murmur dragged Adrian's limp body to the edge of the embankment, and Stolas kneeling over him, opened his black leather jacket. His chest cavity split open, and the tetrahedron of light bolted through Adrian's dead body. The corpse sizzled and sparked, and into the light floated black particles of dust that were lifted from Adrian's chest and absorbed into Stolas's. "It is complete eminence," he said pushing the steaming remains into the slate water.

David's eyes darted over at me and the silver necklace dropped from his hand. He lifted me from the ground and placing his alabaster arms around me he said, "love and loyalty."

Unable to speak and shaking at the sight of Adrian's dead body, semi-amerced and bobbing in the middle of Silver Lake, I held onto David and hated myself even more.

WANDERLUST

April 24, 2003 St. George's Day

What does she think of me now? All this time, I've told her that the only thing that matters is love and loyalty, and she swears that she has both for me. I've thought about this moment so many times. I've thought of wringing his frail little neck. I've broken all the rules for her...and what have I gained if not her love and loyalty? "It has been done my lord," Stolas said. *And are you pleased my bird of prey? Has your thirst for destruction finally been quenched?* **Very good raven. His body will soon be discovered. We must make haste.** "And what of the girl eminence?" Murmur asked nodding toward Autumn who was still crouched in a sitting position near the edge of the dock. **I must speak with her alone. Draw back into the cover of the shadows, and I will join you soon.** I waited until they were out of sight and looking on to my princess, who was still numb with shock, joined her at the water's edge.

The Reign must surely be satisfied with the outcome of the events that have unfolded, but nothing else matters if I have turned her against me. In the end, the jinn always are against me- even if the loving embrace lasts a lifetime- in the afterlife it always vanishes. Make a life with me princess. Stay with me forever. **Autumn I had no choice my love...he was never going to stop. I couldn't allow him**

destroy you. *That is my job.* Her listless brown eyes met mine and she said nothing. *You feel that your heart is broken? It's not. Soon enough you will feel it being torn in half. I feel sorry for you- an emotion that I've never felt until I met you. How is it that with you I am capable of so much?* **He has hurt you for the last time. I won't allow anyone to hurt you- not Adrian, not The Reign, not even myself.** Her eyes widened and narrowed at me. "What do you mean The Reign?" she asked. *My faithful followers who reign over you all.* **I must admit my love that I was not fully forthcoming with you on all accounts. I had to make sure that I could trust you.** "I had a dream about you...it's been months ago...before we went to London even...you took me to hell...you called them The Reign." *If only it were a dream.* **That is part of what I must explain to you my love.** I watched her tremble and I liked it. *You're so pretty when you're vulnerable. I see now why Mara, Lamia, and the slave can't get enough of you.* "You're scaring me David," she whispered and the tears began to stream from the corners of her eyes. *All that makeup that you applied to hide your lie is washing away. Did you honestly think that I didn't know about that? I know everything. I know that you are equally able to love and hate.* **Scaring you is not my intention princess, but we are running out of time. You and I are running out of time together.** "What do you mean?" she gasped locking onto my hands.

    I mean that it is time for the wanderlust to continue. *You will feel a great loss, and at your expense, I will ensure that I feel none.* "Talk to me David...what do you mean? Why are we running out of time together?" I could feel the pleading in her voice- the desperation that swelled inside of her. It turned me on. *You are still wandering blindly, but the time has come for the Morning Star to light your way. I can only speak so much. I can't risk explaining it all.* **Do you still believe that everything that has happened over the past year is merely coincidence? Do you still think that the nightmares and the day trips are just that- a chimera? Do you still experience this world at face value? Pity on you if you do. Have you've learned nothing from me Autumn, or are you still**

wandering- blindly- in lust? I told you from the very beginning that it was all a false reality, but what I did was give you the ability to see the true reality of it all. Don't you see? It was a gift. The falseness arises in the mirrors that distort this world. Everything that you saw, and felt, and thought- was real. It is this world. The vices, the sin, the manipulation, are all around us. They bear their ugly head, every second of every day. Who do you believe makes that all possible? "The devil," she said releasing my hands. *Yours truly.* I smirked at her. **The devil and his followers- the little voice in your head that influence your decisions and present an alluring alternative to all the choices that are right and good. The devil and his demons are everywhere. There is no escape. I liked your illusion to a tesseract by the way. When the devil gains control, you are trapped within yourself- you've allowed him to win.** "And you?" she asked tugging at the beading of her soiled white dress. **I make it all possible.** She buried her face in her hands and shook her head in disbelief. *You are coming undone.* "I don't believe you," she sobbed. *If you didn't then there would be no need for tears.*

Believe in wanderlust. "What is it?" she asked in a state of near hyperventilation. Her agony made my heart skip a beat. I'd thrived off of it for so long, that and her adoration. There was no way that I could completely let go of it now. **I am the fallen angel Autumn my love. Since the beginning of time...the moment I was cast out... I've been wandering. The one that you think is so good...well he has an unique sense of humor I would say. My followers, the angels that defied him, and vowed to follow me, were cast down as well. Two...soon to be three, damned, I've created myself. It's a common misconception that we are bound to hell. The truth is, we are there from time to time, but it is so much better to wander the Earth and gather the jinn ourselves. The funny thing is I'm given all the credit...which I suppose I deserve, but the truth of the matter is that only a fraction of the jinn could be swayed**

without the help of The Reign. Her eyes were not afraid of me. I had pondered many long hours if my revelation would frighten her. She appeared to be more hurt and anything else. *Helpless love, perhaps she will still be loyal despite it all?* "You're telling me, that all this time, I've been in love with the Devil?" she spat. **None other. Only I have the ability to jade your reality. The Reign simply does as they are told.** "What have you done David?" she asked standing and holding onto the dock post for support. She stared out into the lake at the dead body of her ex-love and sobbed even louder. *Should I tell her the truth? No…no I cannot. After all this time, I can't set myself up to fail…to lose her forever. I need her. A fraction of the truth shall suffice.*

 I came to Osnaburg, that much you already know. The moment I saw you Autumn, I knew that I wanted you to be mine. Needless to say, I have the power to make even the strong bend to my will. "What will?" **Destruction, devastation, and ultimately…death.** "Death? I thought you loved me?" she cried. I sprang to my feet. *Stupid girl, if I wanted you dead I would have killed you a long time ago. Or if not I, The Reign would have happily carried you off to hell.* **Of course not my love. I must admit that upon meeting you, yes that is what I wanted.** "What!" she screamed, panting and out of breath. I rose to my feet and meeting her at the edge of water, I placed my arms around her. **Why would I not want that? It would mean having you forever…in hell…with me.** Muffled cries were my response, buried deep in my suit jacket. **But…it only took one night for me to completely fall in love with you. The Reign had their minds set that you would be our next victim, but the day of the track meet when they came to my porch, I told them that I loved you and that I would not allow any harm to come to you.** I clutched her tighter, and if I thought prayer would have worked, I would have dropped to my knees and prayed that she wouldn't leave me. **The Reign was angry, they had learned of the omen proclaimed by Madam Therriot at the festival.** "How did they know about that?" she asked pulling away slightly. *This is going to come as quite a shock.* **She is**

my oracle, and a member of The Reign. "I feel sick," she said holding her stomach and diverting her eyes from mine. *The worst is yet to come.* **I had to have Madam Therriot prophesize if you were the one...my one and only...the princess for my kingdom who would reign with me forever. That day at the festival, she confessed that you would die too soon. She was not referring to Adrian- that I knew- he was only collateral damage. She was referring not to a literal death, but a figurative one.** "I'm not going to die?" she asked anxiously. **All humans must die at some point my love, but just like all the other events in the false reality that the humans live- sometimes the figurative, the things that you can't see, or taste, or smell, are the most damning.** "A figurative death? She followed me a few weeks ago...Madam Therriot. I had gone to St. George's Cathedral to pray... and she was there. She told me that I was already dead." *You died the moment you let me into your heart.* **She can see all things my love. She knew that this day would happen.** "How am I dead David?" she shouted out. I clenched her by the hand. **Because- what we have must now come to an end.** She straightened, and her mouth hung open. "Why? I don't care who you are or what you've done. I've seen that you are capable of love and empathy and goodness. Nothing else matters in this world to me David- just you."

I was hoping that you would say that my love. I will have a princess and the ultimate prophesy will be fulfilled. **If I told you what I've done, it may change your mind.** She shook her head. "Nothing will change how I feel about you. I swore to you my love and my loyalty and I meant it. If nothing else in this fucked up world of mine means anything, you can take that at face value." **It won't change your mind to learn that I've manipulated you and your friends? That I sent Tony Greggory away to Missouri? That I turned Vicki Tinsdale and Ramsey Sanders against you?** "How have you manipulated us? Besides lying about who you are and who your followers are?" She was defensive, and I knew that soon it would elevate. **Humans have a tendency to sin, The Reign** and I have a way of influencing it a bit more. All your friends are sinners Autumn. You dismissed your dreams as nothing more than nightmares, but they were the reality, you were just unable to see it. Lauren Vanderbilt has swollen with pride before your very eyes. She only cares about herself, and can't see past her own nose. Stacy, on the other hand, will follow straight into the fire. Gluttony is a disgusting sin. A nasty and disgraceful habit. Adrian Waters, and how fitting where he now lies, was more of a sloth than I've seen in over a hundred years. He was a complete waste of space, sucking down the air of all the other jinn. Honestly Autumn, you could say that I did the planet a service in finishing off the job. Typically, that is not how we fallen and the damned handle things; we allow the jinn to choose their own downfall- of their own free will. But, I couldn't allow the sloth to ruin you either. Need I go on? Tony, though he may be kind hearted, and certainly sweet on you, is wrathful and unsettled. He's been angry over your situation with Adrian, your lack of reciprocation of his feelings toward you, and most of all- of our relationship. It was easy enough to send him away. His loving counterpart, Vicki, is just as entertaining to Captain Murmur and the Erinyes. They thrive on collecting the souls of the jinn easily influenced by wrath, envy, and jealousy. You must know that your not- so-dear friend Vicki encompasses those sins just as well as Tony Greggory. Last but not least Cameron. "What about Cameron?" Autumn hissed. *That's more like it. Give me the hate baby, because I know that the love is going to follow.* That leaves only greed and lust princess, and I think you know which one was becoming of her. "I read her suicide letter," she said glaring at me. *Oh yea...well I helped her write it.* "She wrote about the raven...about your bird Stolas. She saw him before she died. Everyone sees the raven before they die...if they are joining the damned that is. "You killed her too?" she shrieked. Adrian is one of the three exceptions my love.

We don't kill. We only encourage. Cameron took her life on her own accord. She was vile, treacherous, greedy, and despicable. She was a drug addict worse than, even to this day, you realize; she was immoral and sexually unclean. She deserves to be exactly where she is. "How could you do this?" she asked taking a step back, her feet now beneath the shallow water of the lake. **This is all I know my love.** "So that leaves me...the sin of lust," she said thoughtfully. *My favorite of all the sins.* **Yes, sexual sins are ruled over by the Royal Pair- Mara and Lamia- and their slave. That is why they came to you in your dreams. Your lust for me is like something, in all my years, I have never felt before. You made me fall in love with you Autumn...a feeling that had escaped me since the day I was cast out and damned to wander this world. That is my reality.... eternal wanderlust.** She kicked her feet about in the water for a few moments. "And Cerberus...he is your guardian? He truly is the three headed beast?" *In hell and on Earth, he is my un loyal.* **The loyal one...yes he is the beast from your dreams, and Iago, the bas rouge, he is his hellion offspring.** She nodded.

I couldn't discern if this was all sinking in or if she was in a complete state of shock. **Come to me princess.** I motioned for her to stand next to me on the dock. Surprisingly, she obeyed and joined me without a trace hint of resentment or defiance. **Autumn, if I had it my way I would stay with you...in this way forever...but I can't. I sense we only have a few more moments, so I must make this quick.** *Soon the body will be discovered. I only have a few moments left with her. How do I tell her that the light of her world- her Morning Star- will be lost forever?* **If I could damn myself a thousand times I would to stay in this way, with you, but I can't. In just minutes, several students will wander down that very path and will discover you. The police will not be far behind. I must leave you now...forever.** "Forever?" she gasped clamping her hand over her mouth. "You can't. I won't let you!" **There is no other choice my love.** *The time is not right,* *but rest assured, your time will indeed come.* **I must do what I was damned to do…to wander until the end of time. You've changed things though, princess, now I will wander in lust. If I do have your love and loyalty, you will wander with me until the end…and then we will be together for all of eternity.** "And until then? I can't give you up David. Take me with you please," she begged and threw her forgiving arms around me. *I won't give you up.* **I will be with you forever…as long as you will have me.** "David, please don't do this." She followed after me as I stepped off the deck and wandered toward the dark path leading into the woods. I turned to her, embracing the one soul that I had loved enough to let go. I kissed her, taking in the soft moist lips that I had grown to adore. I would never forget what we shared. I stopped at the path and listened. *I can hear them coming. This is it.* **Your love and your hate, I want it all. All I want is you Autumn. I will always be with you. Don't be afraid.** I looked down on Silver Lake. **I will be there for you through everything that is to come…even cleaning up the mess with the sloth…I will take care of you.** I watched her gaze into my face for the final time and I slyly grinned back at her. *Stay with me forever in wanderlust.* **Remember princess, all I ask is for your love and loyalty.**

Italics indicate David's thoughts; Bold text indicates David's spoken words.

GABRIEL

April 24, 2003- St. George's Day

The flashing lights and sound of the wailing sirens was nauseating. The strobes of red and blue drew closer and standing in the rancid muck lining the narrow embankment of Sliver Lake, I contemplated joining Adrian, face down in the still cold water. Instead, I allowed the gritty mush to squish between my toes and the hem of my white, flowing dress to lie buoyant on the water's edge. I hadn't noticed the wave of bodies spilling out of the grand entrance of the hall and down the trail, my classmates, fellow committee members, and chaperones. I was paralyzed, staring at the lifeless body bobbing in the water until I was shaken by screams- a sound so unforgettable.

"You, out of the water," a husky voice called out to me.

I didn't react. Police or not, they weren't my keeper. I had survived mental and physical attacks, not to mention brutal psychological manipulation from David and The Reign- there was nothing a flesh and blood human could do to scare, hurt, or intimidate me now.

"I said out of the water!" the police man called out again.

THE LONGER YOU WAIT THE SAFER YOU WILL BE MY LOVE. NO RUSH. EVERYTHING IS UP TO YOU NOW. I WILL HELP YOU THROUGH THIS.

"Autumn…Autumn," I heard Stacy and Lauren scream.

I spun around just as they barged through the crowd, pushed their way past the police officer, and fell into my arms. The force of our contact knocked the three of us to the ground. "He's dead. He's dead. He's dead!" I cried into Lauren's shoulder. She stroked my weary head and brushed the matted wet hair out of my face.

"Shush, shush, don't say another word," Lauren whispered to me.

"For God sake, put down your weapons," Stacy cried frantically at the growing number of police officers that had arrived to the crime scene.

"She's in shock," Lauren said angrily. "Come down here and help her. She is a victim too!"

Several of the officers lowered their weapons and with their help, I was able to drag my lead legs out of the mud and up the marshy incline. I was suddenly cold and standing protected between my two friends, my teeth chattered and my hands and knees shook. I could hear the screaming and the concerned outbursts from the crowd of students behind me, until the commotion died into a soft hum and everything slowly faded to black.

I opened my blurred eyes, blinking several times to dissipate the cobwebs that were draped over my swollen eyes. Confused as to why I was sitting in the back seat of an SUV, I immediately reached for the door latch, but to my dismay, it was locked. I gazed out of the misted over window, taking in the horrific sight: the red flares illuminating the gravel walkway David and The Reign had wandered down, there was a balding and chubby cop interviewing Lauren and Stacy, and then the stretcher that was wheeled by my window. The young woman who navigated the gurney slowed as she passed me. With Adrian's lifeless body only inches way, I placed my trembling palm on the window glass and let out a slow and painful moan.

A soft voice from the front seat startled me- I thought I was alone. "I'm sorry for your loss."

I said nothing.

"Autumn Marseille?" a pair of copper eyes questioned through the rear view mirror.

"Yes," I replied cautiously. "Who are you and what am I doing in here?"

With a voice barely above a whisper I made out, "Detective Spenser Gabriel- Sheriff's Office.

I fought to swallow the glob of vomit that pushed its way up my esophagus and wondered how Stacy found pleasure in the sick, habitual feeling. Nervously twirling a wet mess of curls around my index finger, I avoided making eye contact with the Detective in the mirror. What was the story that David told me say? Now, trapped in the back of the Sheriff's vehicle, I was terrified to recollect the chain of events that would undoubtedly keep me out of jail. I was going to jail for sure- I had discovered the body, I had a motive to kill him, and my prints and DNA were all over the crime scene and murder weapon. *The necklace! Where was the necklace?*

STOP IT PRINCESS...YOU'RE FINE. REMEMBER WHAT I TOLD YOU. YOU FAUGHT WITH HIM YESTERDAY AND HE CALLED YOU TO APOLOGIZE. YOU CAME TO THE DANCE WITH A GROUP OF FRIENDS. YOU DECIDED TO GO DOWN TO THE LAKE FOR A SMOKE AND YOU DISCOVERED HIS BODY. THAT IS THE STORY THAT YOU MUST STICK TO MY LOVE. THEY WILL KNOW THAT HE CALLED YOU SO YOU CAN NOT DENY THAT FACT. YOU MENTION NOTHING ABOUT THE NECKLACE. THE WORSE THING THAT WILL BECOME OF ALL THIS IS THAT IT WILL BE EXPOSED THAT YOU WERE SMOKING AGAINST SCHOOL POLICY, BUT YOU MUST ADMIT TO IT AND TAKE WHATEVER PUNISHMENT COMES FROM ST. GEORGE'S ON THAT ACCOUNT. THAT IS YOUR REASON FOR BEING AT THE LAKE.

David's voice comforted me and I bit my lip and tried to focus, with his help, this Detective and the other police officers that were against me didn't have a chance. I closed my eyes again and exhaled heavily. I felt my mind wandering away- to a happier, safer place.

"I'd like to talk to you Miss Marseille about what happened tonight," Detective Gabriel said.

I opened my eyes and reluctantly lifted them to the rearview mirror. Stolas's white pupils drilled deeply back into mine. I shuttered with the fear that only an army of demons could instill.

Gabriel's quiet voice continued, "I know this is difficult for you Miss Marseille but the sooner you show cooperation and tell me what happened, the sooner you can put this terrible tragedy behind you."

I twirled the ends of my hair tighter around my finger. I didn't like his good cop pretending, or the way in which his golden eyes widened and narrowed when he addressed me, or the hushed tone in which he possessed. I snickered and thought about how amusing it was that this was the person who was after both me and my Morning Star.

I TOLD YOU MY LOVE, WE HAVE NOTHING TO FEAR.

"What is it there to know?" my hoarse voice managed to squeak.

"Plenty… like what happened to your face."

The makeup that I had thickly applied must have smeared away, exposing the bruise on the left side of my face. In the midst of the events that transpired, I had forgotten about my fight the previous day with Adrian; it had blended together in a net of hate- the same one I had been snagged in for years. My pruned fingers grazed across my swollen cheekbone. Wincing in pain I shrugged off his questioned, "sports injury- it's nothing really."

A flick and a glimpse of flame was my reply. A thick cloud of blue smoke hovered in the air and all was silent for several agonizing minutes. "A couple of half-smoked cigarettes were found along the edge of the dock," Gabriel finally said pointing toward the small clearing amidst the dense thicket that surrounded the opening of the lake. "Would you like one?" he offered slowly.

I readily accepted and welcomed the harsh smoke which filled my lungs and brought about a sense of calmness to my rattled nerves. I puffed loudly, expelled a muffled cough, and watched as the observing students were ushered toward their vehicles in the parking lot not three hundred meters away. "Would you mind rolling the window down?" I asked nervously. Hanging my bare arm outside, I contemplated tossing the filter into the brush, but instead, decided against it.

VERY GOOD PRINCESS. DON'T GIVE THEM ANY EVIDENCE TO USE AGAINST YOU.

I drew my arm back inside the open window and smashed the butt into the tiny, flip down, ashtray compartment. Taking the lighter out of my dirt stained handbag, I proceeded to set the filter on fire. I would do as David commanded and leave no evidence.

Gabriel's glowing eyes were back in the mirror looking into mine. "Miss Marseille, please, tell me about Adrian. Tell me something. Why did you fight with him? Why were you down at the lake alone? Why do you say that the contusion on your face is nothing? Are you covering for someone? The facts just don't add up." His voice never altered, never strained, never rose. There was an implacable collectiveness, softness, distance which chilled me and made me doubtful and uneasy.

"Why do you have to ask me about this now? He's dead!" I spat. "Can't I just sit here in silence and think about the days that were filled with more love than hate- when we were young and innocent and inexperienced with the evils of the world? Why can't you grant me just that?" I cried lashing out.

"Tell me about those times."

"What is there to tell?"

"What was it like then? Help me understand."

Frustrated, I slammed my fist against the door. "What

was it like? I met Adrian when I was twelve years old. He was beneath me, I knew that even then, but he was so sweet. He had a smile that could light up any room. We attended different schools, but back then we would talk on the phone for hours," I paused wiping the tears from my eyes.

"Go on."

"We would spend every available second together, but my freshman year everything changed," I stopped abruptly looking up into the mirror I had been avoiding. A fire had ignited in Spenser Gabriel's golden eyes. A sudden urge to put a face with the melodramatic voice and amber eyes of the detective rushed over me. I didn't trust him and I longed to know exactly the enemy I was faced with.

"Please continue," his voice prodded.

"Things changed."

"This is not looking good for you Miss Marseille," he replied slowly.

"It's Autumn," I snapped. "Quit calling me Miss Marseille. And what is with you faking concern and politeness? You are just going to use this against me later!"

"That depends," Stolas said, his dark ghastly face twisting in front of mine.

I jumped and pushed myself further back into the fabric of the seat. Stolas glared at me and shot me a gleaming, wicked smile.

"Go away please!" I cried raising my hands in front of me in an effort to push his face away from mine. Instead, my hands landed on the back driver-seat head rest, and the face of many demons evaporated into the cloudy air.

"Autumn?" Gabriel said in a tone hinting of concern.

I didn't reply. My eye lids were clamped shut, I could only scream in horror. An instant later, I felt the swoosh of the car door opening. The muggy air clung to my skin refusing to let go. A hand, almost non-existent, supported me as I stepped down out of the vehicle. Blindly, I wandered with the nemesis, Detective Gabriel, from the Sheriff's SUV, across the marshy grasses which sank beneath my feet. We moved quickly and I fought to keep my eyes closed in fear of opening them to find Stolas and his Legion again.

"Open up," Gabriel called. "Miss Marseille, allow me please," he said lifting me off my feet.

YOU ARE GOING TO BE FINE MY LOVE. HAVE FAITH IN ME. I AM HERE WITH YOU.

Finding courage from David's words, I opened my eyes and groaned at the fact that the detective had secured me in the back of an ambulance. I battled against the EMT personnel as they wrestled to place restraints on my raw wrists. Wildly, I scanned my surroundings and glared up at the orderlies who were busy running wires and configuring the machines that they were connected to.

"Gabriel!" I yelled. "Where is Detective Spenser Gabriel? I am being held here against my will!"

"I'm sorry Autumn," his soft voice said from within the crowd of emergency technicians.

"You're sorry?" I retorted fuming. "You have no right putting me in here!"

As I lay on the stretcher with dozen of tubes running from all surfaces of my body, a figure emerged from the middle of the crowd. He was thin which seemed to make him taller than I guessed he probably was. His sharp, distinct cheekbones framed his heart-shaped face and his amber eyes glistened against his even, fair complexion.

"I'm sorry Autumn," he repeated. "I can't allow you to go home in your condition."

His feminine features matched the softness of not only his tone and demeanor, but his touch as well. I noted this as he placed his slender hand on top of mine. I looked down and nearly fainted. My wrists were spilt open from corner to corner- all I could see was protruding flesh and the red.

"Oh my god! How did that happen?" I wailed, shocked, pain-free, and hysterical.

Gabriel tucked his coffee brown, chin length curly locks behind his ears and smoothed his rose colored tie. "You almost...."

"Finished off the job!" a fiendish, inhuman voice roared. Stolas loomed over me, and I witnessed in disbelief as his chest opened filling the ambulance with his Legion, which multiplied and expanded all around me.

VICISSITUDES

April 28, 2003

I was kept for observation for several days and upon my release, I agreed to accompany Cathy to view the body of Adrian- her son. I had dreaded the inevitable outcome the entire drive into town, and dreaded it more as I stood in the cold blank hallway of the Coroner's Department. The strong smell of rubbing alcohol matched the sterile and diluted hallway in which we stood. White ceilings, white walls, and white tile floors beamed the reflections of the ghostly souls that occupied the inhabitance. Their twisted ash faces glared up at me, and elevating up from their current position, the faces of the dead conjured up speeding winds which whirled around my head like a cyclone. Even though David was gone, his power and the presence of his demons was still very much alive.

Cathy and I stood just inches apart, clutching hands, mustering our courage as the petite Indian medical examiner pushed the glasses up on his pudgy nose and moved closer to the small, dirty windowpane that separated us. His thick voice erupted over the loud speaker positioned above, "Are you ready?"

I squeezed Cathy's trembling hand and placed my arm around her slumped shoulders. The doctor slowly and deliberately rolled the crisp white sheet down exposing Adrian's face and chest. Resting on the metal slab, an expression of tranquility was forever captured on his face. Cathy gasped at the sight of her dead son- her only child-lifeless and still. Collapsing, her wails and sobs echoed down the corridor and filled my heart with regret. If only I had loved instead of hated, maybe Adrian would still be alive. The ligature marks were pronounced around the base of his neck and the pattern of the markings was startling. I could visibly note the small oblong impressions, all identical, that wrapped around the pale flesh underneath his narrow chin. My hand wandered down my own neck and chest. Frantically, I searched my memory of that dreadful night, and remembering that I had not recovered it, I immediately broke into a cold panicking sweat.

CALM DOWN MY LOVE. IT'S NOT THE FIRST TIME YOUR ORNAMENT OF BEAUTY HAS BEEN USED FOR A MORE DEVIOUS PURPOSE. YOU MUST NOT GIVE AWAY SURPRISE OR DRAW UNNECCESSARY ATTENTION TO YOURSELF. I FEAR THAT DETECTIVE IS SUSPICIOUS OF YOU ALREADY. TELL NOTHING THAT I HAVE'NT DIRECTED YOU. IN DUE TIME, THE SILVER NECKLACE WILL BE RETURNED TO YOU, AND I KNOW, WITH YOUR LOVE, IT WILL BE SAFE.

A sudden gust of air raced down the hall and the swoosh of the automatic doors drew me back to reality. My heart jolted with anxiety as Detective Gabriel strolled through the opening and stopping just beyond the sticky sensor pad, he surveyed the lobby, and then the hallway until his eyes fell upon me. The sliding doors closed behind him with a squeak and combing through his wind tousled curls he presented himself to the assistant, flashing his credentials, and was directed to proceed. His long strides afforded him the advantage of approaching much more quickly than I would have liked. Uneasiness pressed against my chest as his amber eyes blankly connected with mine.

"Can I be of assistance Miss Marseille?" he asked with a complete lack of empathy. He placed his hand on Cathy's shoulder and his awkward attempt of condolence only caused her to sob more violently.

"We're fine," I replied. "Leaving actually." I nervously shifted my weight to the other foot and wished that at this exact moment I was somewhere else- anywhere else but here. I understood now why Mason refused to come.

"Such a shame," he said quietly. "I was hoping to ask you a few more questions. Pick your brain a bit about that fateful night. Any new information you could provide would be useful in the investigation.

"I really can't right now," I said. "His mother needs to rest and I am taking her home." Supporting her underneath her chubby arms, I lifted her from the ground and cradled her against me protectively.

"I understand, but when you get a moment please call me." He pulled a business card from the inside pocket of his pinstriped suit jacket.

"Sure," I mumble, pinching it between my fingers.

The loud speaker rumbled to life once more. "You can come in Detective," the medical examiner called.

Gabriel's face twitched slightly and nodding his head to us he said, "I'm sorry for your loss."

"Thank you," Cathy replied in between her tears.

I pulled her away from the unforgiving glass and down the hall toward the exit doors. My raging pulse began to recover as we neared the end of the hallway and glancing back, I noted the strange Detective was still listlessly staring back at me.

Cathy had pleaded for me to stay with her. Things would never be the same without her darling boy she claimed. I suspected she was frightfully lonely, with no one but her cats and her alcoholic husband now. I was alone too. I had my cellphone disconnected, I ignored my landline, and I deleted my email and instant messenger accounts. I was afraid every waking moment and fought sleep every night, paralyzed with the fear of Stolas, Murmur, Mara, Lamia, and their followers; but for several days, even the demons stayed at bay.

Driving back from my daily visit with Cathy, I decided to take a detour from my usual route home and instead of turning right onto Big Bend, I stayed straight and traveled several miles to the edge of the west township line until the street sign- Grace Ave. - came into focus. I applied the brake and drove at a snail's pace in front of the familiar white house with the sprawl wrap around porch. *David where are you? You promised that you'd never leave me.*

PRINCESS I'M HERE. IT'S YOUR CHOICE TO HAVE ME OR NOT.

I shook my head trying to clear the voice that I loved from my head.

BUT THIS IS NOT SMART MY LOVE. YOU SHOULD NOT HAVE COME HERE. UNTIL YOU SPEAK WITH THE DETECTIVE, AND CLEAR ANY DOUBTS THAT HE MAY HAVE, AND SATISFY THE BURDEN OF PROOF, THAT YOU ARE INNOCENT OF ALL POSSIBLE CHARGES; THIS, COMING HERE AND SEARCHING FOR ME IS NOT SAFE.

David's voice disappeared and reluctantly, I accelerated down the road until the house was out of sight. The Duke gas station was on the corner, nestled between a patch of dense woods. It was the same mini-market I had met David at after visiting Adrian in juvenile hall for the first time. It had been a year ago. I wanted the nightmares to cease. I wanted to see David again, but maybe he was right, things would not return to normal until I met with Detective Gabriel. Tired and frustrated I slammed the door of my Audi and making my way across the empty parking lot, I entered the small store. The same Arabic men sat behind the same counter, watching the same tiny TV monitors. The monotony of life was so apparent without the bright illumination that the Morning Star provided.

I grabbed a can of Surge, a sinful soft drink infused with

sugar and caffeine, and shuffled down the dirty aisle which led to the checkout counter. One of the young men behind the counter jumped up and with a smile rang up my purchase.

"One dollar," he said flashing me a toothy, flirtatious grin.

"Let me add a pack of Newports," I replied pointing to the green and white striped box of cigarettes on the shelf behind him.

"Sure," he said reaching for them and scanning the additional purchase along the bar code reader. "Five dollars and twelve cents."

Nodding, I unzipped my pursed and locating the exact change I handed it to the overly eager clerk and began drumming my polished nails on the edge of the counter.

"Can you believe that it's supposed to storm tonight?" the young man asked pointing toward the drive-thru order window. "Get out and enjoy it while it lasts," he said handing me my receipt, soda, and cigarettes.

I followed his gesture and watched as the wind outside shook the leaves of the trees and the sky that just minutes ago was a splendid shade of periwinkle, now had turned a threatening grayish hue. Just then, the familiar sickening knot formed in my stomach, as David walked past the window. It was David! I was certain of it! I could have spotted him in a crowd of thousands. As he glided by, he turned slightly, flashing me a sly smile and continued on out of sight. The Surge can crashed to the floor spewing yellowish green fizz all over the racks of candy and snacks just beneath the counter. I bolted for the sliding doors, making a sharp right as I hit the sidewalk.

"David!" I yelled, chasing the sweet and spicy smell that hung in the air. I sprinted the length of cracked sidewalk along the building and stopped. David was nowhere in sight. The small alley behind the building was dark and frighteningly narrow and isolated, but cautiously, I wandered down it calling out to him. I hated the love I felt for David. I emerged from the alleyway, and found myself on Grace Ave again. I hated that David was right- I would forever be trapped alone, with him, in wanderlust.

REQUIEM

April 30, 2003

The days immediately following my thoughts of reverie- seeing David outside the Duke mini-mart- passed in a blur. I secluded myself in the comfort and safety of my bedroom. Nothing was real anymore. I had been living in a false reality for the past year and I longed only for it to return.

I could not believe that Adrian was dead...that David had killed him. I hated Adrian with every ounce of my being, but I didn't want him dead! Tony had been right all along: I hated that I loved Adrian most of all. Only my own pride and selfishness had kept me attached to him. He filled the void of misplaced hope- a hope that never was meant to be. I had always been afraid to let him go...how would my desires ever be fulfilled? My sun had died and it was my fault, Adrian is dead and it is my fault, if I would have let him go, none of this would have ever happened.

My eyes, incapable of shedding anymore tears, sagged under the immense pressure of denial and grief. I had absolutely nothing left. My dreams, of our child, will be buried today with Adrian and perhaps finally put to rest. The thought of attending his funeral sent a sickening pain through my stomach like a screw slowly being twisted into place. The idea of facing everyone was terrifying. I shuddered as I imagined how they would tightly embrace me, rock me from side to side, whisper hollow reassurances in my ear, and I was the one who stood idly aside and watched him take his last breath. Father Ontari would stand behind his casket and utter falsehoods. *He was a wonderful young man, he was caring and kind, he didn't deserve to die, blah blah blah- the lies.* I loved him for all his faults, all the pain he caused me, all the black secrets we shared; but I hated him more. Over the past several days, Adrian's final moments replayed redundantly in my mind. David's controlled violence and rage. If I had protested, Adrian might still be alive. I could have tried to stop it, but I hadn't. Apart of me felt strangely satisfied that I didn't and I am just as evil as him.

Bitterness had found its way into my soul. David had lied to me from the very beginning. He had manipulated me and I hated him for that. Selfishly, I had poured all of my love into him, and in return, he had hoarded it and wandered away forever. David, my beloved beautiful angel- my radiant Morning Star, was the devil. Satan, Lucifer, or Devil it mattered not, he would always mean the world to me. No matter how much the police, led by the fastidious Detective Gabriel, pried I would never utter a negative thing about David-he forever had my love and loyalty. Sure, he may have had the power of influencing- but I could not bear the fact that he was evil; but even so, it didn't change anything- I still loved him the same anyways.

We were trapped in wanderlust, David and I. I recalled the fire that ignited his already piercing eyes as he described the way in which he latched onto a victim becoming exactly what they want him to be. It devastated me that David had originally sought my demise. He had won complete power over me… he could have destroyed me at any time. His faithful followers, The Reign, had tried to fulfill that plan, but David loved me and he had protected me. Love was not in his nature and hate existed only through him. I was neither afraid of him nor troubled by the demonic nature of his being. He was caught in the vicious cycle of wanderlust for all time. David was gone and he was never coming back.

I watched the ceremony from afar. Every thought and emotion that surfaced within me I fearfully checked- apprehensive that David was influencing me again. I concluded that more so than avoiding the pain and grief of Adrian's burial service, it was my own paranoia regarding the circumstances of his death. I had arrived early; dressed in all black: a knee length pencil skirt, sleeveless top, peep-toe heels, and oversized floppy hat, and positioned myself under a lofty oak tree that was situated nearly 100 meters from the crackling wooden sanctuary. The sun peeked out from time to time behind the clouds which illuminated the pine wood casket that was elevated in front of the sanctuary and surrounded by dozens of potted plants and vibrant floral arrangements.

I was there, leaning against the thick truck of the old oak tree, when the processional of cars flowed in from Main St. through the open wrought iron gates into the cemetery. The cars slowly scooted down the narrow dusty lane, and I studied each face that had come to pay their final respects to a young man that no one had ever respected. I was sure that the entire town had attended to mourn Adrian's death; it was a duty they all felt obligated to pay. One by one, they filed in quietly and took their place on the weathered benches underneath the pavilion. I scoffed witnessing that several mourners dabbed their dry eyes with tissues- the spectacle was soon to commence. The only sorrow that was sincere was that of Cathy- his mother, who knew she had raised a dreadful child, but in a strained motherly way loved him anyway. Mason sat with the other West Virginia boys and stared blankly off into the distance. Cal, Cathy's alcoholic and abusive husband, was in his rusted mini-van working on another pint of Mad Dog.

Wolfgang Amadeus Mozart's Requiem started softly over the dull hum of the mourning congregation. With every syllable of gained momentum of Mozart's greatest masterpiece, the harder it became to breathe. I turned my back to the ceremony and half-way bracing the tree for support, I doubled over in pain. I had allowed the devil into my heart, and Adrian was dead because of my wickedness. I sobbed in self misery and cursed Adrian, cursed myself, but never David. I faintly heard Father Ontari proceed with the Mass.

The sound of footsteps startled me, and I raised my head to see who was approaching. I groaned inwardly as Detective Gabriel closed in upon me.

"Are you alright Autumn?" he asked with genuine concern.

"As well as could be expected. Adrian is dead and apparently I'm the prime suspect in his murder," I retorted.

The young detective tucked his hair behind his ears he replied, "we can continue that conversation another time, now is a time for mourning." He offered an outstretched arm, and for a split second I fantasied about chopping it off. *Stop it David.* He gently led me down the soft grassy hill and through the maze of large tombstones that encircled the open sanctuary. Father Ontari paused mid-hymn, and held his hands up to the heavens to silence the mass.

"Come my child," he said motioning for me to come to him. Detective Gabriel placed my shaking hand into Father Ontari's leathery palm, and I stood at the podium: silent, reflective, and subdued. I fought back the urge to vomit and after several minutes of connecting with the eyes of the fellow mourners I said in a hoarse whisper, "O GOD, who did grant to Saint George strength and constancy in the various torments which he sustained for our holy faith; we beseech you to preserve, through his intercession, our faith from wavering and doubt, so that we may serve you with a sincere heart faithfully unto death. Through Christ our Lord."

I watched Detective Gabriel exit the sanctuary, and before my prayer concluded- with the universal 'amen'- he had already disappeared down the lane. My final plea for forgiveness lifted up and my last words to Adrian muttered; I knelt before his casket with my arms stretched out before me, until his requiem mass ceased and he was finally laid to rest.

EPILOGUE

I remain fearful for the future. David said that we would always be together, so I must hold onto that. My heart cries daily for him- just to catch a glimpse of him would be enough I think to satisfy my broken spirit. He was right...Madam Therriot was right. I will never be able to let him go. I will die too soon.

I look into the eyes of Iago, my bas rouge, and I miss him further. Iago is all of David that tangibly remains. For all intent and purposes I am dead...sure I wake up every morning...I'm still breathing...but I too will live my life in persistent and uncontrollable wanderlust. I stumble through the days with only love and loyalty. I search for him.

A black cloud hovers over my life and I often doubt that he was real. I desperately cherish my memories of him, and deep inside, I know we are still together somehow. He snaked his way into my life and coiled himself tightly around my world. He defined my false reality, and now everything is distant and lifeless without my Morning Star.

I will forever cling to his promise- I will be his princess for all eternity. I have all but accepted the fact that I will be trapped in wanderlust until then- among the living...and I am dead.

ABOUT THE AUTHOR

Madasin Mayfair is a published poet and essayist, debuting her first novel- Wanderlust: Love & Hate- from the highly anticipated Wanderlust series. A 2008 English graduate from Malone University, she is currently a graduate student at Northwestern State University pursuing a Language and Literature Master's degree. Madasin grew up in Osnaburg Township, and currently resides in Massillon, Ohio with her husband, daughter, and German Shepherd Dog.